Wicked rulers band together against the life of the righteous, and condemn the innocent to death.

— Psalm 94

The Hand that Wields the Sword

By
David Standeven

Progressive
RISING PHOENIX PRESS

Text Copyright © 2024 David Standeven, Jr.

All rights reserved.
Published 2024 by Progressive Rising Phoenix Press, LLC
www.progressiverisingphoenix.com

ISBN: 978-1-958640-51-7

Printed in the U.S.A.

Edited by Alicia M. Hesterly.

Front Cover Photo: "A Fantasy Sword Engulfed by Flames and Darkness." Stock Photo ID: 1126875374 By T Studio. Image used under license from Shutterstock.com.

Interior Illustration: "Legendary Sword." Stock Vector ID: 1711886083 By omnimoney. Image used under license from Shutterstock.com.

Book and Cover design by William Speir
Visit: http://www.williamspeir.com

ACKNOWLEDGMENTS

Special thanks to Michael, Marie, Matt, Josephina, Bella, and Susanna, who helped beta-read earlier versions of this story.

Further thanks to all the members of Fort Worth Writers, who offered some excellent critiques that helped me clean up the first act.

A special shout out to Darrell, for answering my query to join Fort Worth Writers.

Above all, special thanks to my wife Amelia who has encouraged my progress even when my own motivation faltered.

TABLE OF CONTENTS

PART 1

The Girl with Eyes of Stars

CHAPTER 1

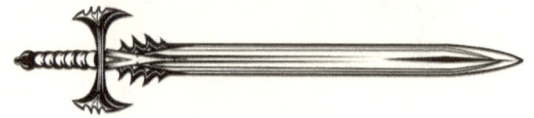

Enna

In the thirteen winters of Vinan's short life, he had never beheld anything like the girl before him in the clearing. The strange girl of the forest who now crouched behind his little sister Kirru.

Her large white eyes stared back at him with a glow akin to a firefly in the night. She made no move towards him, nor did he towards her. His spear rested easy in his hand, unraised, for he could not decide what to make of her. As long as she made no attempt to attack him he could not convince himself to raise his spear nor draw the knife that rested hidden in his furs. If only she would have spoken, moved her hands, mouthed a word... something.

Anything.

When he ignored her eyes she seemed to be but a young girl of nine or ten winters like his little sister Kirru. Her hair's hue was not brown and mud-like like the hair of all Vinan's people, but instead as black as the feathers of a raven. It hung down almost the full length of her back and the ends were crusted in dirt and mud. Aside from the unusual color, the hair upon her crown fell down her head so strangely straight and thin that neither wave nor curl could be seen in it. A dirty grey garment covered her body, a dirty grey garment that perhaps had once been something more but had since been reduced to little more than a tattered rag.

But the eyes... his elder brother Kror had told him that the eyes of the outlanders, like their hair, could be other than brown. He had heard that men beyond the hills had many shades of hair: yellow like the sun, red as blood, or black like that of this girl's. But never eyes of pure ethereal white. He questioned whether she was simply a girl like his sister or something else, a creature much like a girl but not quite one. Perhaps a demon or sprite of the forest like those in the stories his father had used to scare him and Stek to sleep.

And yet, he still could not bring himself to raise his spear against her. She did not move, she made no sign of aggression and only looked back at him with scared curiosity. The memories and fear left by dark tales about forest demons whispered fainter and fainter in Vinan's head the more he watched her.

"Vinan!"

Kirru, his little sister of nine winters, looked back at him with a plea on her face. An unspoken plea to approach and stop gripping his spears so tight.

"Get back!" he shouted.

"*Kirru!*"

The first words from the mouth of the white-eyed girl were carried by a voice as soft and gentle as a wooden flute yet undeniable, urgent, and afraid. Vinan did not know which surprised him more; that the girl spoke, or that she articulated Kirru's name while stretching out her hand with familiarity toward his sister.

He had little time to marvel at this, for a boar burst suddenly into the clearing. Vinan lurched towards Kirru by instinct to put himself between her and the beast and then hurled one of his spears towards the animal. It struck the left hind leg, prompting a

3

cry of pain from the boar. The strange girl ran past Vinan to Kirru and left the boy in the path of the boar's fury.

Vinan had never been so glad in all his life that he had brought both his spears this morning.

The giant, black-furred animal stared at him with feral rage, its curved tusks bared for the killing. Blood dripped from its left hind leg where Vinan's first now-broken spear had struck. Vinan held the point of his second spear forward towards the animal's head. Though he was aware that the spearhead had little chance of piercing the thick bones of the pig's gigantic skull, he kept it forward all the same, hoping to find another chance to strike a weak spot. He wished then that his arms were not the thin ones with which he had been born but mighty thick ones like those of his father or the High Warrior.

In one fell instant the boar charged. Vinan withdrew his spear from the aggressive stance, grasped it with both his hands, and put it between him and the furious beast. But the weapon did little to stifle the animal's charge. Vinan found himself on the ground with his spear broken in the boar's mighty jaws; his hands and the strength of his entire body were all that protected him from the crooked knife-like tusks.

It appeared that now, in the thirteenth spring of his short life and in the year of his own passage, Vinan would meet the Father of All and take his place with the Tribes of the Heavens.

In Vinan's moment of despair, the boar withdrew with a squeal of pain. He noticed pine nettles embedded in its eyes that now dripped with streams of blood. The boar flailed and roared as a flurry of needles flew into its eyes. Vinan rose to his feet and realized that the blinded and incapacitated animal had no more stomach to attack. He pulled the stone knife from his belt, strode to the pathetic creature, and slit its throat in mercy.

"Enna!" Kirru cried.

Vinan had not noticed before now, but the girl of the forest stood bathed in a pulsating aura of pale blue. She glowed like a full moon in the clear night sky as she stood with both hands outstretched. With the threat of the boar now gone she lowered her hands, the blue glow dissipating, and collapsed to the ground exhausted. Kirru ran to the girl to catch her as she fell.

"What was that?" Vinan said in passing wonder.

"She stopped the boar!" Kirru said. "She needs to sleep!"

The girl of the forest bore no marks of the aura, no sign of that mystical presence that had surrounded her only moments ago. By all appearances, what sat upon the ground, cradled in the arms of little Kirru, was but a girl, the same as Vinan's sister.

"Kirru," Vinan said. "Who is she?"

"Enna!" Kirru replied. "I found her in the forest five days ago."

"So, she is your secret friend," he said, realizing why nuts and berries had been disappearing from his mother's food stores. "Is she hurt?"

"No, she is tired."

"How do you know? Has she done this before?"

But Kirru, fully concerned with cradling the girl of the forest in her arms, did not answer.

Vinan contemplated for a moment. He could not bring that girl back to the village. Not now. He only needed to remember the wrath of his mother over little things, let alone something as unusual as this. Further, if he had been shocked by the girl's strange appearance, then the rest of his people would certainly not take it in stride.

Yet he could not leave the girl exposed in the wilderness. Nor Kirru, for that matter, for it was clear to him that she would not leave her friend's side.

He bent down to the girls and lifted the forest child. He found her waif-like body light enough that he knew he could carry her to the cave.

"Kirru," he said. "Come with me."

"Where are we going?" she asked as she followed Vinan.

"To a cave I know."

"Is that where you go when mother and you fight?"

The question made Vinan pause a second. A one-sided beating by his mother could hardly be considered a "fight" but he did not consider it worth correcting Kirru.

"Yes," he replied. "And I want you to keep it a secret. It is our cave now. Our secret."

"Do I need to keep it a secret from Stek too?"

"Stek already knows about it," Vinan replied, brushing a hanging vine of ivy away from his face.

If only Stek were with him now. He could have sent his little brother of eleven winters back to the village to tell their elder brother Kror, who had seen the world beyond the mountains, what had happened. Stek was nigh unmatched in his courage and almost the only person in the world whom Vinan would trust with his life. But without his little brother with him, Vinan had to protect the girls himself.

The cave loomed high above at the height of about twenty full-grown men. A steep winding slope was the only way to it. Loose rocks marked the treacherous path, threatening all but the most cautious climbers with the threat of a fall and broken limbs for their efforts. Vinan scaled it as he had many times before, and even the weight of the girl of the forest did not compromise his footing.

"Wait at the bottom!" he shouted back to Kirru. "I'll come back down and take you up."

"I can do it!" she shot back.

"No! Don't! The rocks are too loose!"

But that did nothing to deter Kirru. She followed him, bent over forward, and trudged upward step by careful step several paces behind Vinan. Vinan did not stop his ascent, lest he lose his own footing but continued to try to dissuade Kirru from hers.

"I'll come back for you!" he said. "You don't have to climb!"

She did not respond but stubbornly took another step, then

6

another. The same spirit of unbending defiance shone in her eyes that had shone many a time in those of their stubborn elder brother Kror. The steepness of the climb sharpened and Kirru bent over to crawl on all fours, grasping handfuls of dirt as she scaled her way to the cave above.

Vinan saw that it did him no good to argue with her. He clutched onto the girl of the forest tighter and moved up step by careful step, ignoring the pain that began to form in his sides and the aches in his legs. That strain was always an accepted part of the climb, one he feared Kirru did not know and could not overcome.

When he reached the summit, he gasped in relief at the feeling of his feet upon somewhat flattened earth. The entrance to the cave laid a few paces ahead but he did not yet enter. He looked back to see that Kirru had not given up and had not fallen to her death. She climbed upwards, straining and panting, while never losing her footing. Vinan, realizing she had made it most of the way up, watched her finish the rest. At the summit, she too succumbed to relief and the need for respite. Her thin body lay sprawled face-up and staring at the sky as her panting gave way to slower and slower breathing.

"You didn't have to climb," Vinan chided Kirru after a few moments. "I would have come back for you."

"I know you would have," she answered with a carefree smile. "I wanted to climb it myself."

"Why?"

She replied with a question Vinan knew not how to answer, "What if you and Stek aren't there one day to come back for me?"

"I will always be there to protect you," he affirmed after a moment's pause. "From anything."

Vinan and Stek had furnished the cave well with sticks and wood they had collected. Five spears built by the two boys rested in one corner beside four sharpened stone knives. There remained only one entrance, one entrance to defend from any beasts of the forest, if they were even able or willing to make the climb.

Vinan put the girl down near the back of the cave and grabbed an armful of the dry sticks. He placed them in the middle of the cave, gathered fungus and dried pine nettles from the cave floor, and placed them at the base of the pile. The flint and orange rock that he carried in his pouch soon ignited the assortment into a blaze.

"Keep the fire going," he said to Kirru. "It will warm her and keep away any animals, if they even make it up to here."

"Where are you going?" she asked.

"Home," he said. "I need to get our father. He'll know what to do."

"You're leaving us here?" she asked.

"That's why I brought you here," he answered. "Up here you'll be safer than down in the forest. Use the spears if you need to. I'll be back as soon as I can."

He looked down at Kirru, still exhausted and breathing heavily from her climb.

"Kirru," he said, "do you have any water?"

"No," she answered.

Vinan knelt down and reached for his deerskin flask.

"Here," he said. "Drink this."

Kirru almost did when she suddenly looked to her left. The girl of the forest had awakened, sat upright, and was looking at the brother and sister with her shining eyes.

"Enna!" Kirru exclaimed.

"*Kirru*," the girl answered in a calm melodic pitch as she looked about to measure her surroundings.

"Did she tell you her name is Enna?" Vinan asked Kirru.

"I called her and she responded," his sister answered.

"You called her... Enna?"

"She looks like an Enna, don't you think?"

Vinan didn't know what she looked like. He simply watched as the girl rose from where he had laid her and walked to Kirru.

She placed her hand on Kirru's head.

"*Kirru,*" she said as she smiled for the first time Vinan had observed.

She began to glow with the same aura as when she had thrown pine nettles into the eyes of the boar. The blue light was unmistakably the same but far fainter than before in the forest. Vinan's fear for Kirru arose at the strange sight, but some instinct within told him it did not threaten his sister. The light soon dissipated and the girl of the forest slowly sat upon the ground.

"Vinan!" Kirru exclaimed. "I'm not tired!"

Vinan saw that Kirru had indeed been refreshed with no sign of her earlier fatigue. He wondered what power or magic could produce such an effect. The power was certainly beyond any power his mother, the High Priestess of his clan, possessed with her myriad herbs and potions.

He then looked at the girl of the forest and saw that she was tired herself. He concluded that the girl had somehow given some of her own energy and life to Kirru. She had done this even though her fatigue was just as great as anyone in the cave.

Vinan moved to her. She regarded him with some fear in her countenance but did not move away from him.

"Thank you," he told her, hoping she would understand.

She did not seem to. As before, in the clearing, she stared at him with neither movement nor sound. He reached for his water flask again and opened it.

"Drink," he said, taking a gulp before offering it to her.

With some hesitation, she took it from his hands and put it to her lips. When she had determined that Vinan had no intention of taking it back from her she drank her fill greedily and then handed it back to him.

"Thank you," he repeated with gratitude. "Thank you for helping Kirru."

He stood up and made sure he was equipped with a flask, knife, and spear before leaving.

"Stay here," he told Kirru. "I'll be back with Kror soon enough. He will know what to do."

As he descended the slopes, he wondered if today would earn him the pride of his clan. A boar slain, a strange but benevolent girl of the forest discovered, and Kirru protected by his hand. It mattered far more to him, though, that his sister was safe where he had left her.

CHAPTER 2

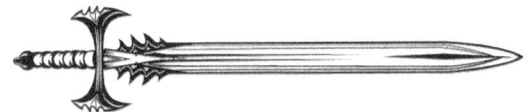

Kror of the Long Knife

Vinan returned to the village and barely anyone noted his presence. The preparations of the coming spring ceremonies were proceeding. With the Rite of the Warrior's Passage only three days away, every boy his age teemed with eagerness to prove his worth. The various clans had arrived at the shrine, the old men instructing the young in the ways of wife-choosing, and the young warriors telling their little brothers what they had to do to take a place as warriors in their clan beside their fathers and kinsmen.

Vinan made his way toward his mother's tent, knowing that the High Priestess would be preparing her ointments and prayers for the young men about to undergo the ritual. Vinan wondered how many of those prayers were meant for him. He knew his mother had no faith in his ability to overcome the trials. She hated his older brother Kror so much that Kror had been one of the few mountainfolk to ever leave the mountains and return—the first one in many generations. But at least he was old enough to care little for her hate. She heaped praise upon his little brother Stek, at least as long as it could humiliate his elder brothers. She doted relentlessly on little Kirru, her only daughter, to the point of smothering.

But Vinan knew in his heart that no genuine love poured from his mother towards any of her four children.

The aromatic scent of burning flowers greeted his nose as he entered the familiar hut. Smoke rose from bowls placed all around the room and an earthen pot simmered in the center beneath a crackling fire. Vinan saw his mother standing at the far end of the hut, resting momentarily as if having finished an exhausting task. She had passed her fiftieth winter some time ago, with the grey strands fast overtaking her crown of acorn hair like red leaves of autumn overtaking the green. Her skin was calloused, her body thin from a life of strenuous activity, and her face hardened from long years surrounded by death.

Across the hut stood Kror like a prowling animal in the dark shadows. In fact, to Vinan's eyes, his brother and mother in this moment appeared as two vicious beasts opposing each other in a deadly standoff. Each bore enough hatred in their stance to tear down the other, yet neither seemed willing to make the first pounce. Vinan judged that he had come at a poor time indeed.

Kror of the Long Knife was a man of nearly twenty-five winters now. His seven years in the outlands had done much to sharpen and harden the once-thin boy Vinan remembered from his childhood. His chin had become defined, his body filled in, his arms thickened, and his eyes cold with icy resolve. It seemed that the land outside the mountains, a land few of the Mountain peoples dared go, had taken much from Kror and given back much in return. The most obvious being the strange long knife of the outlands, as long as a small child, which rested in a leather sheath in Kror's belt.

The most striking of all to Vinan though, was that since his return Kror seemed to fear absolutely nothing.

"What is it, Vinan?" his mother snarled, her hard face staring through him and the necklace of bones around her neck rattling.

12

One question. One question from her was all it took for terror to seize hold of Vinan and for him to forget his purpose entirely. Kror stood still as a stone, smirking with disappointment at his disarmed little brother.

"I... uh, thought supper was ready?" Vinan mumbled.

"Oh, you're done hunting rabbits in the forest?" she asked with mockery. "The little warrior has decided he likes me after all?"

"I have killed a boar!" Vinan forced his tongue that much. "I came to get help carrying it back."

"Why did you kill a boar without my permission?" she asked with agitation. "Bring it back yourself. I have more than enough food here. More work for me, and half of it will probably go to waste."

"The little warrior has much to learn about the world," Kror said with a smirk. "That includes thinking he needs to fear or obey you."

If the ferocity of a look could bring harm, then the one the priestess shot toward her oldest son would have struck him dead where he stood.

"Enough of your talk!" she snapped. "I am tired of your mockery! Do you think that leaving the forest for a few winters gives you power over your mother and priestess?"

"Seeing the truth of the world," Kror replied without a moment's pause, "has shown me how little weight the power of the High Warrior, the priestess, or even mother actually holds."

A lump of dread formed in Vinan's stomach and he wished to slip away in silence. Somehow, through his mother's perverse and sadistic logic, he would be punished for all this. Somehow, this would be his fault. And all because she could no longer strike Kror, who had long ceased to fear her.

He could already see the wrath billowing in his mother's face, the unbridled rage that had been unleashed many times on Vinan and upon Kror in his youth. It terrified Vinan more than even the great boar that had almost gored him earlier that day. For when that wrath was unleashed, no mercy would his mother's hands or staff impart.

And yet Kror just stood there grinning. Almost as if the memory of her blows had lost their power over him, or perhaps he welcomed them. Vinan's eyes noticed Kror's fingers toying with the hilt of his long outland knife, and then he saw the truth in his brother's eyes.

Kror waited for her to strike. He wanted her to strike. He goaded her to strike.

The fear that should have been in Kror, the fear that she had instilled in her children, the fear that pulsed through Vinan as he wished the earth would swallow him... that very fear now showed itself in the mad contorted face of the priestess. The fear of looking into the eyes of a monster capable of taking whatever it wished. Cornered thus, the mother began to weep an exaggerated lament.

"Who are you?" she croaked. "What have you done to my son, Kror?"

"I am still he." he responded in triumph. "And I have returned to bring my people from your clutches. You are nothing and I have returned a great warrior, bringing our people the future by my hand."

"You are no warrior!" she replied. "My father was a warrior! My brothers were warriors! Even the man who slew them, he is a warrior! Your father and all his sons, you will never be warriors!"

"All the warriors you mentioned," Kror smiled, "are dead men."

This was not quite true. The slayer of Vinan's uncles and grandfather not only still lived but remained the High Warrior of the Mountain Peoples. It didn't matter much though, not in a conversation like this.

Vinan found a fire rising within him. Perhaps his brother had emboldened him, or perhaps he had become exhausted from hearing the same tired and over-worn abuse from his mother every day. Regardless of the reason, he found himself speaking against her like he never had the courage to before.

"I will be a warrior in three days!" Vinan proclaimed, his spine tingling with both fear and exhilaration. "And nothing you say will change that! I will be a warrior far better than the dead father you worship!"

He regretted his words almost immediately, for the gaze of his mother's eyes shot towards him with all the fury she held against Kror and him. She ran towards him, fist clenched and staff raised high above her head.

"Enough of your defiance!" she shrieked as she brought down her blows upon him. "You are a little simpering puppy! You will never be the warrior my father was! You are the son of your father! And I am the daughter of the bear!"

Her fist made contact with Vinan's jaw and he tasted blood between his teeth. Her staff came down to strike him and Vinan raised his arms to protect his head. Kror's spear stopped the staff mid-air.

"Strike him again, and I will kill you," Kror said flatly and dispassionately. "It would be a lie for me to say I won't enjoy it."

The priestess backed away, genuine terror in her eyes. She could see just as well as Vinan that Kror meant every word he said. Kror had lost all fear of her. He had lost all fear of slaying her. He had killed any love he had ever held for her, and it was as dead as the father she still loved.

"Why am I cursed?" she wailed as if mourning a dead child. "Why are my sons so ungrateful and wicked to the mother who gave them birth?"

"Because you are the daughter of no bear," Kror answered. "You are but the spawn of a demon, and your own child has come to take his place. Now stay away from Vinan and me if you value your life at all. Go back to your potions and incantations. Drug yourself until you are numb if that gives you solace, for our people will sing my name for generations even when you are long forgotten."

The dark smile upon Kror's face said all else that needed saying. He stood above his cowering mother triumphantly. The beasts in the hut had fought and the winner was decided, the son finally triumphed over his mother.

Vinan, however, wanted no more of this and slunk away. Once outside the hut, he remembered his original purpose and realized he had not fulfilled it. His mother would never listen to him now. He had set himself against her just as Kror had done all those years ago. He did not know what he would do about the girl of the forest. He had no idea what he would tell Kirru. He had no idea if he could find a quiet moment with Kror soon. Perhaps if he waited a bit to sharpen his spear...

"Vinan," the hand of Kror patted him gently on the shoulder, "are you alright?"

Vinan looked up to his brother and saw no darkness in his face. The boyish softness that had been there in the years before Kror left for the outlands had returned. When Vinan looked he saw once again the familiar and kindly brother who had tucked him to sleep while telling him tales of hunts and heroes, the brother whom he had watched take many a beating at the hands of their mother, the brother who had foolishly challenged the High Warrior to combat and failed, the brother who had disappeared for seven years and left Vinan alone to shoulder the wrath of the High Priestess alone, and the brother who Vinan had given up for dead in the outlands until a few months ago.

The brother who assuredly had returned to protect him just as in the old days.

"I am, Kror," Vinan answered, his eyes welling up with water. "I am now."

"You had something to say, didn't you?" Kror asked. "Something you cannot say before her now?"

"There is," happiness filled Vinan as he realized that here

16

was someone he could trust with anything. "A girl in the forest. A girl Kirru found."

"A lost child? Where is she from?"

"I don't know. I can't understand her tongue and her eyes glow."

"They... glow?" Kror asked skeptically.

"Like a firefly."

"Curious..." Kror stared off into the distance.

"Do you know what to do?"

Kror smiled. "Of course I do. Come with me."

Vinan followed Kror towards the hut of the elders, the grey warriors among whom both his father and the High Warrior sat. Kror strode to it with all confidence and none of the timidity of his little brother. Vinan wished he could share in that boldness that flowed through his brother since his return home. Asking anything of the elders was an intimidating thought, to say the least.

"Going somewhere, Kror?"

Dhof the Tree-Jumper asked. He was a nimble young warrior of lean body and a good friend of Kror. Many of the younger warriors were friends of Kror, now that he had seen the outlands and returned to tell the tale.

"To the elders," Kror answered. "I have business there."

"You'll find two fewer there now," Dhof said. "Yark the Fatherless has gone with Bheif to hunt. Who knows when they will return?"

"They have gone?" Kror asked with some surprise. "My father went to hunt with Yark the Fatherless?"

"Now is as good a time as any."

"Probably right," Kror reflected. "I think now is the time for the great hunt."

"Now?" Dhof asked with eyes wide.

"As soon as I speak to the High Warrior."

Dhof nodded in agreement and walked away at a brisk pace.

"Th-the High Warrior?" Vinan stuttered.

17

"Who else would you go to?" Kror asked. "Is he not the leader of our people?"

Of that fact, there was little to dispute; regardless of what the High Priestess believed.

CHAPTER 3

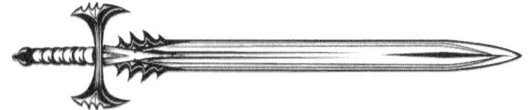

Kin-Slayer

Vinan was surprised by the softness with which the High Warrior treated them, surprised that his mother's enemy bore no hatred against her sons. Vinan had so long avoided the presence of the High Warrior that he had only the stories of his mother and father to form an image of the man in his mind. His father spoke highly of the chieftain, but his mother... well, had he not slain her father and brothers? Few would have looked with favor upon the man in such circumstances, let alone the woman who forgot neither slight nor grudge.

But Vinan found the man to be the ideal of a warrior when he looked upon him. He was tall, broad-shouldered, and crowned with a full head of grey hair. From his strong and pointed chin hung a short beard and his distant grey eyes told a tale of tragedy and triumph. His attire was nigh indistinguishable from the rest of the warriors save for the sapphire necklace he wore beneath his cloak of fur. His spear was as sharp as that of any young man's, though Vinan knew it had seen more use than most of the other spears combined.

It had taken only a short explanation from Kror for the High

Warrior to agree to accompany them to meet the girl. All this time, Vinan thought, he could have put his trust in the High Warrior instead of the High Priestess. Perhaps life would have been easier for him.

Vinan now led the way through the forest brush towards the clearing where he had met the girl. Kror and the High Warrior followed behind and kept pace. They were far away from the village and in a part of the mountains where the silence could be enjoyed in peace. Vinan knew they were not far from the place where he had slain the boar, where he had met the girl.

"Tell me," Kror said, "is this not the ground upon which you fought the previous High Warrior many winters ago?"

"More or less," the High Warrior answered with his voice that was as deep as the rumble of storm thunder.

"Did it please you," Kror asked, "when you killed him?"

"Killing never brings pleasure to any man, unless that man is a monster."

"So, you only killed him to take his place."

"I killed him because he killed my sister. I did not want to become the High Warrior back then."

"So, you did kill him for pleasure?"

"I killed him for vengeance and it brought me no joy. Not when I killed him and not after. I had to bury my sister all the same."

"That is always how the killing goes," Kror mused. "Whether we enjoy it or not, we must do it all the same. It is the way of the world."

Silence descended upon the company for a few moments, a dark silence that was soon broken by the sound of a struggle. Vinan turned around to see his brother and the High Warrior locked in deadly combat. He did not know either who had started it, or why. He could only stand in place with spear in hand and mouth hanging open.

The High Warrior pushed Kror back with the weight of his

body, forcing the young warrior to stumble back to regain his footing. The High Warrior looked to Vinan, doubtlessly seeing the boy's indecision, and pleaded.

"Vinan! You are not part of this! You are better than him! Help me stop this madness!"

But Vinan did not move.

Kror at last drew his long outland knife. As it slid from its hide sheath Vinan saw that it was not made of stone but of a material smooth and grey. It glistened in the light with magnificent beauty and appeared to be sharp on both sides. Vinan could not even imagine at that moment how such a weapon might have been crafted.

The High Warrior renewed his attack. But with one sweeping motion, Kror swung his long knife and cleaved his opponent's spear in two with a clean cut. He then drove his spear into the chieftain's stomach.

"Monster..." the High Warrior choked, "What sorcery have you mastered?"

"One which the people will learn soon enough and which you will not," answered Kror. "Now die knowing that I will be the next High Warrior and that everything you ever loved is now mine!"

Kror shoved the spear deeper in to finish it before pulling it out again. The High Warrior slumped and fell to the forest ground, never to speak again. Vinan only now started to take in all that had just happened.

"Y-you killed him..."

"Of course I did," Kror said dryly as he re-sheathed his long knife. "Truly your eyes can see, Vinan, son of Bheif."

"W-why?!" Vinan exclaimed. "He was going to help us!"

"Because the time has come," Kror answered as darkness descended on his aura, "for us to help ourselves."

Vinan stammered. "Wh-What are you...?"

"The High Warrior, the High Priestess, the old ways... it is all nonsense, Vinan. I returned to help our people, to bring them out of the darkness. To do this I must do some unpleasant things."

Vinan stood still as stone, still reeling in shock.

"In the outlands," Kror continued, "there are those who would kill and enslave our people. There are those who have begun enslaving the hill clans, and there are far more of them planning to join. I returned to give our people the weapons of the enemy, the methods of the enemy, and the savagery of the enemy. I came back so my people would not be swallowed up."

"You murdered the High Warrior!" Vinan protested, leaving aside his question on what it meant to "enslave."

"I did what had to be done!" Kror answered with command. "Vinan, if you want to help our people then you will follow me. Outlanders slew the High Warrior. We will swear vengeance on those outlanders and I will be High Warrior. You will be a warrior at last. My warrior. And I will teach you how to use a blade such as this."

He patted the hilt of his long knife, now sheathed in its place.

It shamed Vinan, but part of him truly wanted to follow Kror. Had he not shown him kindness all those days ago when no one else would? What did he owe his mother or the elders?

But still, he could not. It was not the way of the warrior. Despite his youth, he knew this would not be his way and he would never allow himself to justify it.

"What you are doing," Vinan said at length, "is wrong. I can't do it."

"Then what are you going to do?" Kror asked, amused. "Kill me?"

"No, I will go to the elders and tell them the truth!"

"Curious," interjected the voice of Dhof from a tree limb above, "that you would even show your face before the elders after I watched you slay the High Warrior."

"What?" Vinan asked incredulously.

"Exactly as Dhof said," Kror said. "We both watched you kill him. It is both of our words against yours."

"Y-you would lie? Against me?" Vinan stammered.

"As I said," Kror smiled, "It is time for our people to be remade anew. Anyone that stands in my way must be stopped. I will trample underfoot far more than this before I am finished."

Wrath boiled inside Vinan to the point of bursting. He raised his spear for battle, ready to fight, but then remembered that Dhof lurked in the trees above.

"Stand down, Dhof!" Kror commanded.

To Vinan's surprise, Kror dropped his own spear and stood with his arms outstretched.

"Come on," Kror taunted. "Do it!"

It seemed easy. Too easy. After what Vinan had witnessed today, he could not trust that no further surprise awaited him. He paused, ignoring his first instinct to leap into an attack on Kror, and looked into his brother's eyes.

The look returned again. The same look that had goaded their mother earlier now called to him, daring him to strike. The once gentle face of the protecting older brother was replaced by a demon from the darkest reaches of Vinan's night terrors. A horror overtook Vinan and paralyzed him as he realized one terrifying fact. Kror indeed feared nothing now. Not even killing his little brother.

Vinan lowered his spear and, with much trembling, backed away from Kror slowly.

"As I thought," his brother said with disappointment, "you are still only a cowering little boy afraid of all that our mother has made you fear. I came back to free our people, free them from all that holds them back, to free you from the oppression you never chose. But you are unworthy of it. You love your slavery and will never understand what it means to be free. Not unless I cut you free from it."

"Slavery?" Vinan asked, puzzled by this new outlander word.

"You will learn what that is soon enough," Kror smiled. "Now, go. I give you your life today. Flee into the outlands as I did

23

and witness with your own eyes the truth of mankind. Take the forest girl if you want, because I will have her killed if you don't take her far from here."

"But," Vinan protested, "Kirru will not leave her! If you banish her then you will banish Kirru too!"

"Kirru is old enough to make that choice," Kror answered callously. "If you care so much you should protect them both."

"But Kror," Vinan pleaded, "it is Kirru!"

"What is that to me?"

"She is our little sister!"

"The little sister I never knew. You can thank our mother for that. Kirru is nothing to me. If she will not leave the demon girl's side, then I suppose she will have to accompany you into the wilds as well."

Now Vinan realized that Kror had killed more than the High Warrior in these last seven winters. The brother who cared for him, loved him, and played with him all that time ago was gone forever and replaced with the killer who stood before him.

"Why are you still here?" Kror asked. "If you will not join me, then leave before I begin the hunt for you."

Vinan looked above and saw Dhof standing upon a branch, eagerly awaiting Vinan to make the rash choice. Vinan no longer cared whether he would be a named coward, for he had been named murderer already. He turned and ran before he could give Dhof the desired excuse.

He fled deep into the forest to find Kirru and the girl with eyes of stars. To protect them from whatever evil followed.

***

Stek was not Vinan.

He did not hesitate as his older brother so often did. Uncertainty of his worthiness to stand in the warriors' circle did not torment him. He knew he would be a great warrior someday.

24

His mother also told him as much. She did not punish him as she punished Vinan and had punished Kror. He knew that fact well.

Yet he did not love her any more for it.

A great disturbance began on the edge of the settlement. It started with but one saying like a little spark of firestone and grew, kindling a fire among the ears that heard it and the mouths that repeated it. The flames of the gossip soon reached the ears of Stek, who could only listen in dumb astonishment.

The High Warrior has been murdered.

Stek ran as fast as he could to his family's hut with his spear where it almost always rested, in his hand. He arrived to an empty hut with the items his mother used for her work strewn about. So unlike the usual arrangement, compulsively methodical in its organization, that it unsettled Stek to his core. The disturbance was of such great importance that it had caused his mother to leave her things untidy.

It was almost as unthinkable as the murder of the High Warrior.

He turned to look for where to go next and saw the others gathering towards the Rock of Offering. He ran there as quickly as he could, wondering where his sister, brothers, father, and mother could be at that moment.

The corpse of the High Warrior had been laid upon the Rock of Offering and Kror stood above it mourning. The High Priestess stared towards the sight without making a move, yet the bones that dangled from the staff in her hand still clacked together. The bones were the only noise that dared break the stillness as the bloody corpse lay upon the sacrificial stone.

"Who did this?!" yelled the oldest son of the dead chieftain, a man of just less than thirty winters who was as impressively built as his father had been.

"Warriors and those who would be warriors!" Kror shouted. "Priestesses and maidens! Our High Warrior has been murdered! The one who did this has killed the father of the warriors! The father-killer must die!"

"Who did this?!" the chieftain's son demanded again.

"My own brother," Kror answered. "Vinan, son of Bheif!"

Stek stood stunned as a deer, trying to convince himself he had not heard that. A great tumult erupted from the crowd and chaos reigned before Kror shouted above the din and brought it to silence.

"Yes, Vinan, son of Bheif! My own brother! He has turned his spear on us and done a great murder! I say death to the father-killer! Death to the kin-slayer! He is no brother of mine and I will have his head should I find him!"

Stek could not believe it as he absent-mindedly stumbled closer to the rock. Vinan killing the High Warrior? Vinan murdering anyone? Impossible! Kror was lying!

Why was Kror lying?!

"How?" the son of the High Warrior demanded.

"Yes, Kror!" the High Priestess pressed. "How did my harmless little rabbit hunter kill the mighty High Warrior?"

"Vinan lied to him by sneaking and without warning," Kror answered. "I saw it all. He has made a pact with a demon of the forest!"

"Is it true, Kror?!" asked the High Priestess. "Can it be true?!"

"It is as true as anything you ever taught me," Kror answered in a voice so sinister and low, that Stek believed few besides him had heard it.

The High Priestess froze in terror and the bones upon her staff ceased their clacking.

"All he says is true!" Dhof said from a tree on the edge of the clearing. "I saw it. Vinan killed the High Warrior by gaining his trust."

"Death to the father-killer!" Kror shouted as he raised his fist in the air.

"Lies!" Stek shouted back.

But in the din of confusion, no one listened. No one cared. That which a boy had to say, however true, was of no importance.

Death to the father-killer!

Thus, rang out the cry of the throng.

Death to the father-killer!

The people had chosen their path.

Death to the father-killer!

And condemned the innocent to die.

"Enough!"

The High Warrior's son now spoke to those present, who awaited the words of the grieving son.

"Vengeance will not return my father to us," he began. "We need to bury him and choose a new High Warrior!"

"Why wait for the burial?" Dhof asked.

Silence from the shocked crowd. A violation of the sacred traditions of the mountainfolk, to choose the new High Warrior so soon.

"There is a demon lurking in the forest and outlanders growing ever closer to our home," Dhof went on undaunted. "We need a new chieftain now! And I say that chieftain should be Kror, son of Bheif!"

"Brother of the father-killer?" The High Warrior's son asked with incredulity.

"What my brother did, he did by his own hand," Kror answered. "And I will kill him if he ever shows himself."

Of that, Stek was assured.

"You are not worthy!" the High Warrior's son pressed. "You are the son of the High Priestess! The blood of many is on your grandfather's hands! The blood of my father is on your brother's hands!"

"And your only claim to lead is through the merits of your father."

A voice low, grim, and dark penetrated the assembly. A silver-haired warrior emerged with a bloody spear in hand. Yark the Fatherless stepped and a lump formed in Stek's stomach. Notoriously joyless and pitiless, Yark the Fatherless held his place as one of the most feared old warriors. He had been battered and beaten through the years like many old men but had never been softened with the wizened kindness that many old men possessed. He preferred to make his mark as a man who had earned respect through his deadliness and not from any goodwill the other warriors bore towards him, for there was none to be found.

"Your father did not become High Warrior because he waited for his father to die," Yark continued, his yellow canine eyes glaring at the High Warrior's son. "He took it through merit. He took it through strength. He took it by shedding blood."

A suffocating air fell upon the midst of all as the warriors began to look at those around them with fear and suspicion. All waited for a move, any move, which would spur them into battle with men they regarded as their equals and companions. As if a leg had suddenly been dismembered from the animal that was the tribe, threatening to topple it over and throw it back to the dark days of kin-slaying and war.

The old days of Stek's grandfather.

"I put my claim upon the place of my father," the High Warrior's son said at length. "If anyone wishes to stop me, let them fight me."

"Then I will answer your challenge," Kror answered.

An old warrior stepped forth.

"You will not use your outlander knife!" he declared. "That weapon is forbidden!"

"Let your weapons of the old ways defeat my sword," Kror replied, "and then your way will be shown to be the right one."

"I accept," said the High Warrior's son. "Call the challenge."

This had been directed to the aged warrior. When he didn't move, Kror looked to Yark the Fatherless.

"Begin the challenge," he told the yellow-eyed warrior.

Yark raised his spear.

"Kror, son of Bheif, are you prepared to die?"

"I am."

"Goras, son of Tarak, are you prepared to die?"

"I am."

"Then fight well and die well."

The throng backed away to give the two space for their combat. Goras reached out his hand and a spear flew into it from a sympathizer for his leadership. After inspecting it and feeling its weight in his hand he held it ready and began to position himself against his enemy.

Kror had no spear. Kror asked for no spear. Instead, he reached for his belt and pulled out his long knife from its leather sheath. It slid out with barely a sound. He held it at his side with no care and motioned with the finger of his free hand for Goras to come at him.

Goras charged forward and thrust his spear forward with a feint. Kror sliced the tip of it off with one swipe of his blade and then slammed his fist into his enemy's face. Goras sprawled on the ground helplessly as Kror stood over him, the edge of the long knife pressed against his throat.

Just as quickly as the fight had begun it had ended. The knife of the outlands stood victorious.

"Every good warrior we lose is a victory for our outlander enemies," Kror said to Goras. "Give up and you can help me defeat them."

Goras looked back with defiance in his eyes.

"You don't have to die here!" Kror pleaded. "Death for death and vengeance for vengeance was the way of our forefathers. It does not have to be our way. Don't force me to kill you."

Goras considered for a moment and then nodded in surrender. Kror withdrew the long knife and helped his opponent up by the hand. The son of the old High Warrior raised Kror's arm up and shouted.

"He is our High Warrior! Kror the Long-Knife!"

"Kror the Long-Knife!" Dhof shouted with glee.

"Kror the Long-Knife!" the warriors answered with a single chorus.

The chorus Stek would not share, not only because he was no warrior but because he would never be a warrior if it meant accepting Kror as his leader. He wondered why Vinan had ever loved or thought highly of this older brother, for Stek's eyes only beheld a monster and liar intent on destroying every good thing among their people.

"Brothers and warriors!" Kror announced. "I will lead you forward. I have been to the lands beyond and have lived among the people there. They are a savage people, a cruel people, a murderous people who kill one another every day and every night! They have many laws and yet no laws, for their tribes fight over anything they can regardless of good cause. They all seek to conquer us when they tire of fighting themselves. We cannot let that happen!"

For a moment, Stek's fear of the outlanders almost convinced him to believe Kror's words. But he would never put his trust in Kror. He was not Vinan.

"We will seize the weapons of the enemy and learn how to use them!" Kror continued. "We will learn how to craft them! We will break the enemy before they come for us! We will be the wolves in the night! They will speak of us and they will tremble! At last, we will pour from these mountains and take what is ours! This I swear to you!"

If the admiration for his victory and mercy were notable, the reception to this was overwhelming. The warriors stood united and not one of them felt the need or desire to challenge Kror in this moment. They had decided the High Warrior once and for all among themselves.

But Stek would never accept it.

"Rest now!" Kror said. "Weep and mourn for our lost father. Rest and be ready, for tomorrow we prepare for the coming war against the outlanders."

Priestesses, his shocked mother chief among them, came to retrieve the old High Warrior's body for burial. The crowd dispersed and Kror made to slip away unnoticed. Stek would not let him do so easily. He followed his brother from a distance until they were away from the rest. In a clearing surrounded by a dozen or so mountain pines so old and thick that their nettled branches formed a roof above their heads, his brother, at last, acknowledged him.

"What is it, Stek?" Kror asked as if humoring a small child.

Stek saw no point in interrogating Kror. He already knew what had to be the truth.

"You killed the High Warrior!" he said.

"Of course I did," Kror answered with little concern. "Do you really think you're the only one who can see the obvious? Even Goras could guess as much."

"You murdered him! You lied about Vinan!"

"And is Vinan here to defend himself and challenge me?"

"No," Stek supposed that Vinan was probably too intimidated by their oldest brother to fight him, "but I am!"

"Oh?" Kror smiled at Stek, smiled at him like he would any child. "You think you can take me?"

Stek pointed his spear forward for battle. "I *will* take you."

Stek assumed he had a few seconds to charge while Kror unsheathed his legendary long outlander knife. A few seconds to feint, let Kror prepare for a thrust that would never come, and then run past him to strike him from behind.

But Kror never drew his long knife. His fist landed in Stek's gut and knocked him to the ground on his back. Stek lost all his breath. He held his stomach and whimpered as the pain began to emerge from the shock. Tears of pain involuntarily welled up in his eyes. He wondered if Vinan felt this pain every time their mother struck him.

Kror stood over Stek and kicked his spear away.

31

"It hurts, does it not?" he mocked. "You have never felt what it is to be struck, to be brought down so low, to be shown just how weak you are."

He bent down and grabbed Stek by the throat, lifting him to his feet with strength Stek did not think Kror possessed.

"Vinan and I know that pain and that fear," Kror continued. "We knew it every day for years. It is why Vinan knew not to fight me, though you were not so wise. Our mother's favor has made you weak and stupid just as her beatings have made Vinan reasonable and afraid."

Kror pulled Stek close, so close that Stek's ear was beside his older brother's mouth.

"If you ever wish to challenge me again," Kror whispered, "be ready to die."

Kror threw him back on the ground with violent force and turned away. Stek slammed against the ground back-and-shoulders-first. It was the first time he had ever been humiliated so painfully, and that panged him even more than his impact against the ground. Stek got off his back and scrambled back to his feet, refusing to let Kror leave him in the dirt for long.

"When father returns from the hunt," Stek gasped as his breath returned to him, "he will kill you for this."

"You think he's returning?" Kror asked, almost laughing.

"What?"

"Why do you think he hasn't returned? Yet, Yark the Fatherless is back from the same hunt."

Ridiculous! Was Kror actually implying that he could have their father killed? Was Kror willing to kill their father?

No. That's why Yark the Fatherless had done it. Just one look at Kror's face and Stek could discern that his older brother told the truth.

"Murderer!"

"Murderer?" Kror asked, feigning confusion, "I have no control over our father dying in a hunting accident."

32

Stek gritted his teeth, seething and ready to boil over in wrath. He wanted to lunge at Kror again but knew that it would be useless. He wanted to tell everyone, anyone, but knew he would find only deaf ears. Kror had won and Stek had one final outlet for his spite.

"You... lying..."

Kror smiled.

"...weasel!"

The insult was absurd, childish, and delivered with a cracking voice and streaming tears. But it was the best Stek could conjure in that moment, just the embarrassing taunt of a little boy. And that stung worse than being thrown into the dirt.

Then Kror began to laugh.

"Still a child! At least Vinan controls his tears."

Stek had seen and heard enough. Nothing remained for him here. He needed to find Vinan, find Kirru, and do anything he could to stop this.

He now fled deep into the woods, searching for his only brother.

CHAPTER 4

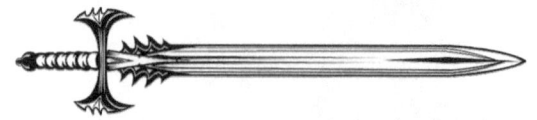

Blow, Wind, Blow

The sun passed over the hills to leave only night behind when Stek arrived at the cave where Vinan took his refuge. Vinan prepared himself to throw his spear at the approaching shadow but hesitated when he saw it was a boy. He then recognized the shape and the gait of his younger brother climbing up to their shared secret cave.

"Stek!" Vinan said, so enthusiastically that he almost broke his whisper.

The shadow recoiled and raised his spear to his shoulder. Vinan emerged from his hiding spot among the rocks and held his arms outstretched. The moon rested at half-circle, enough to illuminate him in a shining white aura.

"It's me, Stek!" he repeated in a loud whisper.

"Vinan," Stek answered in the same hushed voice. "You're alive!"

"Alive?" Vinan asked, puzzled. "What's happened?"

"Kror is High Warrior."

"Impossible."

"No, Vinan. Kror is High Warrior and you are marked for

death."

"How?"

"He came back to the village with the High Warrior and told everyone you killed him."

Stek proceeded to recount the events of Kror's return with the High Warrior's remains. When he spoke of what Kror had told him about Bheif and the hunt, nausea overwhelmed Vinan as the last hope of deliverance he held was taken from him. The final great law that he thought Kror might not transgress, kin-slaying, had been irrevocably violated.

Nothing left remained, that Kror would not destroy or taint.

"God of Warriors," Vinan breathed heavily. "Even father?"

"He was not lying," Stek said.

"No," Vinan agreed, shaking as ice tingled his spine, "I watched him kill the High Warrior. He would not stop there."

"We have to go back!" Stek said. "We have to go back and kill him!"

"No," Vinan said. "He'll just kill us both."

"We have to get Kirru!"

"Kirru is safe with me."

Stek was quiet a moment.

"Kirru is up in the cave," Vinan continued. "She doesn't know about any of this!"

He paused for a moment to think, and Stek stayed silent.

"We can't tell her," Vinan realized. "We can't tell her any of this."

"We can't let her go back!" Stek countered.

"No," Vinan agreed. "I will not let her near Kror. Never again."

Stek nodded, "I will help you protect her, even if it means killing Kror."

Vinan nodded and considered his options. He had to keep Stek away from Kror at all costs. He looked to the starlit silhouettes of the eastern hills from whence the sun would rise the

35

next morning, staring into the distance away from his home in the mountains and the entire world he had ever known in his short life. He considered that Kror had gone that way and lived to return. He pointed to the horizon, the black bumps of hills that were as unknown to him as his future.

"We leave for the eastern hills tomorrow," he said to Stek.

"But we don't know what is out there," Stek protested.

"We know what lies for us the other way," Vinan retorted. "Kror, his lies, and his outlander knife."

"But there are more knives in the outlands, and men carrying them."

"But none of them are our enemies."

Not yet, Vinan thought to himself. In his heart, he dreaded that some of Kror's words were true. A vast land that bore men of lies and their smooth knives filled him with fear for Kirru, for Stek, and for himself. It was still better than the other choices.

"If we stay here," he told Stek, "Kror will find us. We have to get as far from here as we can and take Kirru someplace where she will be safe from Kror."

Where you will be safe from Kror, Vinan thought. He knew that Stek would want to kill Kror as long as he had the chance to try it. A dead Stek could not protect Kirru.

"All right," Stek agreed. "We will go that way. I hope you know where we are going."

"I don't," Vinan said. "I only know we go that way towards the rising sun. We will find out where to go when we learn what's out there."

"Well, at least you'll have me to keep you from getting killed."

Vinan laughed quietly. Each joked constantly that they would protect or save the other one day. It occurred to Vinan that the time for it may come soon.

"We need to sleep," Vinan said. "We have a long day's journey tomorrow."

"You have food?" Stek asked.

"Only what I carried with me this morning, and three rabbits I killed and skinned. You?"

"I got some before I found you," Stek answered with satisfaction at his own foresight. "Dried meat, nuts, and seeds."

"Good," Vinan said. "That will help. The girl knows how to survive in the wilds, so maybe she knows something."

"The girl?"

It was then that Vinan realized he had never told his brother of the forest girl.

"There is a wild girl we found," he said. "She is with Kirru in the cave."

"You left Kirru with her?"

"The girl protected Kirru from a boar. Kirru is safe."

"Good. Because if she hurts Kirru I will kill her."

"I don't think she is who we need to protect Kirru from."

"Does she speak?"

"Not much. I don't think she can speak as we do."

"So, you know nothing about her."

"Only that, when we found her in the wilds, I saw her protect Kirru and Kirru thinks of her as a friend. That's good enough for me."

Stek paused for a moment then spoke at length. "If it's good enough for you then it's good enough for me."

"Let's go try to get some sleep," Vinan said as he turned back to climb the remainder of the slope. "Have you rested today?"

"If you are trying to get me to take the first watch," Stek replied, rolling his eyes, "I'll do it."

Vinan had yet to enter the cave and talk to Kirru since fleeing Kror. He had looked inside earlier to ensure the girls were still safe but he escaped their notice due to the cover of darkness. He could not face Kirru yet, not without knowing what to tell her or what he planned to do next. But that uncertainty had since dissipated.

He entered the cave to see a nervous and trembling Kirru clutching one of the spears behind the fire, and the girl of the forest standing beside her. Both girls relaxed when they saw it was Vinan, even if the girl of the forest looked past him to observe Stek.

"Vinan! Stek!" Kirru exclaimed. "You're back!"

"Yes," he said. "It took everyone a while to decide what to do with the girl."

"Can she live with us?" she asked with excitement overflowing. "Are we bringing her home?"

Vinan had done his best to prepare himself for this moment, and it still had not been enough. The sorrow bled through his expression and Kirru noticed.

"Kirru," he said, trying to look at her while ignoring the disappointed face of his sister, "We can't bring her back home."

"Why not?" she pleaded indignantly. "Why can't we bring her back?"

"Kirru..."

"It's not right!" She wailed. "She needs a home! We can't leave her out here!"

"Kirru! Listen!"

It was one of the few times Vinan had ever raised his voice in anger to his sister. It silenced her as effectively as it put him ill at ease.

"She doesn't belong with us," he said, his voice returning to softness. "She has a home out there, and we need to take her there."

"Can't we just make our home hers too?"

"The High Warrior won't allow it," Vinan omitted entirely that a new High Warrior had arisen. "We need to bring her to her home. The only thing we can do for her is bring her back to her people. Stek and I are leaving with her tomorrow."

"I'm coming with you!" she demanded, as if any doubt remained she would.

"Of course," Vinan said. "She trusts you. We need that trust."

"We are going to the outlands?" she asked with excitement. "Where Kror went?"

Kirru had only lived through two winters when Kror had departed. She had no memory of him in the time before the darkness and, it seemed, no idea of what he had become. Vinan resolved that she would never meet him again.

"Yes," he answered her. "We will find her home, wherever it is."

"It will be a journey!" she exclaimed, almost giggling. "It will be like in father's stories! When heroes go to the outlands and have adventures! We are going on an adventure!"

"Yes," he smiled. "It will be an adventure."

The questions from her came like a winter avalanche. Fear, excitement, and joy were all present in the quivering voice of the little girl who was unknowingly about to leave her home for the last time.

"What are the outlanders like? Are there really mountains of fire and a lake so big you can't see the other side? Are there monsters out there? Will I need to learn how to use these spears?"

"Kirru..." Vinan interrupted.

She fell silent for a brief moment, long enough for him to clasp her hands in his and look with confidence into her eyes.

"I will always be there to protect you," he promised, "from everything we will face."

At that moment, lightning cracked and illuminated the night sky. A sudden downpour covered the mountains in a torrent of spring rain. Vinan, after recovering from his shock, realized that Kirru trembled in Enna's arms. Vinan knew it was no use to convince the little girl that she was safe in the dry cave, so he began to sing an old song, a lullaby that his mother had once sung to him in the days when her arms covered him in embraces instead of striking him with blows.

Howls the wind in the nettles of the pines
What does it ask of me?
In loud and labored pains, it whines
If only it could speak to me
But all I hear are its pain in untold signs

Blow, wind, blow!
If only your words my ears could understand
If only I could know what you withstand
But I hear only your howls of pain
As they cry through the falling rain
So, blow, wind, blow!

Oh, child in the sky, who has made you cry?
Oh, maiden in the air, what great sorrow do you bear?
Oh, warrior of the winds, how great your wounds must be
That I can hear your cry break an ancient tree
Shout down the forest no more, come and speak to me

Blow, wind, blow!
If only your words my ears could understand
If only I could know what you withstand
But I hear only your howls of pain
As they cry through the falling rain
So, blow, wind, blow!

CHAPTER 5

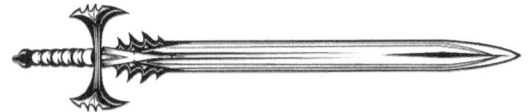

Outlanders

inan, Stek, Kirru, and the girl with eyes bright as stars left the home of the mountain clans and descended into the hilled forest. This land sprouted lush with fruits and teemed with game even more than the inhabited mountains that towered far above it. Vinan and Stek found plentiful rabbits, squirrels, and eggs from bird nests to feed themselves and the two girls with little difficulty. The girl of the forest, or "Enna" as Kirru named her, proved herself adept at discovering all sorts of roots, berries, and nuts to accompany the roasted meat obtained by the two boys. Kirru followed, talked to the girl, endured, and did not complain once. For this, both her brothers were both grateful and ashamed of their own constant gripes.

Vinan and Stek, who knew the true reason for their exile, forced themselves on with purpose. They had been driven from their home, their hopes shattered by a hideous and dark truth, and had watched the ideal of a warrior's virtue dismantled before their eyes. Everything they held dear had been taken from them violently only days ago.

Everything except their only sister. Their only sister who,

despite her smallness and seeming frailty, trudged ever onwards with even greater determination than them. It humbled them to see her so determined to bring "Enna" safely to her home, a home her brothers had fabricated in a desperate lie, even as they both pressed themselves to go on step by painful step.

The morning in the forest came with both the girls still safe and sleeping peacefully as cool dew sent from the gods above lay upon the leaves. Vinan rose and drank some of it before taking up his spear. He found Stek leaning against a tree, with his eyes carrying the signs of a long struggle to keep awake during his night watch.

"Did you see anything?" Vinan asked.

"No," said Stek, "just the forest."

"No wolves or great cats?"

"No. A few small cats too afraid to come near"

"Strange..." Vinan pondered.

"What?" Stek asked with a yawn.

"We have not seen a sign of wolves in days."

"Good."

"We have seen very few great cats or deer too."

"Good! We don't need deer for food. The rabbits, the fish, and the squirrels will be more than enough."

"But, Stek, listen," Vinan, slightly annoyed, raised his voice slightly. "Why are they not down here? The land is full of food for them."

"Maybe because the land beyond the mountains is cursed and only the wolves and great cats are smart enough to know that."

"Stek..."

"Why have our people never left the mountains?" Stek retorted. "Why is Kror the only one to do it and come back?!"

Vinan held his tongue for a minute. He saw Stek's face full of wrath, the pain of betrayal and hatred directed at a brother who he had been told was brave and kind, a brother Vinan had both loved and admired.

But that had been so long ago. Long ago in the days before Kror had ventured into these unknown lands and returned as an evil shade bringing back only lies and death.

"Stek..."

Vinan did not know what to tell him. In truth, he felt everything Stek did and perhaps more due to the love and respect he once carried for Kror. He had been there to see Kror commit murder and had been the one to suffer for it. He hated Kror for this and, though he did not wish to admit it to himself, wished for a chance to destroy him and his memory forever.

"I will kill him, Vinan!" Stek promised as he fought back his tears. "I will return one day and see everything made right!"

"We can't," Vinan replied with a shake of his head.

"How can you say that?!" Stek wept. "How can you not want to kill him after all he did to you?! To Kirru?!"

"I do want to kill him!" Vinan exclaimed.

This silenced Stek, so Vinan continued on more quietly and held nothing back.

"I want to break Kror's spear and drive his long grey knife through his black heart. Just as he did to the High Warrior. I want to push Dhof from the top of one of his tall trees and watch him fall to the ground and break his neck. I want to slay Yark the Fatherless and tell every warrior in the mountains the truth until it is sung for a hundred winters."

He now trembled uncontrollably and found himself unable to continue. Stek stepped back but remained silent. Vinan collected his nerves, took a deep breath, and regained control of his quivering voice.

"But we can't, Stek. We have Kirru to protect. We can't let anything hurt her!"

Stek nodded. "You're right. I'm sorry."

"Don't be. Get some rest."

"Are you hunting for morning food?"

"Don't worry!" Vinan finally found the ability to muster a

smile on his face. "I at least know how to catch and kill rabbits."

He ventured into the woods to find his prey and morning meal. The day was still young and he was fresh and ready for whatever it provided him in this hunt. Should the rabbits here elude his grasp, he would find eggs from a bird's nest. Though he had never mastered tree-jumping like the liar Dhof, he could climb one with ease when needed. Regardless of what the morning brought him, he would return to the others with food before long.

Vinan had gone some way when he noticed some unusually large prints on the soft forest ground and inspected them closer. He determined quickly that these were not the marks of deer, cats, or wolves. No, this was the size of a grown man's but shaped unlike any foot or shoe Vinan had ever seen. The shape rounded entirely at where the toes should have been and there appeared to be some sort of hoof-like mark in place of a heel. He studied it a while before inspecting others and observing that they were like the first set. He followed them.

They soon led him to a smoothed trail upon which he could see many prints, prints the size of men's shoes. Some were faint, perhaps weeks old, while others were perhaps as fresh as a day or two ago.

There were other men nearby, outlander men of whom he had no knowledge. Were they twisted as Kror? Had Kror learned his evil from their ways?

It did not matter. He had to return to Stek and warn him. He and the others would have to go on concealed from the eyes of these men. Perhaps there was nothing wicked about these outlanders, but Vinan was not yet willing to take that chance. He had to go back now even without any food.

A twig snapped behind him and he froze. Something jumped out from the brush behind him. He raised his spear and turned to face it.

Vinan looked to the clearing and saw the girl of the forest.

"*Vinan!*" she exclaimed, pointing frantically back at the way he had come. *"Kirru! Stek! Stek! Kirru!"*

Vinan looked down at her and saw fear, terror, and panic in her face as she tried to lead him back to the camp. She tugged furiously at his fur overcoat and he saw a large bruise on her face. Blood covered her hands and had burrowed under her long sharp nails.

But not her blood.

Vinan's heart stopped for a moment before reawakening with a fiery whirlwind of anger, pounding at the speed of a running deer. He gave himself into the pull of the girl and followed her through the woods. He held his spear ready and grasped it tight as he followed her through the growth of the forest. He had no sense of his own fatigue then, for his mind only focused on finding Kirru and Stek. He let the strange child of the forest lead him back the way he came.

Until she stopped without warning.

A man stood in their path, a tall and strong man. His body was as large as a thick tree, his arms and legs as wide around as the limbs of the oldest of the great oaks, his face scarred by the edges of many blades over many years, his hair cut so close to his scalp that Vinan could not determine its color, and his eyes were dark and pitiless. In his hand, he held a long shining grey knife like the one Kror possessed.

"Another one?" The man mused as he swung his long knife in the air.

Vinan pointed his spear, his rabbit-hunting spear, at the outlander before him. He positioned himself in a stance ready to strike.

"Listen, boy," the man said without concern. "I don't want to hurt you if I don't have to. Drop your spear and come with me."

"Go away, outlander!" Vinan shouted, attempting to sound in command. "I have no time for you!"

"I have no time for you, boy," the outlander shot back. "I have dealt with one like you already this day. It always ends the same, slavery for the mountain savages like you."

Slavery, Vinan thought to himself. That word again. What did Kror mean by it? What did this outlander mean by it?

Vinan worried for Stek and Kirru, fearing that perhaps Stek had been the other "one like him". Then he noticed the girl of the forest beside him, her face filled with hate, crouched on all fours like a forest cat prepared to pounce.

Horror overcame Vinan as he pieced it all together. Fear for Kirru and Stek overwhelmed him, sending tingling cold down his spine and filling his gut with fire. The urgency with which he intended to return to Stek and Kirru was greater than any he had ever felt in his life. Hate boiled within him and he directed it towards the outlander who stood in his path, between him and his two siblings.

The outlander smiled, doubtless noticing all this in Vinan's expression and stance.

"If you *ever* want to see your two little friends again," he said. "I suggest you come with me. Put down your spear."

He delivered this goading with all the iciness of a cold knife slipping into a throat, measured and calculated, to trick Vinan into revealing his attachments.

And it worked.

"So," the outlander grinned. "You do know the other two. Capturing them was so easy. The boy tried his best to fight but was no match for us."

The thought of the impulsive Stek fighting men twice his size filled Vinan with terror. Kror had let him live that one time, but would outlanders give the boy the same chance?

"The little girl, though," the outlander's eyes bored into Vinan's, "she cried so much that we had to strike her face to silence her."

It did not matter that Vinan knew exactly the man's gambit. He charged him anyway full of fury and bloodlust. He would kill the man before him. He would kill anyone who hurt Stek or Kirru.

46

The man welcomed Vinan's charge and swung his great knife. Vinan resisted his instinct to raise his spear to block the blow, instead ducking beneath the heavy blade and jabbing his spear point toward the man's lower body. His opponent had foreseen this though and stepped aside to avoid it. Vinan and the man, having both struck and missed, regained their footing.

They stood still with their eyes locked on each other. They circled each other with their weapons aloft. Each waiting for the other to give him an opening, each waiting for the other to attempt to strike, and each waiting for the other to let down his guard.

Vinan knew all the advantages were in the hands of his enemy. The man opposite him had the advantage of size, possessed a better weapon, and carried in his face a tale of many years of combat. A tale told by the mosaic of scars on his cheek, his forehead, his forearms, and even one across the front of his throat that must have almost killed him. Vinan knew he could not match a man who had waged such a battle with death and still lived. When he locked eyes with his enemy, the icy ruthlessness of death within the dark orbs struck Vinan with indescribable terror.

It was the same soulless evil that glared in the eyes of Kror and Yark the Fatherless.

As fate would have it, neither Vinan nor his unknown enemy would be the first to strike. The man with the long knife yelled in pain and Vinan looked down and saw the strange girl biting viciously at his exposed calf. Her eyes burned furiously like the white fires the gods used to forge the earth when all had been but darkness.

Vinan did not waste this chance. He leapt and stabbed again, and this time his spear made contact with the man's body. The tip sunk into the shoulder of the arm in which the man held his great knife and Vinan pulled it out so his enemy could bleed and he could strike again.

But he would not be given that opportunity.

"GAAAAHHH!" yelled the frenzied outlander. "Forest demons! Die all of you!!!"

The wounded man violently shook the girl off his leg and then kicked her in the face. For the first time, Vinan saw the girl cry in pain as she held her hands to her bleeding mouth. But he had no time to attend to her. With the man's main arm unable to swing his great knife, he threw it aside and charged Vinan like a great boar. Vinan raised his spear to jab again, but the man proved too swift. His large body crashed into Vinan's and pinned the boy to a tree.

Vinan yelled in pain and dropped his spear as the bark dug into his back and the bulky frame crushed his stomach. The man backed away one step and smashed his fist into Vinan's face. Vinan tasted blood in his mouth and smelled it everywhere as he felt it dripping from his nose. The world went black, his mind went numb, and a painful sleep began to overtake him as he surrendered himself to his inevitable defeat.

"I had thought of taking you alive as a slave," the outlander panted, "but now I think I'll just kill you here."

He unsheathed a small knife from his belt, a straight dagger made of the same shining grey material as the larger knife and held Vinan by the hair. The boy was too exhausted and beaten to fight back and could only stand there meekly with his throat exposed. Despite all his desire to fight on, Vinan had no strength at this moment to oppose his imminent slaughter.

And then the arm of the outlander froze midair. Try as he did to move it and the knife it held, he could not. He cursed with anger.

The girl of the forest stood behind him, her arm outstretched. The mysterious blue aura surrounded her again. Her face stared with resolve at Vinan and the outlander as a stream of blood streamed down her mouth where she had been struck. She focused with everything she had to hold the knife-bearing arm of the outlander in place.

"What?" the outlander screeched in terror. "What is this sorcery?!"

"*Vinan!*" the girl shouted.

Vinan found the strength and will to break free. He drew his own stone knife from his belt and plunged it into the outlander's belly. He slid the blade to the side until it came out of the man's torso with a clean slice.

All at once the man fell to the ground choking on his blood, the girl's blue aura dissipated as she fell to her knees exhausted, and Vinan realized he had killed his first man. He had always thought that if the day came when he needed to slay a man it would be as easy as killing a rabbit or boar. He had been gravely mistaken. Nausea and exhaustion overcame him at last and he fell to the ground. The thought of the terror-stricken faces of Kirru and Stek were the last phantoms that flashed through his fevered imagination before the embrace of darkness.

CHAPTER 6

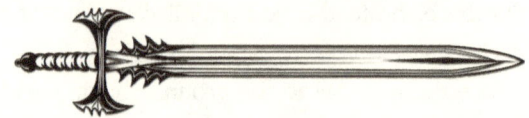

Resolve of the Defeated

Vinan opened his eyes to a shining blue light. The girl of the forest sat beside him bathed in the aura of mystic blue once more, her hand resting on his head. When he came to, the girl slowly removed her hand and the light faded. His eyes beheld now only the blackness of the cave. They adjusted to the darkness quickly, taking in what they could just as his awakening mind followed suit.

Night had fallen over the land. The entrance to this cave was ten paces from Vinan and only slivers of starlight from outside allowed him to determine this. Only one other shadow cast itself in the cave, the shadow of the forest girl.

Kirru and Stek were nowhere to be seen.

He knew well the deadliness of the night, the time when wolves prowled in the shadows. He knew that even the strongest warriors in any clan lacked the ability to fight a pack in the darkness. If he emerged from the cave to expose himself, the chance that he would be torn apart and eaten by the beasts of the night would be high indeed.

But Kirru and Stek, dead or alive, were outside the safety of this cave. Outside, where the flesh-eating wolves prowled with impunity.

He rushed out of the cave, mindless of the perils of the night. The full moon illuminated the forest with a pale glow amid the deep blue sky of the early dawn. Vinan looked around and could only find the trees, the moon, the stars, and the shapes of the bushes. Neither man nor vicious beast could his eyes observe, and his ears only heard the nightly chirping of the mating insects. He did not recognize this place and no clear path showed itself despite the high season of the moon.

The girl of the forest walked up beside him and pointed.

"*Vinan*," she said, pointing and walking past him with purpose. "*Kirru, Stek!*"

Vinan followed her. He followed through the moonlit forest and back to the camp from the morning, where last he left his brother and sister.

No one remained at the camp. The remnants of the previous night's fire were scattered throughout. Stek's furs, torn and sliced, lay on the ground. Three spears were broken and another was in the dirt unused. Stek's stone knife had been discarded nearby like the bones of a devoured rabbit.

But of Stek or Kirru there was no living sign.

I have dealt with one of you already this day! The outlander had told him.

So, you do know the other two! He had jeered.

The boy tried his best but was no match for us! He had gloated.

Now it was clear what the man had meant before his death. Never in his life had Vinan hated anyone with such intensity and fury. The outlander he had slain was surely just one of a race of demons.

Kror had been right about the outlanders all along. He knew what they were and that they needed to be defeated with spears and knives. He had perhaps been right to return home and incite his people to war against these monsters. And yet, knowing all this, Kror had sent his siblings into this cruel land among these cruel people.

Vinan, overwhelmed by his solitude at that moment, fell to his knees. He wept over the wickedness of the outlanders, the betrayal of his brother panged his gut, and the loss of Kirru and Stek devastated what remained of his spirit. The weight of his failure crushed him like the cascade of a mountain rockslide.

The tears flowed as the voices of Kror and his mother rang in his head. Even now, he imagined the opposing forces of Kror and his mother standing over him

Kror's smile cut him down. *You are still only a cowering little boy afraid of all that our mother has made you fear.*

You are no warrior! You will never be the warrior my father was! Screamed back the ghostly howl of the High Priestess.

I came back to free our people from that which holds them back, Kror said with a contrasting calm, *to free you from the oppression you never chose. But you are unworthy of it.*

Unworthy indeed.

Unworthy of becoming a warrior.

Unworthy of protecting anyone.

The memory of his broken promise to Kirru struck him harder than the bloody blows of the outlander.

I will always be there to protect you, he had told her, *from anything we will face.*

And yet here he wept, in a forest over the remnants of his last camp. Kirru had been taken far away if she was even still alive. Stek had tried his best to protect her and failed. Maybe he still lived, maybe not. Nothing remained certain anymore, nothing except the fact that if Vinan did not rescue the two of them, no one would.

And yet here he knelt, weeping like a lost child while Kirru and Stek needed his help. No greater warrior would guide him, no one to run to for help this time, no band of warriors to call upon to save his skin. Him, his knife, the one unbroken spear that still lay on the ground, and the strange girl of the forest to whom he could barely communicate...

It would have to be enough.

The girl of the forest stood a ways off, looking back at him and pointing towards the trees. Vinan wiped his eyes and arose to his feet, ashamed further that, unlike him, she had not lost sight of their purpose. He collected the spear and Stek's knife, assuming that more weapons were better than fewer. Ready as ever he would be to pursue Stek's and Kirru's captors, he pushed aside all thoughts of the smirking Kror in his mind. His resolve and purpose seemed weak and wavering compared to that of the warriors of myth and legends but it drove him forward all the same. Perhaps he could never aspire to the heights of the heroes of legend, but that mattered no more and seemed a flippant concern now. What mattered was that he would be the one to chase the men who had taken Kirru and Stek. He would be the one who would deliver them from the clutches of the outlanders.

He would have to be enough.

"*Vinan!*" sang the voice both familiar and musical with otherworldly beauty.

Vinan walked to the girl, Enna was her name, and understood that several sets of tracks led in the direction she was leading him. This had to be the way to Stek and Kirru.

"*Stek! Kirru!*" Enna looked to Vinan with pleading on her face.

"Yes, Enna," said Vinan. "Stek and Kirru. Let's go!"

He ran down the trail, trusting that Enna could keep pace with him. If she could heal wounds, restore strength to the weary, and project objects with her mind, what other surprises did she possess waiting to be used at the needed moment? His only remaining ally and he could not imagine a better one. He believed the gods had sent her to aid him.

She would have to be enough.

They ran into the night, pursuing the outlanders who had spirited Stek and Kirru away. Vinan would keep his promise to Kirru. While he still breathed, he would fight to protect her and Stek. He would save them, or he would die in the attempt.

For that was the only path left to him.

PART 2

The Swordsman and the Sage

CHAPTER 7

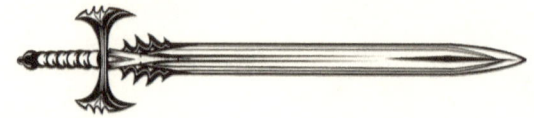

The Shai of Kodumaa

Night descended upon the hills. Another day passed with Vinan and Enna pursuing the slavers. Another day and still they had not caught up to the captors of Stek and Kirru.

They swiftly followed the tracks until they led to a worn dirt path. The path cut through the forest like the slit mark of a knife blade on skin; trampled upon by the feet of men, the hooves of animals, and straight groove lines that made Vinan wonder if there were strange snakes in these hills and lowlands. Vinan followed Enna down the dirt path and she continued to lead him onwards as if she knew exactly where she was going. For two days they chased the captors down the path, pausing only for food, water, and a few hours rest in the night some distance away from the path.

For two days they followed thus, with little sign of gaining ground on the men they followed. As with the previous night, Vinan and Enna diverted from the path during the rapid approach of dusk to find a place to rest. Clearings became more common now and the undergrowth of the forest less thick. Tree stumps cut as if by blade rested intermittently among the thick trees of the rest of the forest.

And the howls of the wolves grew more distant with each passing night, their shadows among the trees no longer present or a worry to Vinan. What he hunted now was far more dangerous than the wolves and had taken more from him than those animals ever had.

Vinan went to the usual task of lighting a fire with his flint, twigs, and dried plants while Enna left again to pick the wild berries. How she found them so easily and quickly was unknown to Vinan, but he was glad she did. She always brought far more than he knew he was capable of and it was not a task he had ever enjoyed.

The fire soon sparked to life and Vinan roasted a squirrel from a quick morning hunt. The girl returned carrying large round, green-skinned fruit that Vinan had never seen before. He followed her example by biting into it directly and found it to be far harder than berries, with the fibers of the fruit resisting the chewing of his teeth. Mild sweetness and tartness made the fruit pleasant to the taste and complemented the unusually fat squirrel. It would be enough food for the night; enough to carry on tomorrow.

The sounds of steps in the darkness put an immediate end to Vinan's thoughts of sleep. He listened and quickly realized they were the steps of a man. He grabbed his spear and ducked into the darkness. He crouched behind a tree and readied himself for anyone or anything that would approach his camp.

But Enna strangely did not move, nor did she betray any fear or concern.

The stranger soon entered the light of the fire, a well-built man with a strong square jaw. He was old enough to have passed on from youth but not so old for his age to decrease his strength. His hair, though browned with wear and beginning to gray, still had enough of the golden yellow from its younger days that it could be noticed even in the faint campfire light. It was long, but tied in a tail behind the man's scalp so it would not flow freely. A roughly trimmed and red-tinted beard covered his face.

He was dressed similarly to the other outlanders Vinan had fought but with clothes of far more sturdy quality. The hides that covered his legs and torso were cut and crafted with more mastery than Vinan imagined possible: seemingly soft yet sturdy and unlikely to wear easily. A cape covered his body down to his knees, doubtless providing a cover from cold winds. His shoes, though faded and covered in dust, were black and came almost to his knees.

And in his belt, he carried a long knife of his own, the largest Vinan had seen yet. It had a handle so smooth Vinan could almost imagine how it felt without laying a hand on it. The grey material on it reflected so clearly the lights of the stars and the fire that Vinan could not help but stare and wonder what the blade looked like inside its leather skin.

The outlander sat by the fire next to Enna and began to warm himself.

"Hello, little one," he said. "Is this your fire?"

Enna just stared speechless at the outlander with her luminous white eyes glowing at him. She warmed herself beside the stranger with what Vinan thought was surprising peace.

"Speak you a tongue of men?" the outlander asked her.

Enna cast her head down and did not answer.

"I see," the stranger sighed. "It was too great a thing for which to hope. Perhaps you should tell your friend he can come out and stop his hiding."

Vinan froze where he stood. How did the outlander know he was hiding here? Did he know or was he just using a trick to lure any possible attackers out?

Then the man turned his head straight to Vinan.

"If I wished you dead," the outlander declared, "I would have made you so already. Come out, friend. I do not long remain friends with those who think they can point a spear at my back."

Vinan emerged from the shadows; his spear raised.

"Why do you call me friend?" he asked. "I know you not."

"You do not trust easily, En'Shai," said the outlander. "Good. That will protect you in these savage lands. Sit by the fire if you want to stay warm. Stand there with spear pointed at me if not."

"The last outlanders I met," Vinan replied, "tried to kill me."

"Worse," answered the outlander, "they took someone from you."

"How-" Vinan raised his spear ready to strike. "How do you know that?"

"It shines in your eyes, En'Shai," the man answered. "It is written in your face and it is sung in the feared trembling of your voice. Some men took someone dear to you, and you are chasing those men. Who was it they took from you?"

"My brother," Vinan answered with a croak, "and my sister. They took them and are carrying them down the path."

"Down the road and to the settlement where the three rivers merge," the outlander said. "The slavers will take them first there, and then to Qiriq."

"Qiriq?"

"A rotten place of filth and slavery," the man replied. "It is the center of slavery in these western lands."

"I don't care what the place is," Vinan said. "I will follow them there if it means getting Stek and Kirru back."

"I believe you, En'Shai," the man nodded. "I believe you."

He reached into one of his pouches and pulled out a strip of dried meat. He chewed it, seeming not to care that Vinan stood only feet from him with his spear still raised aloft. Vinan watched the man's hands and ensured that they did not go anywhere near the long knife that hung from his belt.

"The sword interests you, En'Shai?" asked the man.

"Sword..." Vinan repeated slowly.

The man's left hand slid down to the handle.

"It is a masterwork and among the best of its kind," he said.

"There is no shame in you wanting to look at it."

"Sword," Vinan repeated. "That is what these things are named?"

The man looked surprised. "You have never seen one before today, En'Shai?"

"No," Vinan answered, remembering Kror, "I have seen others like it, and I have seen the pain they bring."

"The sword brings no pain, En'Shai," scoffed the man. "It is but a soulless weapon."

"My brother returned to my people with one," Vinan shot back. "Nothing but evil came with it and my people became like beasts."

"Then they were already like beasts and held darkness in their hearts."

Vinan bit his tongue. Not only did he want to further hear what the outlander had to say, but he was still too wary of the man to let his guard down in an impassioned argument. He listened attentively as the man continued.

"The sword brings no pain," repeated the outlander. "Only the man who carries it can do that. In the hands of a good man, it is but a tool to defend both that man and those he loves. In the hands of a wicked one, many innocent suffer and perish."

The man rose to his feet and turned to Vinan. The boy remained trained on him, looking for any sign of an incoming attack.

"If you wish to save your brethren from the slavers," the outlander said, "you will need a weapon that can match theirs. That primitive spear will break the moment a sword strikes it."

The man looked into Vinan's eyes.

"But you know that already," he said.

He pulled back his cape slowly, his eyes moving between Vinan's eyes and the tip of the boy's spear, to reveal a second smaller sword on the right side of his belt. He unlatched the sheathed weapon and offered it to Vinan hilt-first.

"Take it," he said. "You will need it when the time comes."

Vinan warily grasped the handle with his left hand and pulled the blade out as he had seen Kror do. The soft sliding of metal against leather heralded the unsheathing of a weapon of silver hue. It rested light in Vinan's hand, far lighter than he had expected. He moved it around in the air slowly and examined it. He understood now why the outlanders were so fond of the weapon. So simple, so easy, and so deadly.

Perhaps it would be wise to take one if it meant he could use it against the slavers.

Vinan held the sword in his hand for a few moments and nodded with reluctance. The outlander tossed the sheath to him.

"I took it from a man who tried to rob me," he told Vinan. "I hope you make better use of it than he did, I will help you learn to master it."

"You will help me?!" Vinan asked with surprise and skepticism.

"Perilous is the way for you two alone," the man answered. "Full is the land of men who would hurt both of you."

"Yes," Vinan agreed, staring back at the man. "The land is full of evil men."

"Is it always your way, En'Shai," the man asked, "to threaten men with the gifts they have given you?"

Vinan looked at the sword in his own hand with some embarrassment.

"Why would you help me?" Vinan pressed.

"Why does the girl help you?" the outlander retorted. "Why does anyone help anyone in this world full of lies and betrayal?"

Silence hung over the camp for a moment, punctuated only by the crackling of the fire which the girl continued to feed with twigs.

"I will help you, En'Shai," the outlander said, "because it is right to help those in need. I will help you because long ago no one helped me."

61

Vinan quietly assented and lowered his weapons, both the old and the new. He took up the sheath and latched it to his belt. He slid the sword into it and found satisfaction from how naturally the two items had been made for each other.

The boy, the girl, and the outlander sat around the fire amidst the towering shadows of the trees. The man chewed on dried meat from his pouch and took a drink from his flask. He offered it to Vinan.

"Drink only a little, En'Shai," he said. "It quiets the ghosts that haunt your dreams and it stills the mind for sleep. But drink too much and you will sleep too long, so be careful."

With hesitation, Vinan drank from the pouch and forced the burning liquid down his throat. Uneasiness took hold of his stomach as it went down, and very quickly his mind began to sedate itself and a gentle numbness took hold. He drifted ever closer to sleep as his muscles relaxed and the fire of battle left his bones.

But the ghosts remained. The voices of a captive Stek and Kirru, if anything, screamed louder for Vinan to save them as he collapsed into a dazed and dreamless sleep.

CHAPTER 8

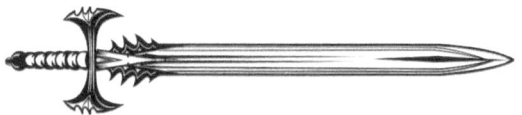

Lessons through Bruises

The morning came with the deep blue sky of early dawn. Vinan awoke with a slight throb in his head unlike any he had ever felt. He forced his limbs to move and his body to stand erect, rising to meet the new day. Another day to relentlessly pursue the captors of his brother and sister.

He took a drink from his water pouch. His head began to clear as he took in the daylight and his surroundings. He remained at the same site of the camp where the outlander and Enna had been the night before. The embers of the fire were long dead and cold, leaving behind only a pile of ashes. The outlander had awakened and was currently rolling up his blanket. He took notice of Vinan's rising in stride.

"So, En'Shai," he said, "you also are disciplined to rise with the sun."

"Is there any other time to awaken?" Vinan asked.

"Not when a man has someone to follow, no," replied the outlander.

Vinan ensured that all he needed was on him and was ready to go. The outlander folded up his blanket into a small square and put it in a small sack that was slung over his shoulder.

"I should thank you," Vinan said.

"You are right to do so," the outlander replied, "but I need no thanks. It is only fitting that I do something worthy of the sword I carry, for once."

"Have you a name?" Vinan asked, realizing he did not know the man's own.

"Does it matter, En'Shai?" the outlander replied.

"I would like to know who you are."

"You need not my name," the outlander said as he walked back to the path. "All who know my name are long dead."

"Then what do I call you?" Vinan pressed as he followed the man.

"Has the girl a name?"

"Enna. Her name is Enna."

"Is it? She told you this?"

"It is her name," Vinan insisted.

"Very well, En'Shai. Then Enna is her name. You are the one who knows more of strange, white-eyed girls of the forest."

"Wait," Vinan realized, "are you saying there are no others like her in the outlands?"

"En'Shai," the swordsman answered, "for many years I have travelled the world. I have seen deserts so hot they can roast a man alive, lands of ice where no creature or plant can live, mountains that spew fire and black smoke, and blood-stained cities built by ancient men who worshipped strange demons. And yet, in all this, I have never seen anyone like this girl. There are some things in this life that we cannot understand and never will. I am still mystified that your tongue is so close to that of the civilized men in this region."

Vinan followed the outlander quietly for a while until they made it back to the path. All the while, he wondered where Enna was.

Until his outlander companion stopped suddenly.

64

"Your friend Enna awaits us," he said.

There she stood in the middle of the path, like a specter, looking down the way the slavers had gone with their catch. Her pure, white eyes glowed ahead of them like bright stars in the near darkness of the early morning. She waited for Vinan and the outlander to approach her and, when they did, she pointed down the road.

"*Kirru*," she said. "*Stek*."

"Yes, Enna," Vinan said. "We will get Kirru and Stek back. I promise."

The outlander tapped him on the shoulder to offer a piece of dried meat. "You will need this if you intend to catch them, En'Shai."

Vinan accepted the strip and bit into its tough meat with savor. "Thank you."

"Thank my horse for dying of exhaustion and being only good for meat," said the outlander.

"Horse?"

"An animal of which you should pray the slavers don't have many. Let us go."

He strode forward a few steps ahead of Vinan and Enna before stopping.

"En'Shai," he said, "if you wish to call me by a name then call me Shai. I will help you save your people, so I ask that you honor the memory of mine."

"Understood," Vinan nodded. "Then let's go, Shai."

For that entire day, the three traveled swiftly through the woods, the swordsman leading the way without hesitation. Vinan, though battered by his last fight and having far shorter legs than his new companion, had little trouble following. The ground in this forest proved far less treacherous without all the rocks and slopes of the high mountains that Vinan only days ago had called his home. The girl likewise showed little sign of tiring and continued on, ever hunched over and twitching like an anxious and wary animal.

There were few rests taken by any of them. The swordsman moved rapidly and only stopped for moments at a time to drink from his water sack. Vinan kept pace and did the same, though the sword that hung at his side proved a small annoyance through the trek. The girl came and went as she pleased, running off and returning with berries she devoured as she rejoined Vinan and the swordsman.

The sun had almost set, leaving only an orange light among the trees, when the swordsman stopped.

"This is far enough, En'Shai."

"No," Vinan answered with agitation. "I don't need to stop yet!"

The swordsman remained unmoved. "We must make camp before the night falls."

"We must go until we catch them!" Vinan shouted as he moved to walk past.

"And we will, En'Shai," said the swordsman as his hand clasped Vinan's shoulder, "but not this night."

"We need to go," Vinan protested. "We need to gain ground while they rest."

"They must have set up camp a while ago, En'Shai. We have pressed on two or more hours after."

Vinan could argue no further, and the swordsman's grip on his shoulder may have played a part in that. He relaxed and turned to the swordsman.

"Then let's set up camp and rest," he agreed.

The swordsman nodded. "Find some wood, En'Shai. We will need a fire to keep away any beasts."

Vinan threw himself into the task with fervor. The sun had still not yet set by the time he had found enough brush, twigs, and branches to start the fire. The swordsman took two black fire rocks out of a pouch and scraped them together until their sparks ignited the pile that Vinan had assembled.

The girl approached Vinan with her hands full of blackberries and offered them to him. Vinan looked at the lush fruit for a moment and accepted them.

"The girl seems a blessing to you, En'Shai," said the outlander.

"Before I met you," Vinan answered with his mouth full, "she was all I had left."

"Be grateful, then," the swordsman said. "Some men have only their wits and their sword upon which to rely in this cruel world. Fortune has blessed you that you should be aided thus."

"If this is fortune's blessing," Vinan asked, "then what is it like to feel her curse?"

"To lose your entire land and be driven into the wilderness. To have no friend to comfort you, no ally to aid you, and no means to ever fulfill your vengeance."

"What of being driven from your home by your faithless brother, and then losing your sister and your brother because you could not protect them?"

"You will save Kirru and Stek, En'Shai," answered the man. "You will save them because you have what my people once called Pneu'Shaii, the soul of the warrior. I see it in you as you walk yourself to near exhaustion."

"You see nothing in me," Vinan retorted. "I could not save them without help. It's as my mother always said. I am but a weak and scared rabbit-hunter, unworthy to ever be a warrior."

"Then your mother is a fool, En'Shai, and you are as great a fool," the swordsman scoffed with disgust. "I see a boy before me with the courage of a hero, if only he could not fear his own shadow."

"Then you are blind and know nothing of me," Vinan mumbled.

He sullenly reached for his pouch full of dried meat, but suddenly received a sharp kick in the side. He voiced his pain momentarily and Enna gasped with shock. He held his stomach and rolled on his back while trying to suppress voicing his pain any further. The swordsman's boot pressed down on his chest.

"No, En'Shai. You will have your chance to eat. Now you must fight for your food."

"What?!" Vinan groaned defiantly through gritted teeth. "Get your foot off me!"

"If you wish to save your brother and sister," said the swordsman, "then I must prepare you for it. As it is, you are still far from ready..."

He lifted his boot off the boy and backed away two steps. "... Far from ready."

"Get up, En'Shai!" he commanded, drawing his sword from his leather sheath. "Get up and fight for your right to eat! If you want to save your brother and sister then you should learn to use your sword now."

Vinan pressed his palms upon the dirt, dug his fingers into the ground angrily, and pushed down to lift himself to his feet. With little grace or skill, he drew his small sword from its leather scabbard. He stood in defiance to the swordsman for a moment and then transferred the sword to his left hand. He looked around frantically to try to find his spear.

At that moment, the swordsman struck. He lurched forward with the speed of a fleeing deer and his blade came swinging down towards Vinan's skull. In desperation, the boy lifted his own sword above his head. He clutched it with both his hands and exerted all the strength he could muster to keep his opponent's sword back.

"Your first mistake, En'Shai, is that you must never underestimate the weapon you possess in favor of a weapon you do not possess."

The pressure bearing down on Vinan's blade did not cease, so the two of them remained with their swords locked in position.

"Your second mistake, En'Shai," the swordsman continued, "is that you must never take your eyes away from your enemies."

At that moment Vinan realized the lesson. The swordsman

68

was teaching him in a painful manner unlikely to be forgotten. Certainty rose in him, the certainty that he would never make these mistakes again. He could not...

"And your third mistake, En'Shai..."

His knee slammed into Vinan's exposed stomach. As the boy sought to regain his wind and footing, the swordsman gave a restrained blow with the palm of his hand to send him falling to the ground.

"...is that you should never forget that you are in a battle!"

With a new determination, Vinan jumped immediately to his feet. He finally saw where his spear lay on the ground and knew that he had to reach it. Even though the swordsman stood between them, he had to reach it.

Seeking to imitate the swordsman, he lifted his own sword and held it straight ahead at his opponent. He readied himself to fight on these terms. He had no choice.

The swordsman recognized Vinan's renewed spirit and prepared himself. He held his sword sideways at the height of his head, planting his feet flat on the ground with his knees bent. Vinan guessed this to be a ready position, a defensive stance to prepare for any attack that could come. Vinan chose to give the swordsman his attack.

Vinan jumped forward with a feint and swung the sword. He stopped halfway with the blade directly before him as the swordsman stepped aside to ready a counterstrike. Vinan pulled his sword back, rushed, and swung. The swordsman's blade met Vinan's mid-swing and brushed it aside. Vinan now saw that the path to his spear was open, and so he ran towards it.

A forceful strike from the side sent him crashing to the dirt. The voice of the swordsman was all the boy could hear as he pulled himself up.

"Never accept bait, En'Shai! I left that opening so you could take it. It is the first trick most fighters learn."

Vinan ignored the sting of the berating and lifted his sword again. He positioned it forward, locked eyes on the swordsman, and began to step to the side. The swordsman followed his every move with his sword poised similarly. The two stood circling, each barely out of reach with the blades hovering less than an arm's length apart.

"You want your spear, En'Shai?"

Vinan did not move.

"Then take it. I will give it to you freely this once."

The swordsman stepped back and left the way to the spear open. Vinan kept his sword up and sidestepped slowly towards the weapon, never taking his eyes from the swordsman. He reached the spear and, to his surprise, the swordsman let him reach for it without making a move. Vinan repositioned himself with his sword in his right hand and spear in his left and began another attack.

He led with his spear, positioning it as if to throw, yet holding on to it tightly. The swordsman stepped out of the way and swung his sword back for a counterattack. Vinan pulled his spear back, changed his footing, and brought his sword up to block his opponent's. Cold steel clanged as their blades clashed midair.

This was the opportunity Vinan had been waiting for and he did not waste it. He thrust his spear forward, straight at the stomach of his opponent.

But the swordsman gracefully and quickly stepped aside while disengaging his blade. Vinan fell forward to the ground. Before he could recover, he felt the swordsman's boot flat on his back pressing his body into the earth.

"I knew the spear would do you little good, En'Shai. Unfocused determination will not be enough to save the ones you love and neither will it put more weapons in your hands. Only skill learned through pain can do that."

The boot was removed from the boy's back.

"You may eat now. My lesson tonight is finished."

Vinan pulled himself to his feet and sauntered back to the encampment. Despite the pain and the bruises, Vinan could not let the lesson go un-thanked.

"Thank you."

The swordsman turned, a faint smile cracking through his lips for the first time, and nodded to Vinan.

"You learned, En'Shai. That is thanks enough."

The night wore on as the cracking of the fire intensified. Neither Vinan nor the swordsman cooked anything upon it, choosing instead to eat the dried meats from their pouches. The fire would instead serve to warm and drive away whatever creatures prowled about in the unfamiliar darkness. Enna sat close by, ate berries, and watched it intently until she fell asleep.

Vinan spent a while rubbing his bruises and gnawing on the dried meat before he spoke to the swordsman again.

"How much longer must we go through this forest?"

"Three days, En'Shai."

"Then comes the green treeless lands?"

"Not treeless, cleared flatland for farms"

"Farms?"

"Where men have cleared the forest to grow food."

"But the forest already gives food."

"Not enough for those in cities."

"Cities?"

The swordsman paused, realizing how little the boy he accompanied knew of the world.

"Have you villages where you are from, En'Shai?" he asked.

"Yes," Vinan answered.

"Well then," said the swordsman, "a city is a great village with many more people. We are going to Qiriq, the only large city on this side of the grasslands."

"Are there more cities beyond the grasslands?"

"Yes, En'Shai," said the swordsman with a somber voice. "My home once had many."

The weight with which the swordsman said this convinced Vinan to ask him no more about it. There was a sorrow and anger in the man's voice that Vinan perceived, but for which he dared not reach. Instead, Vinan slowly ate the meat from his pouch and tried to rest.

Though he had walked all day, his legs were not what hurt most. His pride and confidence that he could defeat the captors himself had been destroyed. What remained was determination, determination to match his new companion and teacher in combat. Until he could fight back with skill, he could not save Kirru and Stek.

And with these thoughts still swirling in his mind, Vinan's exhaustion overcame his anxiety to take him into the sweet embrace of a deep sleep.

***

There were no words exchanged at dawn as the three continued their trek. Vinan was awakened by a slight kick from the swordsman's boot then greeted with another handful of forest berries from Enna. This time Vinan took a few, shoved them into his mouth, and pulled himself up from the ground. He had no time to waste fighting off the morning weariness. Kirru and Stek were still far from being found and the swordsman was already beginning to leave. Vinan strode after him hurriedly and the girl followed.

The swordsman marched onwards as the sky turned from black to dark blue, then to blood red and bright yellow, and finally to true daylight. Vinan and the girl silently kept pace without a mumble or whimper. When morning hunger took hold of the boy, he fumbled in his bag to find some of his dry meat and ate a piece—all the while without even pausing a moment. If the swordsman did not stop, then neither would Vinan. Not until Kirru and Stek were with him again and safe.

The swordsman stopped around mid-morning to drink from his water sack. Vinan took the opportunity to sit a moment and do the same. His spirits were refreshed and his strength replenished as he saw the sunlight between the trees illuminate the forest with a beauty that calmed him for a few moments. It was little respite while his brother and sister still needed his rescue, but it was the first he had enjoyed in several days.

Vinan saw the girl looking at his water sack with pleading on her face. It had not occurred to him until now that she too needed water and did not have a sack of her own, so he gave her some of his. She gulped much of it down without pause.

The speechlessness among the three was broken by the swordsman.

"When she finishes, En'Shai, we will continue. We cannot be far from the main road, and from there we will reach the river and much more water."

Vinan nodded. He took back his water and slung it over his shoulder when the girl gratefully handed it back to him. He stood up again and walked to the swordsman.

"Let's go."

It was not long before they came across a dirt path even smoother than the last Vinan had seen. Brown earth cut through the green forest and in it many prints of hooves and lines continued to bewilder him. Hooves, even unusual ones, were something he knew well from the elk and deer, but these straight lines without end were still inexplicable to him. What creature could leave such a mark? Were these the tracks of some strange sort of snake that could leave such heavy grooves in the dirt? Who could say? Perhaps it was best to ask the swordsman, who was already on his knees inspecting the trail.

"Look, En'Shai. Seven to eight mounted men passed through here this morning. I believe they are the ones we seek."

Vinan got on his knees and looked to where the swordsman pointed. Though the tracks were fresh enough to be from that morning, they looked like hooves to him.

"Men on horses?" he asked.

"Yes, En'Shai. They have a wagon as well, which is likely where Stek, Kirru, and any other captives are kept."

He pointed to the grooves that Vinan had noticed before. The boy saw no point yet in asking about this "wagon" and chose instead to rise to his feet.

"Then we need to move now," he said. "We are close."

"Yes, En'Shai," the swordsman said as he stood up, "and they will stop before long. There is a village some miles down the river where they will water their horses and sleep. We can overcome whoever is left to watch the slave carts and then your brother and sister will be free."

Vinan found himself ready to continue on with all haste as a new excitement filled and drove him. He looked back to the girl and saw—to his surprise—that she was hiding behind a tree by the side of the path. He motioned for her to come out. She shook her head violently. Vinan motioned again, but more earnestly. The girl, unmoved, continued to resist.

"Come!" he pleaded

"*No!*" she answered.

Vinan stood as still as if he had seen the dead High Warrior approach him.

"What is it, En'Shai?"

The voice of the swordsman was enough to snap Vinan out of his shock, but not enough to allow him to speak clearly.

"Th-The g-girl... she speaks!"

"Well, En'Shai, she is a girl. And she does possess a tongue."

"That's not what I meant," Vinan protested. "This is the first time she has said anything except names."

"She understands your speech it would seem," the swordsman retorted. "Curious indeed."

The girl moved before the other two heard what approached them. She cocked her head to the side and her face was overcome with terror.

"*No!*" her voice cracked, filled with terror. "*No! No!*"

She slunk back into the forest just as Vinan heard the swift approach of hooved beasts. The swordsman planted his feet in the road and placed his hand upon his sword's hilt. As he stood waiting with the stoic look of death in his eyes, he appeared as Vinan had always imagined the God of Warriors would look if he were to take flesh. The boy took his position behind the swordsman and kept his spear ready, not prepared to draw his sword just yet.

Three men came into sight, three men sitting on the backs of large, long-faced beasts. The hooves of the beasts trampled upon the dirt with the sound of thunder as they approached, and their speed was such that Vinan guessed that he would be trampled where he stood. Yet, the swordsman did not move and kept his hand on the handle of his sword.

The three men pulled back on leather straps they held in their hands and their animals stopped short of Vinan and the swordsman. All three wore clothing like Vinan had seen on the swordsman and the slavers, and they too carried swords on their belts. The first man, raven-haired with a pointed jaw, rode in the front and center. As he was the first to pull back his animal's straps and the other men did the same as him, Vinan reckoned him to be the leader. The man to his right was crowned with a scalp of short black hair and carried two smaller swords on his right and left. The third man—to the first man's left—was white-skinned, yellow-haired, golden-bearded, and larger than either of his two companions. A gigantic and ornate sword the size of Vinan himself was borne by this last man and Vinan was unsettled by the piercing glare from his black eyes.

"Are you lost, traveler?" asked the first man after he and his companions had stopped. "You are a long way from anywhere civilized."

Vinan noticed that at that moment the man shot him a look. He also noticed the second man watching him and the swordsman without looking away for even a moment. The third man meanwhile seemed entirely fixated on the swordsman.

"I could ask you the same," answered the unmoved swordsman. "There is little business for anyone up that road. Only mountain folk and wild animals lie that way."

"I see you know all about the mountain folk," said the first man as he glanced at Vinan again. "Is he your guide?"

"No," Vinan answered. "He is mine."

"And why," asked the first man puzzled, "would a mountain boy need a guide in these lands?"

"We of the mountains do not go down into these lands," said Vinan. "There is too much evil here."

"Then why are you here?" asked the second man, in a curious tone that was far more pleasant than Vinan had expected.

"Because when an evil takes something from you," Vinan answered with defiance, "it is only natural to take it back. And I have something that was taken from me."

The third man slowly took his gaze from the swordsman and watched Vinan with a stone-cold glare.

"Well then," said the first man with a mirthful smile, "we will continue on and wish you good omens to that end."

"May no harm come to you or those you meet," returned the swordsman. "The world is uncertain these days indeed."

"Indeed," answered the leader. "Though if it is slavers you pursue, I would be careful. The trade is most profitable and those involved can afford almost any blade they desire to protect their precious goods."

He looked at Vinan conspicuously, as if he wanted Vinan to notice.

"I fear not the blades of animals and cowards that steal children to be sold in the slave markets," the swordsman shot back with a dark smile full of bloodlust. "And neither does En'Shai."

"The Shaii' of Kodumaa lacked no courage," said the third man at long last with a flat voice, "yet they were all destroyed and scattered as dust in the wind."

76

The swordsman looked back to him with dark recognition.

"Kodumaa is no more," said the swordsman, "but the Shaii' remain as long as I draw breath."

"If that is what you wish to believe," the third man scoffed, "then believe it. I put my faith in numbers and steel, not the idea of chivalry and faith in dead religion."

The two stared at each other for a brief and tense moment that seemed an eternity. Vinan held his spear ready for the duel that seemed only one move away but never came as the second man spoke again to break the silence.

"Courage is not without its own reward, Shai of Kodumaa. But choose your battles with care, lest you find yourself in one you cannot win. I wish you well as long as our blades never cross."

"Indeed," said the first man, "that would be unfortunate, not to mention unpleasant. It is time we left for our business."

He kicked his animal in the side and steered it around the swordsman to proceed down the path, giving the two no more heed. The second man followed in like manner, but the third passed by without ever taking his eyes off the swordsman. He turned his head back to the path and followed his companions after a long, meditative stare.

"Who were they?" Vinan asked the swordsman when they were gone.

"I do not know, En'Shai. Nor do I have any idea as to their business here."

"What were those beasts they rode on?"

This almost snapped the swordsman from staring down the path and he now had a look of some amusement.

"That, En'Shai, was a horse. Had we two of our own, we would have caught up with the slavers by now. There may be some in the village down the path."

"But," said Vinan, "I do not know how to ride one."

"Then I will teach you, En'Shai. It is not difficult."

Vinan only wondered what harsh, bruising lessons awaited in

learning how to master a horse with the swordsman. Still, the beast and the thought of riding one fascinated him. The idea that he could travel at such speed was unimaginable but moments before. He thought of what great distances he could cover with such an animal and the knowledge of how to ride it. It was almost enough to make him forget of Stek and Kirru for a moment until he had a striking realization.

"We need to go now!" he said to the swordsman. "If the slavers have horses of their own, then we cannot lose a moment."

"Yes, En'Shai. Drink some water and we will continue."

Vinan did not want to drink, but he knew he needed it. When he poured the water into his mouth it relieved the parched dryness and gave him new energy he did not realize he was lacking. He heard a sound behind him and saw the star-eyed girl emerge and crawl slowly towards him.

"Ah," the swordsman said as he recapped his own water skin, "there she is. It seems that she fears men most. I understand that all too well. Are you ready to go?"

"Yes." Vinan answered.

"Good. Now tell me, En'Shai, do you remember what I taught you about your sword?"

"Yes."

"Good. Remember it well. You may need to use it soon."

Vinan anticipated with eagerness the moment when he finally would, for then he would finally be within sight of Kirru and Stek. He could see them again and he would be close to saving them. He would be together with them, never to let them fall into peril again.

Or so he believed then, in that fleeting yet sweet moment of hope.

CHAPTER 9

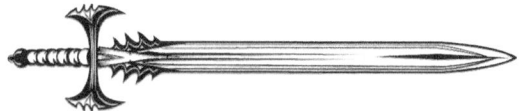

The Town on the Edge of Civilization

Vinan and the swordsman encountered no one else as they walked down the road, though many prints upon it were only days fresh. Before long they found the road lined with many stumps of felled trees cut straight in a manner that only a sharp blade could have done. As Vinan listened to the sound of Enna following just out of sight through the low brush, he knew that other men could not be far away.

The sun set as Vinan began to hear sounds of other life in the distance. The glimmer of light in the dusk, together with the mingled smells of burning wood and meat, drove him on faster. His pace began to exceed that of the swordsman until they were beside each other.

"No rest tonight, En'Shai?"

"No," Vinan answered. "Not until we are there."

The swordsman said no more.

The first men they met were a rough, muscled, and dirty bunch. There were perhaps ten or twelve in number—with beards long and grimy—resting by a hut and eating the contents of a large pot from their wooden bowls. Tools rested beside the men, tools made of a long wood handle and an odd blade that would have not appeared a blade were it not for its rounded edge. Most only looked at the swordsman and Vinan briefly and then continued to eat their supper. But one of them stood up and approached.

"Are you heading to the town?" he asked in a deep voice.

"We are," the swordsman answered. "Is it still there?"

"It is. Are you looking for a roof?"

"If there is one."

"There should be." The man ran his hand through his grey beard. "Many slavers and settlers have been coming through here as of late."

"There has been at least one party of them today, it would seem."

The man's hardened blue eyes narrowed.

"You are following them?" he asked.

"That is our business," the swordsman answered. "Just as the wood you cut is yours."

"As you say," said the woodcutter. "Then I will leave you to your business and go back to mine."

The swordsman nodded and turned back to the trail. Vinan followed while looking back quickly to see that the woodsman was watching him with particular interest while continuing to scratch at his beard. Vinan thought nothing of it, assuming that his own appearance was enough to turn heads among these outlanders. Had they ever seen one of his kind from the high mountains? Unlikely. Only the warriors ventured out and Vinan doubted they ever came this far. Except for Kror.

Kror.

It seemed like years since Vinan had last given any thought to his elder brother, though it had only been a few days. The betrayal still simmered deep and constantly within the boy's heart, but his mind had devoted little energy to it since Stek and Kirru had been taken away. With a goal so plain before him, there was no time left for Vinan to dwell on that smoldering wrath, ever twisting like a dagger in his heart.

"You are going with much purpose, En'Shai. Is something the matter?"

The swordsman's question made Vinan realize that he had picked up his pace to where he was almost running ahead of his companion.

"No," Vinan answered. "I only know they must be so close now."

"I hope the same, En'Shai. Perhaps we will not need to use our blades."

"Why not?"

"It might be wiser to see if we can come to an agreement with the slavers. I have gold to pay them with, if they will take it."

Vinan found himself sickened by the thought.

"Buy Stek and Kirru back?! Like animals?"

"I do not like it either, En'Shai. But starting a fight in this town may not be in our favor. The trade brings profit to many. We will have few friends, if any."

Anger rose within Vinan when he recalled Stek's retelling of how many of his own people had chosen to cast him out and follow Kror.

"It seems it is always the many," he mumbled, "who choose their evil that crushes the few."

"That may be so, En'Shai. But our only concern is getting back your brother and sister. The fewer enemies we make for ourselves, the easier this will be."

"What if we have to fight?"

"Then we will fight."

No further words were spoken between the two until they came to the town. Though she stayed out of sight, Vinan knew that Enna lingered just off the road. He could faintly detect her strides in the growth and her darting among the trees and he knew that no matter how much she wished to avoid the company of other men in these lands, she would not remain far from him and

81

the swordsman until Kirru was safe again.

***

The town was built of wood. Logs for the walls of the huts, planks for the roofs, and great sawed beams to support everything. The main path through was a trampled quagmire of mud and manure where many men and their beasts shoved their way through, without mind to those around them. Vinan, for the first time, laid his eyes on the "carts" of which the swordsman had spoken; wood boxes upon round wooden wheels pulled by beasts, some of which were horses and some of which were large horned animals. All of the carts carried cargo in their back—almost all of it wood—but Vinan did not spot any holding Stek or Kirru.

As he and the swordsman walked through the main causeway they came to a stone bridge. Vinan looked over the edge and saw a rushing river below larger than any stream he had seen in the mountains. Floating on the surface of the river were more wooden things built and manned by the men of the outlands, pointed, cart-like constructions that sat upon the water as a bird would. Within them sat men transporting more wood and sacks of other goods.

The swordsman must have noticed Vinan's fascination with them as he stopped beside the boy.

"Boats, En'Shai. They are used for traveling up and down the river. Come."

Vinan made haste to follow the swordsman as he continued past the bridge and through the town. A short time after they crossed the bridge, the swordsman entered one of the huts through a thick oaken door. Vinan looked around the smoke-filled inside and took note of the rough men—like those he had seen in the wood camp outside the town—relaxing, drinking out of tankards, and joking with the women serving them the tankards. Vinan noticed almost immediately how many women were in this place. They seemed to all be here serving drinks rather than

82

anywhere else in the town. Come to think of it, he had seen no women or girls in the town before now.

The swordsman walked to the back of the house, reached into his pocket, pulled out a brass coin, and placed it on a ledge in the back.

"Something to drink," he said.

The man behind the ledge—bald, of middle age, muscular, and bearing a wisp of a beard on his chin—picked up the coin to examine it. He appeared to be satisfied with it, but his eye first caught a look at Vinan and then focused on the boy.

"We don't serve ale to his kind," he said.

"Children or mountain folk?" asked the swordsman.

"Neither."

The swordsman glared at the man unamused as silence hung heavy between the two men. Vinan also noticed that those closest to him were quieting and beginning to take notice. He hoped the swordsman was not in a rash mood, as there were many strong men under the roof; some of whom eyed him and the swordsman closely and cautiously.

The swordsman broke the building tension around them with a good-natured laugh.

"I will have ale for myself," he said to the bald man, "and two mugs of water. Is that acceptable in this establishment?"

"It is."

The man behind the ledge grabbed two mugs and dipped them into a wooden barrel. He took another and dipped it into the barrel beside, which was filled with a yellow-brown liquid. All three were set before the swordsman, who passed one of the water-filled vessels to Vinan. The two drank with much relish, as they slaked their parched throats and forgot—for one sweet moment—all the wretched circumstances that had brought them here. Though Vinan erstwhile would have thought the water stale and odd to the taste, it was as pleasant now as the coolest mountain spring.

"You spend time with the mountain folk?" asked the man

behind the ledge to the swordsman.

"Only this one," the swordsman answered while tilting his head to Vinan, "though it seems there are others who spend more time than is good for you or for them."

"Don't know much about that. I only provide drinks and women here."

"Indeed. Then you would not know if any came to town today."

"Maybe they did, maybe they didn't. There are many men I serve every day."

"If it is another coin you are after, then you have already failed. You would not hint at it unless they had come through."

"I could argue contrary-wise, but that'd be a waste of my time. Yes, a party came through the town. They left shortly after, down the river."

This interested the swordsman. "So, the river takes slaves to Qiriq now?"

"It does," was the man's answer. "It's far safer than the plains roads, especially now that the Raq hordes roam the grasslands. The merchants may lose a shipment to the rapids now and again when the rains are heavy, but they find it worth the risk."

The swordsman's expression darkened with furrowed brows and his eyes glaring like two wrathful flames.

"The Raqs are at Qiriq?" he asked with an icy voice.

"Not yet," the man said indifferently. "The city pays them to stay away. Pays them in gold and slaves."

The swordsman muttered a curse in an unfamiliar tongue and took a deep gulp of his remaining ale.

"Did the slavers have two children with them?" Vinan asked earnestly.

The ale-man was taken aback and stayed silent for a moment.

"Did they?" Vinan asked again.

The ale-man hesitated, still apparently surprised that the mountain boy would speak to him.

"Answer his question." The swordsman commanded.

"They did," the ale-man finally said with a nod, "a boy much like this one and a little girl."

Vinan's heart leapt in his chest.

"Were they hurt?" He asked with a cracking voice. "Were they alright?"

The man opened his mouth for a second as if hesitating whether to answer, then he looked to the swordsman and the answer spilled out quickly.

"The boy's face had been beaten and he was tied tight in the cart. The girl was weeping as if begging for help but did not seem hurt otherwise."

Vinan frantically turned to leave, but the swordsman's sudden iron grip on his shoulder stopped him.

"Many thanks," the swordsman said to the innkeeper as he placed another coin on the ledge. "I hope you have as quiet an evening as we will once you bring me another ale."

"Not now, En'Shai," he whispered to Vinan after the ale-man gave the ale and left them. "The slavers took a boat and are out of our reach at the moment."

"Then we need to go now and catch them!" Vinan whispered back frantically.

"Do you know how to pilot a boat, En'Shai?"

The question confused Vinan, who stood dumbfounded.

The swordsman pressed. "Do you have a boat here we can use or the coin to buy one?"

"You know I don't," Vinan answered with indignation.

"Correct," said the swordsman. "Look at yourself, En'Shai. You are more exhausted than I am, and I am in need of rest as is. We cannot catch them now even if we tried. I need a little time and rest if I am to even invent a plan that will catch them. I still need the strength to rescue them when we reach them."

Vinan was in utter disbelief at what he was hearing from this man he considered a far stronger and better warrior than himself.

"So, we are going to sit here and do nothing?" he asked.

"Not nothing, En'Shai. We are going to sleep once I get a room. Give me time to talk to one of these women for a while."

"If it is a boat you need," a young female voice interjected, "I might be able to help you."

Vinan almost jumped with a start, unaware that another sat so close listening to the swordsman and himself. She was a young girl of perhaps fourteen or fifteen winters, slender, red-haired, with small eyes of deep blue. She wore simple clothes of a white tunic, a pair of grey wool trousers, a pair of hide boots, and a loose white hood over her head. She stood behind Vinan and the swordsman calmly but not without indifference, paying special attention both to Vinan and the sword of the outlander.

"Oh," said the swordsman. "You finally decided to join us and stop listening in?"

"I only heard you were after a boat..." she started.

"You are not as good at hiding as you think you are," the swordsman interrupted. "And you are too young to be in a place like this selling anything."

"I came in to overhear the goings-on," she replied, "and heard what I needed to hear. You need a boat and my father has one that can take you to Qiriq."

"Right," said the swordsman. "Your father. Tell him he should know better than to let his daughter into places like this."

But Vinan did not share in his companion's distrust. He believed he noticed something in her blue eyes, a pleading desire for the two of them to come with her, a fear that they would not, and sadness over something she could not help.

"Can't we hear what she has to say?" Vinan asked the swordsman.

"En'Shai," the swordsman answered, "there is something you should learn well as a boy before you make terrible mistakes as a man. Always and all around you are those who want to sell you something. Never take what they offer without knowing what it is first."

He motioned to a plump and sultry golden-haired woman from across the room and brandished a coin in plain view. She began to walk over to him, trying her best to conceal her eagerness.

"This girl before us claims much and has little to show for it," he continued. "Her story is good, too good to believe. But this woman..."

The portly woman now stood before the swordsman. She reached for the coin but he teasingly withdrew it from her reach while keeping it in plain sight.

"This woman knows what she wants and has a clear price. It is one I am willing to pay."

He rose from his seat and the woman pointed to the ceiling with a smile. The swordsman nodded in return before looking back to Vinan.

"Inspect the girl's offer if you are willing to trust it, En'Shai," he said. "I have some business with this woman for a time."

The swordsman followed the woman up some wooden steps into an upper level of the establishment, one Vinan hadn't noticed before now. Vinan was left alone with the red-haired girl and at a loss over what to say to her. Fortunately, she made the first utterance.

"Your companion is not the trusting type," she observed.

"I'm not either," Vinan replied. "People out here have given me little reason to trust anyone."

"But you trust him?" she asked.

"He..."

Vinan paused for a moment to consider her well-made point.

"He hasn't taken anything from me yet," he said. "He gave me food and this sword. That's far better than what others have done."

"Well," she reflected, "you both are strangers in these lands so it would make sense that you would help each other. You both are heading to Qiriq?"

"If that's where the slavers are going," he replied.

"Why do you follow slavers?"

Vinan wondered if he had said too much. He remembered the warning about the trade bringing profit to the people here. But perhaps she was different. She had compassion in her countenance and seemed to care about his troubles. She had a kindness in her eyes that put Vinan at ease and made him believe in the goodness of her intentions.

But, after all, he had thought the very same of Kror...

"They took someone you love, didn't they?" she pressed.

"What do you think of slavers?" he asked back coldly.

Her hand grabbed his shoulder and pulled him closer to her. Vinan was surprised to find himself not resisting and allowed her to pull his ear beside her mouth.

"I would kill every one of them, if I could," she answered back with a violent whisper. "Dealers in human misery, crushers of the spirit, and killers of children. Snakes that would not be missed if we could cut all their throats!"

She let go of him and backed away a step.

"Now," she continued, "if you trust me and want to come with me then tell me your name."

"Vinan, son of Bheif," he replied. "And yours?"

"Crissa, daughter of my father," she answered. "Should we wait for your friend to finish or would you like to see the boat now?"

Vinan thought for a moment.

"Maybe it's best to go now," he said. "I'm sure I have time to look so I can tell him it is real."

"Does your friend have a name?"

"He refused to give it to me."

"And you still trust him?"

88

"I don't see why not." Vinan shrugged. "He is almost the only help I have in these lands."

"Almost?"

Vinan reflected for a moment, then decided that if Crissa was worth trusting here then there was no point concealing Enna from her. Enna could not be left behind.

"Come with me," he beckoned, "I have something to show you."

Vinan and Crissa left the inn. He led her behind it and into the passages between the wooden huts. It was quiet there, isolated from the noise of the townsfolk drinking and taking part in whatever pleasures they enjoyed after the sunset. Vinan walked in the unlit alley towards the edge of town where he sensed that Enna would be lurking.

As it happened, she stalked closer than he guessed. He found her sitting in the alley gnawing on the carcass of a freshly strangled squirrel. She acknowledged his coming with a glance of her bright orbs and continued her dinner, taking notice of but showing little concern for Crissa.

"W-what is she?" Crissa asked, stupefied.

"You also don't know?" Vinan asked.

"Did she come from your mountains?"

Vinan sighed. "No one seems to know anything of her, and she hides from everyone. She is with me and is my sister's friend."

"She is following the slavers with you?"

Vinan nodded. "Following the slavers until Kirru and Stek are free again."

"A touching story," said a voice at the edge of the darkness, "and enough to make me want to help you."

There, where Vinan had entered the alley, now stood the first of the three men who had spoken with himself and the swordsman. Though he made no move towards them, Vinan could see—even in the darkness—the man's hand resting upon the hilt of the sword on his belt. Enna did not wait for Vinan to act and sprinted towards the other side of the alley. This ended up a very brief attempt, as another man emerged in the shadows to block that escape. Vinan lifted his spear as the girl frantically looked back and forth between the two men at either side of the passage.

"Curious," the first man said as he looked at Enna, "magnificently curious."

"Crissa," Vinan whispered, "what..."

He looked to where she had stood in shock.

Crissa was gone. Gone as if she had never been with him. Vinan was angry with himself for having told her so much. Now he knew not what she would do with all he had told her or to whom she would tell it in return. After Kror he should have known better, should have kept up his guard like his swordsman companion. But he had allowed himself to trust again. His guard had dropped for the last time and he would not let it drop before the man in the alley.

"Get out of my way!" he demanded of the man.

But the man slowly held up his hand.

"Wait, boy," he answered. "I have something to say to you."

Vinan stood his ground and stared blankly at the man. When he saw the man's stance was relaxed he looked back to the girl, who was still in the alley behind him. Vinan recognized the shape of the man in the shadows behind her as the second man from earlier who held the two smaller swords. He had neither moved nor drawn weapons so Vinan saw no danger yet in listening.

As long as he kept his own weapons ready.

"Then say it," he said. "But who are you?"

"I am Ancar, and men pay me for work I do. Who are you?"

"I am Vinan, son of Bheif. And I search for something that was taken from me."

"What sort of thing is that?"

"That is my own concern."

"I see," said Ancar with much interest. "You aren't the trusting type."

"Most men I've met are not worth trusting."

"That is unfortunate. Will you at least listen to what I have to say?"

"I will listen, and that is all I promise."

Vinan pretended to relax his stance and did not drop his guard. He remained aware of the man behind him and the fact that Ancar's hand still rested on his sword's hilt.

"That man you travel with," Ancar began, "is not someone you want to accompany. He is a doomed man who many would pay to have killed."

"Why?" Vinan asked.

"The reasons are far larger than you or I and do not matter. What matters is that it will not go well for you if you intertwine your fate with his."

As an answer, this was nothing. No, it was less than nothing.

"You haven't answered me," Vinan said with his voice slightly raised.

"Very well," Ancar sighed with annoyance. "It is because he is the last Shai of Kodumaa."

"And why should he be killed for that?" Vinan asked. "I don't even know what that means."

"It should not matter to you," the second man answered. "There are many others who will come forward to kill him because they will be paid well."

A sickening sensation churned in Vinan's stomach as he began to further understand the laws of the world outside his mountains. He would not bow to, stand for, or take part in such practices. Not while he lived.

"Then I will stop them," he said with determination.

Ancar's voice took on a soft condescending tone. "Boy, you do not understand…"

"No!" Vinan interrupted. "As long as the swordsman helps me find what I seek, then I stand with him and will kill any who try to stop us."

"You may find yourself pitted against us very soon," Ancar warned. "Sooner than you think."

"I do not care!"

The man in the back of the alley took a step forward and drew his blades. Enna darted at him and tried to slip past, only to find herself caught by his arm. She frantically kicked and squirmed to no avail. Her teeth sunk into her captor's arm but bit only the thick leather sleeves he wore.

Vinan turned his back to Ancar and crouched low to the ground. He pointed his spear directly forward with his right hand while his left grabbed a handful of dirt.

"Don't do anything stupid, boy," Ancar warned. "You have already given us the girl. Come with us. We will sell her as a curiosity and you will earn half the money. We can help you find what you seek far better than the last Shai of Kodumaa can."

A chill ran down Vinan's spine as he realized the work Ancar and his men did. Just more armed slavers making a living off the misery of captives. It was men like them who had taken Kirru and Stek from him.

He sprung up on his legs and leapt at the girl's captor. A shower of dirt pelted the man in the face and eyes as he dropped the girl to avoid Vinan's spear.

"Enna!" Vinan shouted. "Go!"

Now free, she ran to the boy's side.

"*Vinan!*" she cried.

He pushed her shoulder as he held his spear up against the disoriented man.

"Go!" he commanded.

She seemed to understand and obeyed. He followed her past the man and out of the alley just as Ancar drew his sword and began to give them chase. They were behind the drinking house when the noises of a woman screaming, men shouting, and things being thrown sounded above them. A figure jumped from the window above and landed on the soft earth on his back. As he sprung quickly to his feet, Vinan recognized the swordsman, who looked barely worse for wear, even though he seemed a bit dazed and his belt was undone.

Ancar was almost upon them with his sword ready to hack when he let out a cry of pain, dropped his sword, and clutched his leg. His hand was pressed over a hole, trying to limit the flow of blood from a wound caused by a thin straight dagger. The owner of the dagger emerged completely from the shadows and ran straight for Vinan.

"Quick!" shouted Crissa. "This way!"

Before Vinan had time to react to Crissa's reappearance, the swordsman grabbed him by the shoulder.

"The other man is in the inn!" He bellowed. "Run, En'Shai!"

Vinan and Enna followed the swordsman and Crissa as they ran quickly from the commotion behind them. The four of them ran through the dark, winding alley and then stumbled back into the street. They darted down the way, heedless of the few wayward men who staggered there. Vinan could feel the curious eyes of the men upon him and the girl. But the men only watched as the three ran past, whether from fear, intoxication, or lack of interest, Vinan could not guess, and neither did he care. He continued to run behind Crissa and the swordsman, his heart thumping at the pace of a fleeing deer. The only concern rushing through his mind was to escape Ancar and this town.

"To the docks!" shouted Crissa. "Follow me!"

Before them lay the docks, a construction of wooden planks and poles to which many boats were tied. Crissa ran towards a small boat where a bearded old man stood like a watchful specter in the light of the moon and the single lamp that burned upon the vessel's prow.

"Crissa!" the old man shouted at their approach, stepping forward with his staff raised.

"They're with me!" she cried. "Get underway!"

Without question, the old man leapt into action with far more vigor than Vinan thought possible. The ropes binding the boat to the docks were quickly undone and the vessel was already floating away when Vinan and Enna jumped on after Crissa and the swordsman.

The boat sailed away from the town, down the river, and into the night. The old man handed Crissa a wooden paddle, leaving her to steer as he unfurled the cloth sails. The boat gained speed with the wind and the current and Vinan could no longer see the lights of the town. All that remained was the moon, the stars, and the single lantern on the prow. Ancar and his men were long gone, fast becoming distant memories of the wretched town.

The old man, his task complete, took hold of another wooden oar that lay on the deck and aided Crissa by steering on the opposite side of the boat. As Vinan and Enna recovered their breath and their nerves, the old man looked to his companion.

"What were you running from, Crissa?" he asked.

"Slavers," she replied short of breath, "these two were in danger."

She nodded to Vinan and Enna. The old man betrayed some surprise when he beheld Enna but Vinan found himself used to it now. He had become certain that no one in these outlands would know the mystery of Enna's people, if they even existed.

"And who are you, who accompany these children?" he asked the swordsman.

"I, old Raq," the swordsman answered with an icy, underlying hostility, "am the last Shai of Kodumaa. I help those innocent in need of protection, for no one else will."

A tense moment followed upon that deck as the two men stared each other down. The silence that hung in the air was as conspicuous as the death wails of a wounded boar, suffocating all sense of ease among the other three passengers of the boat.

"Then protect them, Shai of Kodumaa," the old man answered earnestly. "Protect them well, for the world is cruel. My daughter and I will take you where you need to go."

"Qiriq," Vinan said. "We need to go to Qiriq."

"Why?" the old man asked. "You will find nothing there but suffering and more slavers."

"Because," Vinan answered, "my brother and sister were taken there by slavers and I swear... I swear by the God of the Warriors and the Forests that I will save them!"

The old man nodded.

"And you will, brave little warrior," he said softly. "I believe you will."

He looked back at Crissa. "We will go back to Qiriq then. I pray these three find more there than we ever did."

Vinan did not know the old man and barely knew his daughter, but if Stek and Kirru were in Qiriq then he was certain that he would find more there than they ever had. And no one, whether Ancar or anyone else, would stop him now.

CHAPTER 10

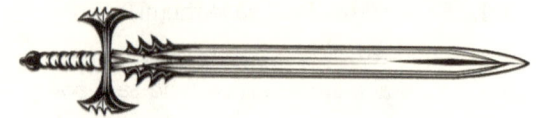

Warriors of Now and Long Ago

T he boat was swept down the river all night with the oars of the pilots guiding it. Vinan, tired though he remained from the excitement, could not sleep well. The rocking of the boat dizzied his brain and turned his stomach like meat over a fire.

He continued to fear the pursuit of the three men. At times he imagined he saw the piercing glare of the third man in the shadowed trees. To add to Vinan's fatigue, a sickness lingered in his stomach from the rocking of the boat on the river's strong current. More than once he leaned over the boat's side to choke and cough up nothing or to splash his face with the icy water. Eventually, he picked up another oar to assist the other three in keeping the boat in the center of the river.

When the town was far out of sight and the first bits of dawn began to turn the sky from black to deep blue, Vinan slept for several hours in a small doorless cabin in the back. The roof of the wooden hut was enough to block out the sun and ease his ability to rest. The swordsman remained outside to help Crissa and her father steer the vessel as Enna sat on the deck staring into the unknown. Vinan, finally somewhat used to the turbulence of the voyage, settled in, and made up for lost sleep from the night.

Vinan awoke at dusk well rested and observed that the boat was still going down the river just as it had been that morning. He walked out of the cabin to see the swordsman and Enna guiding the boat while Crissa slept peacefully on the deck with the old man resting beside her.

"Awake at last?" he asked Vinan.

He was a man of perhaps sixty years of age, strong and well-built. His skin was tanned from many years in the unshaded sun and his beard was full grey from the hardships he had endured beneath that sun. He wore simple white garments like his daughter and held a staff that Vinan suspected was less for support and more to give the impression of feebleness. Vinan was not fooled by it for he was reminded of the old warriors of his people; old warriors whose fire for battle or hunt would burn long after the brighter and hotter flames of the young warriors were extinguished from the eagerness of youth.

And the old warrior that sat upon the deck of the riverboat had much fire still left in him.

"Yes," Vinan answered. "I thought I'd rest and prepare myself."

"En'Shai is unused to the rocking of a boat upon the waters," the swordsman observed as he stroked the water back with his oar.

"You have stayed awake all this time?" Vinan asked him.

"I have," the swordsman answered without turning. "The boat must stay clear of the rocks and the banks."

Vinan watched the swordsman at his task for a moment.

"Let me do it!" Vinan insisted. "I will steer the boat while you rest."

"You have never even been on a boat before now, En'Shai."

"No," said Vinan, "But I have watched you and can do it."

"Have you learned to fight with your sword from fighting with me once, En'Shai? Even then, you are better at the sword than at the oar. You have at least used your sword."

"The task of directing a boat away from the rocks and the shallows," the old man interjected, "is not a difficult one. Hardly the fine art of swordsmanship."

"And what," said the swordsman with visible annoyance, "would an old Raq warrior know of the art of swordsmanship?"

"Far more than you might think, Shai of Kodumaa."

"Do not speak those words," the swordsman shot the old man a murderous glare. "Do not ever speak them again."

"May I ask a question?" Vinan cautiously asked the swordsman.

"You have just asked one, En'Shai. You may ask another."

Vinan ignored the swordsman's deadpan mockery and asked his question.

"What is Kodumaa?"

"Nothing now," the swordsman said while going back to his task of steering the boat. "A land that was once a revered home for honorable men but was destroyed from within before the Raqs swept in and burned the shell of what remained to dust and ashes."

"The Raqs?" asked Vinan.

"Vicious warlords," the swordsman answered. "Warriors of the Great Raq and his sons who sought to rule the world and all men who live in it. They slaughtered many and slew entire peoples in their rampage."

Vinan looked at the old man, wondering if he was capable of such things.

"Your friend is not entirely wrong," the old man said. "The Raqs were horsemen who rode the great grass plains. Warriors of the saddle from the oldest man to the youngest eager boy. The Great Raq prophesied that we could find new homes, more food, and greener lands to the west. So, we followed him."

"They followed him," the swordsman continued, "followed him past the great grass plain and to lands that had never heard of them. They crushed kingdoms, toppled empires, and cut a path of death through the lands they found."

"Kodumaa was your home?" Vinan asked.

"Yes, En'shai, Kodumaa was my home. It was visited by Farken-Raq who demanded they surrender. The Shaii' were too proud to submit so they fought the Raq's army. Their courage was not enough to win and the once-great land was brought to total ruin."

"Is that how you remember it?" asked the old man.

"It is what happened," the swordsman answered.

"I rode with Farken-Raq," the old man said. "I rode with him from the great grass plain to Kodumaa. I still remember his grief when he held his father, the Great Raq, in his arms; killed by poison and treachery delivered by the honorable Shaii' of Kodumaa."

"Lies," the swordsman sneered.

"I battled the Shaii' in their land," the old man continued. "I saw no great warriors. Only people pretending to be because their ancestors had been centuries before."

The swordsman drew his weapon and pointed it at the old man, appearing to disregard the fact that Crissa had dropped her oar to reach beneath her garments.

"Speak of Kodumaa or the Shaii' again," the swordsman warned, "and I will kill you where you stand!"

The old Raq nodded. "As you wish, Shai of Kodumaa."

The Shai of Kodumaa put his blade away, and Crissa moved her hand away from her concealed one beneath her garments. The two went back to their task of guiding the boat without a single word exchanged and the old Raq rested as if nothing had ever occurred. Enna slept peacefully where she lay, unmoved by the commotion and the conversation.

It was a seemingly eternal time of silence and reflection before Vinan spoke again.

"If Shai is warrior, then what is En'Shai?" he asked the

swordsman.

"It is what you are," the Shai said. "In the old tongue of Kodumaa it means 'little warrior', for it was what we called any boy who was not yet Shai."

"What was needed to become Shai?" Vinan said.

"Years of training, service to the One God, and an oath to always act with honor."

"One God?"

"Yes, the One God who created everything; the One God who existed when nothing else yet existed."

"What of other gods? Was there a warrior god the Shaii' called on for courage?"

"There are no other gods, En'Shai. And even the one we have is uncaring of the evil in his world."

Vinan was surprised and confused. "So, you do not pray for guidance in battle?"

"All I know of battle I learned through lessons and battle itself. I have no need of prayers that will bring me nothing."

"I pray every day that my brother and sister are returned," Vinan retorted, "and that I am able to save them when the time comes."

"You may be ready by that time, En'Shai. We shall see. Do you remember all the lessons I have taught you thus far?"

"Yes."

"Good. For you will need to learn more before you are ready to fight men with your sword."

"How old were you," Vinan asked with curiosity, "when Kodumaa fell?"

"What does it matter, En'Shai?"

"How long has it been?" Vinan asked.

"Not long enough to forget," the Shai answered.

"Why are you alive when the rest of your brothers are dead?" Vinan pressed.

"I wish on some days that I had joined them, En'Shai," the

Shai reminisced. "Instead, I must live in a world with no justice, among men with no honor, and with only a memory of my home left."

"Your home?" Vinan asked. "All that is left at my home are my wicked mother and my faithless brother! Forget your home as I have forgotten mine."

Vinan had barely time to draw his sword and raise it in defense, so quick was the attack of the Shai. So quick that Vinan did not have time to wonder how he had cast aside his oar and begun his attack so rapidly. Now the gilded sword of Kodumaa was pressing down on his own as the Shai's wrath-filled eyes bore into his.

"Vinan!" Crissa shouted.

"No, Crissa!" her father commanded. "Wait!"

"Now, En'Shai," the Shai said, "that is enough talk. Prove to me you have forgotten your home!"

The two pulled back their blades.

"Prove to me you are a warrior!" the Shai commanded.

He was upon Vinan again and the boy had to jump to the side to avoid his opponent's sword.

"Prove to me that you are ready to save your brother and sister!" the Shai taunted.

Vinan backed away quickly, dancing around the mast and jumping across the hull to dodge the Shai's assault. He glanced off a strike from the Shai's blade with his own and almost lost his footing on the rocking boat. Fear of capsizing the humble vessel did not deter the Shai from pressing furiously against Vinan.

"You will have to fight in all manner of unforeseen places," the Shai said. "You can never assume the enemy is not close!"

He lunged again and Vinan sidestepped him again, almost falling off the boat into the rushing current of the river.

"You show promise, En'Shai," the Shai said. "But you still fight like a mountain savage."

He finally knocked Vinan down onto the deck. The gilded

101

sword of Kodumaa was held to Vinan's throat.

"That, En'Shai, is why I will never forget Kodumaa. It taught me all I will teach you. Does it matter how weak the Shaii' were in their last days or that I was young and only a few years a Shai before the reckoning? I mastered the blade regardless and will outlive all who destroyed my home!"

Vinan and the Shai stared at each other for a moment that seemed to pass for an epoch. They regained their breaths, the wrath in the Shai's face subsided, and Vinan waited patiently for the blade to be removed from his throat.

"Have you made your point?" asked the old Raq.

He sat at the prow of the boat, steering it down the river as the lone oarsman. Crissa and the now-awake Enna stood in the rear of the boat, beyond the reach of the impromptu martial lesson. A wide berth had been given to the two combatants, and neither had noticed until now—so fully did the heat of battle take their focus.

"My lesson is finished En'Shai. Now help our guests with the boat."

The Shai retired to the little cabin and would not be seen again until long after the sun departed. Vinan remained on deck, sheathed his sword, and took up an oar to help the old Raq.

"You don't have to," Crissa said.

"No," Vinan said. "If you are taking me to Qiriq then I should help you."

"Do you even know how to use it?"

"How hard can it be?"

Despite how easy it looked, despite his longing to do it well, and despite an innate desire to show Crissa he could do it, Vinan soon found himself over-steering the boat so that it veered towards one shore and then to the opposite. Over-correction followed over-correction and left the old Raq countering Vinan's spirited yet unskilled strokes. Vinan tried to adjust but soon began to fear that he had made the steering more difficult than if he had left the old man to do it alone. Yet, he had to learn to do it right. It was now or never. He had to help in any way he could. Kirru and Stek waited for him in Qiriq.

A hand touched his shoulder.

"It's alright, Vinan," said Crissa softly. "We can do it."

She placed her hand on the oar's handle beside Vinan's. Her soft and gentle touch disarmed him a moment yet he was loath to surrender the oar to her. He almost wanted to fight her for it, to prove that he could do it.

"Please," she pleaded, "you don't need to. We will get you to Qiriq. I promise."

Vinan realized he was proving nothing to Crissa except that he was a stubborn tribal fool who could not steer a boat and was too slow to realize it. He let go of the oar, letting it slip out of his hand, and backed away. Deflated and defeated, he sauntered to the side of the boat to look to the shore, to the endless wall of pine, and away from Crissa.

He could see his mother towering over him, reminding him of all that he would never do. He could picture Kror taunting him for being weak and insufficient. After all, he could not stand up to his own mother, he could not protect his brother and sister, could not master a sword, and he could not even steer a boat.

He silenced his mother and Kror in his head. He was tired of their taunting. Here, in the outlands, they could hurt him no more.

"Vinan?" Crissa asked.

Vinan looked to Crissa, realizing only now with utter embarrassment that tears were streaming down his face. He wiped them away with his forearm and sniffled, sniffled like a little boy of five winters with snot dripping from his nose. Crissa's face was overwhelmed with pity and fear.

"Are you...? Did I...?"

She struggled to ask the right question as if trying to discern what could have caused a fierce mountain warrior to weep.

"Thank you," a mortified Vinan croaked, "for taking us to

Qiriq."

She dropped the oar, ignoring her father's stern look that told her to leave the boy alone, and walked to Vinan.

"What is it, Vinan?" she asked. "Was I wrong to take away the oar?"

"No," he answered. "It's better that you steer the boat."

"Please," she pleaded, "is something wrong?"

"Nothing you can help," he sighed.

He looked at her wounded face, wounded not because of his words but because she clearly feared she had hurt him in her attempt to show kindness. Vinan found himself mortified that he had been the cause of so much grief.

"I'm sorry," he said. "I... I..."

"You don't have to apologize," she interrupted. "I won't ask you again."

She turned around to where she had dropped the oar.

"My mother," Vinan blurted out.

Crissa stopped and turned back to him.

"I was thinking of my mother," he said.

"Is... is she dead?" Crissa asked, terrified.

"If only she was!" Vinan replied with tearful anger as an invisible rock lifted itself from his chest.

Crissa stood stunned, mouth agape, as if unable to comprehend that anyone could think such a thing.

"How, how could you say that?" she asked.

"Because," Vinan answered with his whole body trembling, "she is as evil as my brother Kror. It would have been better if she had died while Kirru was a baby!"

"You don't know that!" Crissa protested.

"I do! And I wish I never had a mother!"

"I never had a mother," Crissa said.

Silence befell the deck for a moment of agony.

"I never knew my mother," Crissa repeated more softly. "She died when I was too little to remember. All my life I've wondered, dreamt, what it was like to feel the softness of a mother's touch and to hear the lullabies of a mother singing me to sleep."

"I," Vinan struggled to remember, "I never knew such things from my mother. Her touch was to strike me and her usual lullaby was a scream of anger."

Crissa suddenly threw her arms around Vinan as he stood there paralyzed. Unwilling to break away and unable to return her embrace, he stood dumbly still.

"You don't need to fear anything," she told him through sobs. "It doesn't matter what your mother or brother did to you. You will save your sister and brother and I will help you."

Vinan still stood dumbstruck.

"I promise you, Vinan," she continued, "I will help you find them. Even if it means going past Qiriq or into the darkest dungeons of the world. I will help you find Kirru and Stek again."

The old Raq rose from the boat's prow and approached the children.

"Crissa," he said, putting his hand on Crissa's shoulder, "it is time you rested. You are too tired for any more work today."

Crissa separated herself from Vinan, looked to her father, and nodded. She retired to the cabin to leave three on deck.

"The girl has a good heart," the old Raq said. "I hope she has not given the mountain warrior too much grief?"

"None, none at all," Vinan replied.

"That is good," the old Raq answered. "Practice with the sword while you are awake. I can take you to Qiriq. What you need to concern yourself with, is what you will do when you get there."

Vinan nodded and turned to the empty front of the ship.

"Vinan," said the old man.

Vinan turned back to him.

"Those who betrayed and hurt you as a child were left behind many miles ago," the Raq said. "What you must fear now are the ones that stand between you and your brother and sister."

It was true. Here, in the outlands, his mother and Kror could hurt him no more. In these lands were Stek and Kirru, friends and allies to help him, enemies to overcome, and great deeds he had yet to do to win his brother and sister back. In these lands, Vinan, son of Bheif could become whatever man he chose to become.

Provided he lived long enough to do so.

Vinan walked to the prow of the ship and drew his sword. He held it in his hand and balanced it. He swung it to slash the air and the whistle of steel sounded around him. He balanced his feet upon the rocking deck as he held his sword the way the Shai held his, swung the sword as the Shai swung his, and moved his body just as he had seen the Shai do. He knew his imitation was not perfect, he knew it would not be as quick, but he knew he could remember the motions. He was resolved to get them right and let the speed come later.

Vinan continued this dance as the bright yellow sun set over the river and night fell all around the boat that carried the five travelers ever closer to Qiriq.

CHAPTER 11

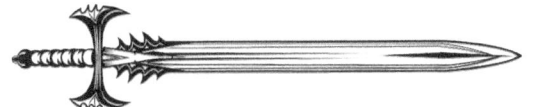

The Rapids

For two days the boat continued down the river. Crissa, her father, and the Shai took their turns at the oars. Enna began to help on the second day and demonstrated incredible adeptness at the task. Vinan heeded the advice of the old Raq and chose to not offer his help at the oars any further, spending most of his restless time on the boat practicing with his sword. The Shai sparred with him intermittently and taught Vinan the footwork and the techniques of blade handling that had been passed to him. In these lessons, the Shai showed far more patience than before and did not subject Vinan to another humiliation. It appeared he had driven his point home to the boy.

Vinan had learned much in the times both he and the Shai were awake. He had learned the best ways to hold his blade, common attacks he would face and how to defeat them, and even some tricks of the wrist to surprise a less skilled enemy. Overall, Vinan found the concepts of the sword similar to those of the spear with some very important differences. He knew he was no master of this new weapon yet, but now he felt he could use it well enough to protect himself and perhaps save Kirru and Stek.

He had also learned more from Crissa and her father. That he was the only family she had ever known, that they had traveled many lands when she was little and he was stronger and more violent, and that they had lived in Qiriq for the last five years. The boat was how they survived, delivering goods to Qiriq and the river settlements in exchange for coins and goods they needed. Vinan also learned that this journey down the river was the easier one. Going back upstream against the current was harder work. Crissa's father often found men in Qiriq who wished to journey to the settlements and offered them passage in exchange for their help. The boat, though humble and worn by the years of use, was the prize possession of Crissa and her father.

The boat would also have been well stocked with food and provisions, had there been only two aboard. Vinan and the Shai very quickly realized the limitations of their hosts' and partook sparingly of the offered food. Enna seemed to understand the fact as well but rarely ate as it was. The old Raq ensured his guests that there was enough food to make it to Qiriq with some to spare and the Shai seemed to agree provided that Qiriq was where he remembered it. Vinan hoped, for the sake of Kirru and of Stek, that Qiriq was where the Shai remembered it.

On the morning of the third day, a warm morning without the familiar cool bite of the mountain air, Vinan noticed Enna at the back of the boat. She was staring as if watching, expecting, waiting for... something. He looked to the river and saw nothing but the current they followed, the pines that lined the dwindling forest, or the rocks that lay by the shore. He dismissed it as nothing for the moment and continued towards the prow to practice more with his blade.

"We approach the rapids," the old man said as Vinan passed. "They will be rough today if the rains are any guide."

"How much longer until Qiriq?" Vinan asked.

"Only three more days down the river," said the old Raq. "Three more days and we will be at the harbor of the city."

"Where will I go then to find the slavers?" Vinan asked.

"The markets. Any slave deemed worth buying will be sold to a merchant in the markets."

"And if they are not worth buying?"

The Raq paused for a moment. "Your brother and your sister... have they any ailments?"

"No."

"Are they crippled?"

"No."

"Have they scars on their face?"

"No."

"Then merchants will buy them. I only fear the thought of them being bought before we arrive."

"What if they are?"

"Then it will prove much more difficult to find them."

A sense of haste formed a lump in Vinan's gut. His heart began to pound like the war drums of his people. The boat could not sail quickly enough for him, even though it now sped down the river faster than it ever had.

Something suddenly whizzed by Vinan's head and hit the deck of the boat. Another sped by and buried its head in the wall of the cabin.

"Get down!"

The old Raq grabbed Vinan and threw him to the deck with an incredible show of strength for a man his age. More projectiles flew past and Vinan saw that they were like small spears, launched with enough speed to penetrate flesh and organs had they hit anyone. These were the "arrows" of the outlanders. He and the old man stayed crouched down to use the hull as cover. Vinan looked to the opposite bank of the river and saw men on horses galloping at the pace of the boat. Most had sheathed swords but a few carried bent bows of wood with which they fired arrows at the boat. Vinan observed that arrows were coming from the opposite side as well...

"*Vinan!*" Enna shouted from the back of the boat.

"We have pursuers!" Crissa shrieked from the cover of the cabin.

The Shai, already crouching opposite Vinan and the Raq, drew his blade and shouted to Vinan.

"We are being attacked, En'Shai! Prepare to fight!"

Arrows pricked the boat for a few more moments but ceased flying when none hit their mark. Vinan saw the boat beginning to veer without anyone to steer it. Soon it would crash on a rock or end up on the shore with the horsemen.

"*Vinan!*" Enna shouted from the back of the boat.

Vinan attempted to leap towards one of the dropped oars but was pulled down immediately by his shoulder.

"Stay down!" shouted the old man.

"We need to steer the boat!" Vinan protested.

"And get an arrow in your chest?"

"We'll be on the rocks soon if someone doesn't steer!"

"*Vinan!*" Enna shouted frantically from the back of the boat.

The Shai took notice of her cries and sprinted to her. Arrows were fired at him and all missed him, instead peppering the side of the cabin with their shafts.

"En'Shai! Come see this!"

Vinan crawled quickly to the Shai and Enna and looked to where the girl pointed. He saw that there were two boats in pursuit. They were larger than the humble vessel of the old Raq and much faster with their sails unfurled to catch the wind.

"We are being chased by other boats!"

Vinan shouted back to Crissa and her father. The two of them shared a look of realization that they would have to manage the ship regardless of the threat of the arrows.

Another landed on the deck beside the Shai.

"Survive the arrows until our pursuers come, En'Shai. We will not outrun that boat no matter how hard the old man and the girl try."

David Standeven

Another arrow struck the back of the boat near the Shai.

"Are you ready to kill, En'Shai?"

Vinan gripped his sword tight.

"No mercy and no surrender," he assured the Shai.

Two more arrows missed the Shai, and one landed near Enna. The girl took notice of the arrows, as if only just realizing their existence, and walked with inhuman serenity to the front of the boat. Arrows landed near Vinan and the Shai, near Crissa and her father as they tried to handle the boat, but none were launched at Enna.

"They aren't shooting at her!" Vinan exclaimed.

"They are trying to capture her En'Shai. They're not going to risk killing her."

Two more arrows landed near Vinan and the Shai.

"Get down, En'Shai!" The Shai ducked at last behind the hull and a barrel for cover. "Our time is not yet."

"Look!" Vinan exclaimed as he pointed at Enna.

The blue aura glowed about her once more, with more brilliance than Vinan had ever witnessed. She stretched her arms out to their full length and stood still as the mast in the center of the boat. Myriad small stones emerged from the water and floated mid-air above the boat. Terrified curses came from both shores. Crissa dropped her oar to stare speechless and dumbstruck. Her father stood silent in awe.

Enna made a sweeping motion with her right hand and stones flew to the right shore. She made a sweeping motion with her left hand and stones flew to the left shore. Men fell from their horses with cries of pain as their companions rode away from them and the hail of river rocks.

"Did you know she could do that, En'Shai?" the Shai asked.

"Not like this," Vinan gasped.

An arrow struck Enna in the shoulder and she let out a cry of pain as she fell to the deck.

"Enna!"

111

Vinan yelled as he ran to her. An arrow landed at his feet and he looked to the source. One of the mounted woodsmen held a curved wooden bow, carried a full quiver of arrows, and had another arrow already nocked upon the string. Vinan dove to the fallen Enna as the arrow sailed past his head. He cradled the girl in his arms and studied the arrow that had pierced her.

"Vinan..." she gasped with exhaustion.

"Don't pull the arrow out!" shouted the old Raq. "You'll only hurt her worse!"

"Look!" Crissa shouted.

The bowman had ridden ahead to a rock that overlooked the river. As the boat approached Vinan saw all too well the significance. Once the boat passed beneath the rock the bowman would have a clear shot from above of all five in the boat.

There was no time to get to the cabin. The rock was fast approaching. Vinan noticed his spear next to him on the deck. His only spear.

The boat now sailed beneath the outcropping. The bowman began to nock his arrow.

Vinan pointed the spear straight up and threw it. The weapon hit its mark, the shoulder of the bowman, and the archer released his arrow too early as he fell forward down the cliff and into the water.

The arrows ceased at last. Vinan had slain the last bowman and the only one whom Enna had not struck down.

"Good throw!" shouted Crissa triumphantly.

"En'Shai!"

The pursuing boats were finally upon them. Vinan heard Ancar shouting from one of the sterns.

"You five come with me! We'll board the boat!"

Vinan drew his sword and rushed to defend the back of the boat. He arrived late to the fray, for the Shai had struck down the first two boarders with the fury of a feral beast. Despite the ever-increasing turbulence of the boat as it was buffeted by the white

David Standeven

foam rapids, the warrior of Kodumaa danced a ferocious dance of war. His blade slashed through the wet air, slicing flesh, and letting blood. Ever he hacked and ever did men from the other boat fall slain on the deck or into the rushing white river below.

Vinan fought cautiously and unimpressively by comparison. He warded off the men who tried to board from the other boat by using the full reach of his sword. He quickly discovered that the swords the men used were of brittle metal far inferior to the one he and the Shai held. He also learned with much relief that the men who held them were woefully unskilled even compared to him. Confidence in his own abilities rose within Vinan as he mocked the men.

"Afraid of a wild mountain boy?" he taunted. "Come get me, you outlander weaklings!"

"Forget the boy!" Ancar shouted. "The girl is who we want! Just kill him!"

Three men on the boat looked at one another and smiled. Together they jumped across from their boat. Vinan stabbed one in the stomach mid-jump, barely having time to remove it and send the man into the river when the other two landed.

The Shai was entirely focused on the men on the other boat, luring them close and butchering them, his bloodlust fully unleashed and far surpassed anything Vinan had ever witnessed from his own people. It was as if the god of war was here and determined to destroy all the men on that one pursuing vessel.

Vinan was on his own against the two men who had made it aboard.

He rushed them without hesitation. Though the first man managed to get his sword up to block Vinan's blow, Vinan's momentum caught him off balance and drove him back. Vinan glimpsed that the other man was entirely unready for his sudden attack, still settling his footing and fumbling with his weapon. Vinan pushed the first man away and drove his sword into the unprepared man's chest. He pulled his sword out again just as the

113

other man recovered and swung. The swing missed Vinan barely. Vinan now raised his blade to block the next swing and caught it midair.

The man used his superior brute force to push Vinan back. Vinan found himself on his back foot and deflecting an unskilled but furious series of sword strikes, his newfound skill with a sword and his few short years in the mountains being all that kept him alive at this moment. There was no chance to take back the initiative, no help from Enna or the Shai, and no room left for him to back away. His back was pressed against the side of the boat, his sword locked against his enemies, with the greater strength of the man pressing down on him. The rough iron sword of the settler cleaving Vinan's skull seemed inevitable.

There was a thud and the man dropped his sword, letting Vinan go and staggering in a daze. Crissa stood behind him with the oar with which she had struck his head.

"Now!" she yelled.

Vinan buried his sword up to the hilt in the man's gut. He withdrew it and pushed the dying man overboard into the waters below.

"Crissa!" the old Raq shouted. "The rapids!"

Before the little boat, a formation of rocks emerged, worse than any they had encountered yet. They seemed to have sharp knife-like points pointing directly against any boat heading downstream. Worse, the formation spanned nearly half the width of the river and before the boat. They had to steer left to avoid it and fast.

Crissa ran to her father and worked with all her might to avoid the jagged edges of the rocks even as the rushing rapids tried to push the boat towards them. The boat sailed closer to the formation, appearing as if its side would strike the rocks. Vinan wanted to aid them, but quickly surmised that he would only get in their way.

The clamor of clanging swords did not cease for even a

114

moment as the Shai, like an insatiable god of war, continued his battle with Ancar and his men. The boat directly behind theirs had lost too many men to the blade of Kodumaa and all its skeleton could manage was trying to survive the river. In this, they failed as the hull of their vessel was soon wrecked upon the rocky shores. The men who clung on desperately were fortunate to have survived and had long lost interest in capturing anyone. The other boat was adjacent to that of the Raq's, its crew diminished but with Ancar leading from the prow. Sword drawn and a bandage around his leg, he looked to the Shai as if ready to fight at last.

"Look out!" came a voice from Ancar's boat.

Vinan looked to the boat to see a pallid-faced Ancar looking downstream to the rock formation. It was then that Vinan realized what Ancar just had. The boat of slavers was headed directly towards the jagged edges where it had no hope of staying intact. If the pursued boat barely missed the rocks, then it would be free. If the pursuing boat could not displace its prey soon, it would be wrecked far worse than its companion boat.

"Push them!" Ancar yelled. "Push them to the shore!"

He jumped across close to where the Shai stood. The Shai shoved his blade into the chest of one more man, pulled it out, and swung at Ancar. The slaver was forced to raise his own sword to defend himself. Vinan approached while clinging tight to the side of the rocking boat with one hand while his other carried his now bloodied sword.

Crissa steered the boat hard on his side to angle it through the opening in the rocks. She and her father pushed their oars with all their might against the jutting edges of stone. It was not enough. They could not overcome the current and the rocks after all.

And then the current began to shift. The boat floated away from the rocks, against all reason, as if the river decided in one instant to spare them.

Enna stood upon the deck, shining in a blue light. The arrow that had pierced her shoulder lay upon the deck. She outstretched her right hand and pulled at the air as if struggling with an invisible force. Her face was contorted with pain and the muscles in her body seemed strained nearly to the breaking point. It was then that Vinan and Crissa realized that the girl of the forest was shifting the current, pulling at the water through some force or power known only to her. And she was pushing herself to her limits to do so.

"What are you?" Crissa whispered in awe.

Enna collapsed to the deck as the front half of the boat narrowly and safely passed through the opening in the rocks. Vinan looked ahead to see a slow current with no white water in sight and breathed a sigh of needed relief.

They had survived the rapids.

The sounds of wood cracking and men screaming in terror assaulted their ears. The slaver boat was dashed upon the rocks and split into a thousand pieces. Vinan looked away, not wishing to watch the dying moments of men he could not help. The punishment for their deeds had come with little warning and no respite.

Ancar's own judgment came but a moment later. The Shai effortlessly pushed Ancar's sword aside and drove his own into the man's throat. When the Shai pulled the blade out, the slaver slumped over and fell gracelessly into the water.

"No!" The second man screamed from the bank.

Vinan looked to the right shore and saw the man he had forgotten. He was sitting mounted on his horse with a pained look of loss and anger. Vinan, however, could see that the man had lost all will to fight. He turned his horse and spurred it into the woods, abandoning his followers. The other riders—seeing no reason to continue—dispersed.

Vinan looked to the opposite bank and saw that the men on that side were doing the same. All except the golden-bearded third man, who sat motionless atop his horse and stared at the boat as it passed. Vinan watched the man until he was out of sight. It unsettled him that the man made no movement but continued to watch them like a hungry wolf. Out of all Ancar's men, this last was the only one Vinan truly feared.

The swordsman broke the silence of the struggle's aftermath.

"It is over, En'Shai," he said in a calm voice, so unlike his earlier blood fury. "We are safe for now."

Vinan sighed, sat down on the deck, and caught his breath.

"Are you hurt?" the Shai asked.

Vinan looked down at his arms and saw many little scratches that had drawn blood. He wiped them and saw that the letting was barely a trickle.

"Not much," he answered.

"Here, En'Shai," the Shai pulled some white linen out of his pouch. "Press this against the scratch to stop the bleeding. We can't risk you getting infected."

Vinan pressed as commanded and wrapped the most serious cuts in the cloth. He made his way back to the middle of the deck where Crissa and her father continued their work of steering the boat onwards.

"We did it," Crissa gasped. "The slavers cannot touch us now."

Vinan was distracted by the sight of the girl of the forest, crumpled on the floor of the boat.

"Enna!" he cried.

He knelt beside her. She was trembling, breathing heavily as if she were trying to hold onto every possible bit of air she could. Her hands were icy cold yet her forehead burned like fire. When he raised her arm he found it limp and cold as a dead trout.

"Enna!" Vinan frantically grasped the girl's shoulders. "Can you hear me, Enna?!"

She turned her head to him slowly and looked at him in a daze.

"*Vinan...*"

Vinan cradled her in his arms and held her close. He pressed her to his chest to warm her frigid body, but it did little good. Were it not for her heavy breathing Vinan would have feared that her end had come. That was something he could not abide, not while Kirru remained captive to slavers. He would reunite the girls. He and Enna would see Stek and Kirru again.

"Vinan."

Crissa's father stood over him. The Old Raq knelt down and put his hand on the girl's forehead.

"She is exhausted, and perhaps even ill," he said. "She needs to rest in the cabin."

He gently took Enna from Vinan and walked to the cabin with the girl nestled in his arms like a small babe. He held her as he had no doubt held Crissa long ago when he left the path of war-riding for the gentle life of raising his daughter. Vinan felt Enna was safe with the old warrior, and hoped she would wake again. After all, she had used her powers and exhausted herself before and she had always recovered after some sleep.

This time would surely be no different.

"You fear for the girl, En'Shai? You weep for her."

Vinan put his hand to his cheek and felt the water. He quickly wiped it away along with the same that had formed in his eyes.

"Does it ever get easier?" He asked the Shai.

"Does what get easier?"

"The fear... The nerves," Vinan held his right hand in front of his face and saw that it was shaking uncontrollably. "Does it ever become easy to forget that you have killed men?"

"No," the Shai said grimly. "It does not. You only become used to the terror, callous to the blood, and numb to the pain."

This was not what the boy had wanted to hear.

"So, I will always be afraid," he said downcast.

"You fear because it is in your nature," replied the Shai. "You fear because you have goodness in you and hate the suffering that fighting brings."

He put his hand on Vinan's shoulder. "You fear, En'Shai, because you are not evil like those slavers or wayward as I have become."

The Shai then reached for one of his two water skins and held it out to Vinan. The boy recognized it as the one with the liquid that tasted like fire. He shook his head to decline it but the Shai shoved it at him.

"Drink a little. It will help you sleep tonight."

Vinan reached out and did as the Shai said. He tried to swallow it quickly to avoid the taste but that caused the burn to only intensify in his throat and his chest. Coughing and with tears in his eyes, he choked a mouthful down.

"Do not drink it so fast!" said the Shai as he took the skin back. "Many good and noble men are destroyed by taking in too much of this drink."

Vinan was already beginning to feel it take effect. His eyes began to close even against his will, his head became like a giant rock he wished to put down, and he could barely feel his hands. He rose to his feet while he still had use of them—and stumbled to the cabin. There he slept for many hours beside Enna as the Shai and the others steered the boat through the night.

CHAPTER 12

The Huntsman

The full light of the sun shone brightly on the deck and through the door of the cabin when Vinan awoke. Enna lay on the floor, shivering and coughing uncontrollably. Vinan rose from where he lay to take hold of her. She was as cold as an icy mountain stream and the shaking did not cease.

The boy tried to gain her attention, to see if she still was conscious.

"Enna!"

"*Vinan...*"

As if in a daze, she struggled to focus on his face. Her eyelids opened and closed as if with pain. She coughed again as if her lungs were filled with liquid.

Vinan placed her down gently. He stumbled onto the deck frantically and found the Shai steering the boat. The old Raq rested upon the deck beside the exhausted Crissa. The daughter of the Raq took notice of Vinan as he worriedly looked for help.

"What is it, Vinan?" she asked.

"Enna is sick!" he replied.

The old Raq arose and walked quickly to the cabin. He knelt

beside the girl of the forest, felt her forehead and cheeks, clasped her quaking hands firmly, threw a fur blanket over her, and withdrew with a sigh.

"She is very ill," he said. "She needs a fire, food, and medicine now."

He picked up an oar and walked to the Shai.

"We need to go ashore," he said.

The Shai nodded and soon the boat had run aground on the mud-lined banks. The Shai, the Raq, Crissa, and Vinan all jumped off to push the vessel to dry ground. Without a word shared among them, the old man returned to the boat with a bundled Enna while the other three quickly assembled and lit a fire.

The Raq placed the bundled Enna beside the fire. He dripped some water from his water skin into the palm of his hand and placed some crushed leaves from his pouch into it. He opened the girl's mouth gently and poured the mixture in.

"Do you know what blackberries are, Vinan?" the old warrior asked.

"Black berries?" Vinan said, confused.

"I'll get them," Crissa interjected. "They must grow here."

"It is too dangerous," the old Raq answered. "Vinan has lived his whole life in the wild."

"But he doesn't know what to look for," she protested.

"I'll go," Vinan said. "You can come with me to get these blackberries. I will protect you."

The old Raq looked to the resolute boy, to his fearless daughter, and then back to Vinan. He sighed with the realization that he could not protect his daughter forever.

"Go then," he said. "I will tend to the girl and our swordsman friend will guard the boat. Come back the moment you run into danger and no later than sunset."

Crissa nodded and walked away towards the forest.

"Vinan!" said the old Raq.

Vinan stopped.

"Protect my daughter, please."

The vulnerability in the tone of the old warrior cut to Vinan's heart.

"I will," the boy answered with a cracking voice, remembering that he promised the same to Kirru and Stek.

He followed after Crissa with due haste.

"Be careful, En'Shai," the Shai said as he passed. "Be wary of any more men you may find and do not let yourself be seen. Come back here the moment you find anything."

Vinan soon caught up to Crissa a short distance into the forest, a forest unlike anything Vinan had ever seen. He sensed that care had been taken to keep it wild, a care that resembled the inner woods by the villages of the mountain peoples. Paths carefully crafted to not appear as paths led into clearings as if enticing the wandering animal or wayfarer deeper in.

The touch of man lingered close.

"Careful," he said quietly to Crissa.

"Why?" she asked.

"Something seems wrong."

"You smell it?"

He shook his head. "I sense it. We need to be careful."

She nodded and continued on with Vinan watching her every step. The more they continued, the more Vinan's unease rose. The forest in which they walked seemed to be crafted for wild animals to walk where they now walked. There was a sterility around them that removed the untamed spontaneity and savagery of an overgrown forest that knew no man.

"You didn't need to come," Crissa said at length.

She turned to him and smiled. "But I'm glad you did."

Before she took another step forward, Vinan noticed something wrong about where her foot was about to land, a loose collection of grass upon the forest ground.

"Wait!" he shouted, pulling her backward with a sudden jerk.

He threw Crissa away from the spot and backed away slowly.

"It's a trap," he said, bending down to lift a rock from the ground. "Step on it and..."

He threw the rock with full might at the spot. The loosely assembled grass caved in to leave a hole exposed. Vinan and Crissa stepped forward and looked down. Sharp wooden spikes jutted upward within a pit five feet deep.

"You'd be impaled," Vinan finished.

"Why would someone make this?" Crissa asked, horrified.

"To kill beasts," Vinan answered. "We did the same where I'm from."

Something whizzed from the trees and struck the ground near Vinan's feet. Vinan jumped back and darted behind a tree, catching only a glimpse of the arrow. Crissa followed his lead and regained her trembling breath while resting upon the trunk.

"A hunter," she panted. "Why..."

Vinan shushed her. He waited and listened. He heard nothing. He waited and listened again. There was a faint sound of wood creaking and leaves shaking, of a man moving branch to branch as Dhof the tree-jumper always did.

"There is a man in the trees above us," he whispered.

"How are we going to get away?" Crissa replied in a whisper.

"Run!"

Vinan ran as fast as he could back the way he came. He had only run about ten feet when he heard a rustling of leaves and Crissa scream behind him. He turned to see her caught in a net hanging from the limb of a tree.

"Crissa!" he shouted.

"Go Vinan!" she shouted back. "Get back to the boat!"

Vinan drew his knife to cut her down but another arrow whizzed by and landed mere inches from his feet.

"Run, you fool!" Crissa shouted.

Vinan ran back to the boats, dodging behind trees and changing direction erratically so the next arrows would miss. His heart raced too fast for him to notice that no more arrows followed. The forest thinned and opened before him, his feet trod upon sand instead of leaves, and the two men who were his companions watched his worried approach in readiness.

"Hide!" he shouted to them.

"What is it, En'Shai?" the Shai asked.

Vinan climbed into the boat and panted. "Arrows! Traps! Men in trees!"

"Vinan! Where's Crissa?!" the Raq demanded.

"Alive in a snare!" Vinan shouted back.

Undeterred by all this, the Shai stepped forward towards the forest.

"Stay your arrows!" he commanded. "We are not here to infringe on you or your hunting grounds."

"Be ye gone then!" answered a gruff voice from high in the trees. "There is nothing here fer ye!"

"We only seek to pass through to track down some slavers," said the old Raq. "We will be gone as soon as we can."

"That time be now!" Said the same voice from seemingly somewhere else than it had been before. "Go before I fire at ye to kill!"

"There is a girl with us who is ill and requires rest and medicine," said the old Raq. "Have the hunters of the lowlands lost all sense of pity and hospitality since I last passed through here?"

There was a space of a few moments where no one spoke. Finally, a man emerged from the trees and walked towards the swordsman; a short man with a long and scraggly grey-brown beard. He was clad in the skin of bucks, roughly cut and tanned by his own calloused hands. He held a bent piece of shaved wood with a long twine stretching from one end to the other, and he carried in his back a great many arrows.

"When last ye passed these lands," he said," that must have been a long time ago. The slavers and their rotten ilk have taken everything. I be the last of the hunters who still live 'round here."

"You have my condolences, last hunter," said the Shai with uncharacteristic gentility. "I too know what it is to be the last man of your kind. We will leave this place in peace when the girl with us is strong enough."

And with that, he pointed to the girl, who lay on the ground in the throes of a fevered and disturbed sleep. The hunter walked past the Shai and knelt by her. He removed his hide glove from his right hand and touched her forehead.

"She be struck with strong fever," he said. "She needs better than ye can give her."

He lifted her in his arms and looked to the old Raq. "I will take ye in until she be strong. Call out yer wild mountain boy."

The Shai nodded. "Come out, En'Shai! And keep your sword low."

Vinan walked out slowly, obeying the swordsman. The hunter observed Vinan with a watchful eye and then relaxed his gaze to turn around and head back into the woods.

"Follow him," said the Shai to Vinan. "This place is his home and we are guests."

Vinan did so warily as the party walked the same way Vinan and Crissa had done the first time. They walked past the trap that had ensnared Crissa, now empty with twine cut by a dagger. Vinan looked for her to no avail and hoped she had not walked into a spiked pit.

The hunter stopped suddenly.

"I know where ye be," he said aloud.

"Crissa!" Said the old Raq. "Come down from there! This man is not our enemy."

Two small, booted feet landed on the leaf-covered ground as Crissa jumped from a limb behind the others.

"I don't trust those who shoot at me," she said with an icy glare.

"That be no concern of mine," said the hunter. "I be takin' this girl to my cabin. Yer welcome to stay with the others and eat or stay out here with the traps."

Crissa scoffed and then sheathed her dagger. She walked alongside her father as they proceeded to the hunter's cabin. All stayed silent in their approach, and Vinan took the opportunity of walking a safe path to look for other snares the hunter had placed.

He found many as they continued: a bit of exposed rope tied to a tree limb and leading somewhere Vinan could not determine, a conspicuous pile of leaves no doubt concealing something painful for an unsuspecting animal, and a hunk of old meat left to hang from a branch. None of these could have fooled anyone who knew to look for them, and Vinan even considered how much better he would have laid them, but it was clear to him that the snares were meant to catch beasts and not men. No man familiar with a hunt would fall for these. Perhaps outlanders unfamiliar with the forest would.

After some minutes of walking through the woods, Vinan could see no more traps. Before them stood a hut made entirely of wooden logs, sturdier than those they had seen in the river town. The hunter pushed open a thick wooden door and entered.

When they were inside the cabin Vinan realized how well-built it was, for it held in the warmth of fire far better than any of the ones in the town could. The fire burned in an enclosed pit of stone that funneled the smoke through the roof and out of the cabin. An earthen pot rested over the flames, emanating the savory scent of broth. The smell reawakened Vinan's repressed hunger and distracted him momentarily from the sickness of Enna or his brother and sister waiting for his rescue.

The hunter placed Enna down gently upon a bear pelt and threw furs over her.

"She needs water," he said. "She will be sweating heavy until the sickness passes."

Vinan immediately opened his water skin and put it to the girl's lips. She kept conscious enough to drink from it through heavy breaths. She looked to the ceiling in a fevered daze as her mouth released the almost empty skin.

"Do you have a well near?" the Shai asked.

"Outside on the west end of the hut," the hunter answered. "It be cold and from a spring."

"Give me any flasks that need filling," the Shai said to his companions.

Vinan gave his freely to the Shai while the old Raq unslung his own from his hip and handed it over. Crissa made no move and said nothing as the Shai approached her on his way towards the door of the hut.

"Yours is filled?" the Shai asked her.

"Full enough," she answered.

"As you wish it." he said as he left the others alone in the cabin.

Vinan watched over Enna intently, taking no note of the hunter scooping hot venison soup into carved wooden bowls and sharing little of the Raq's desire to rest. The old warrior curled up in a corner of the hut and threw a blanket over himself with a seeming relief to be under a roof on dry land. His daughter sat beside Vinan and accepted two bowls from the hunter. She placed one beside the disinterested Vinan and cradled the second one in her hands.

"You can't always save everyone," she said.

Vinan looked at her.

"When we were in the forest," she continued. "You would have died trying to save me, if the hunter had meant to kill you. You should have run."

"I will never sacrifice someone to save myself," Vinan protested.

"Think like that," Crissa said, "and you will sacrifice yourself for nothing. You will leave your siblings enslaved. You sometimes need to choose who to leave and who to save."

"I do not need to choose between protecting you and my brother and sister." Vinan said.

127

"I can protect myself," Crissa retorted. "Your little Kirru cannot. Do not die before you have the chance to save her."

"I will always fight to protect you, your father, Enna, or even the Shai if he needs it," Vinan said determinedly. "Unlike the people of these outlands, I do not hold life cheap. I never will."

"Then don't throw your own away because of some stupid sense of warrior's honor," Crissa finished. "You are too brave and good to die for no reason."

"I be listening to the girl if I were ye," the hunter interjected. "In these forests, a hunter survives. Battles, honor, and great deeds be left to the pretty stories."

"Enough of this," said the old Raq. "Eat, rest, and be thankful we are all alive. Let the talk of heroism come when we have found the enslaved children."

"We will not find the enslaved children if we stay here long," said the Shai, who had entered so quietly the others had barely noticed. "We have at least two more days until we reach Qiriq. Who knows where they will be by then? Who knows where they are now?"

"So, you want to leave immediately?" the old Raq asked.

"If we can," the Shai answered. "Otherwise, as soon as the four of us who will go on are rested."

"Wait!" Vinan rose to his feet. "Are you saying we leave Enna behind?!"

The Shai looked at the hunter. "Will she be safe here?"

"As safe as anyone be in this world, I suppose," the hunter sighed.

"Then, yes, En'Shai," the Shai looked back at Vinan. "We are continuing without her."

"But," Vinan protested, "she helped us..."

"And we should be forever grateful to her," the Shai cut him off. "We must keep moving."

"Her power," Vinan said. "You saw what it did! If we had her with us then..."

"Then she would use it again and need to be cared for again." the Shai interrupted a second time. "Look at her En'Shai! I do not know what she possesses but I can see that this is what it does to her. She cannot do such things without straining herself, and now she is sick with high fever. You can either go to Qiriq and leave her here for now, or you can wait days for her to recover. By then, who knows where Stek and Kirru will be?"

Vinan looked around the room to the others. The old Raq had already risen back to his feet as if ready to continue the journey, only the bowl in his hand indicated any intention to remain in the hut for any time. He looked to Crissa, still sitting, and cradling a bowl of soup in her hands. A sorrowful but resigned expression was on her face as she looked back at Vinan.

"You can't always save everyone," she repeated.

Vinan cast his eyes to Enna, who breathed heavily under a thick layer of furs. Beads of sweat formed on her forehead as she lay next to the fire. Vinan forced himself to admit that she would not recover soon, but too great was the fever to wait for it to pass. He resigned himself to this fact, let out a sigh, and conceded.

"I will return here," he said, "when we have gotten back Kirru and Stek."

"I do not doubt it, En'Shai," said the Shai.

"Vinan!" Crissa said sharply.

Vinan looked down to see her holding out a bowl of the hot soup, teeming with chunks of meat, roots, and herbs in a brown broth.

"Eat this before we go," she said.

Vinan accepted the soup.

CHAPTER 13

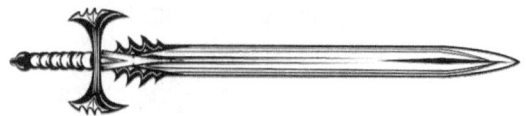

Strange Companionships

V inan swung wide at the Shai, and his sword was stopped
mid-swing by the Kodumaa blade. Without hesitating a
moment, he leaned his weight to the left. The whole boat
tilted with him. The Shai was not deterred by the trick and bent his
body into it, throwing his left fist at Vinan's face. Vinan released
his sword and jumped back, missing the Shai's strike, and
struggling to stay balanced as the boat rocked side to side. He bent
himself into the next sway and moved around the mast with the
hope of getting behind the Shai. The flitting hope proved vain as
the Shai stopped his sword again. The battle, now reduced to the
brute strength and direct swordsmanship of the combatants, ended
in a familiar fashion.

With Vinan pinned to the deck.

"Well attempted, En'Shai," gasped the Shai. "You have done
very well on this unstable footing."

Vinan hardly felt any pride in this, for not once in all their
sparring had he ever touched the Shai with his blade. Even as his
mentor removed his blade and walked away to refresh himself,
Vinan remained lying on the deck, staring up at the clouds that

moved across the blue sky. He closed his eyes and saw Kirru weeping, terrified and lost, with no one to help her. He thought of Stek and his hard-headedness, hoping that his brother had not gotten himself killed in a hopeless escape.

"Get up," said the old man. "You and the Shai have rocked this boat enough and I need the deck to…"

He stopped. Vinan realized with embarrassment that the waters of frustration had swelled in his eyes, ready to stream down his cheeks. There was no way the wizened Raq had not noticed. Vinan scrambled to his feet and made his way to the prow of the boat to stare down the river ahead. He wiped his wet eyes and rubbed the dripping tears from his cheeks.

"Vinan…"

Vinan did not turn to face Crissa, who had come up behind him. He could not look at her like this. He could not let anyone see him like this.

"We had to leave Enna behind, Vinan," she continued. "If we had waited behind…"

"It's not about her," he croaked.

Silence hung in the air, disturbed only by the creaking of the boat and the rushing of the river's current.

Crissa sighed. "You miss them don't you?"

Vinan looked down at the sword he held in his hand. "What if I can't save them?"

"Vinan?"

"What if I can't save them?" he repeated. "I'm not strong enough."

Her hand took hold of his shoulder with a surprisingly firm grip.

"No," she said, "you are the bravest brother a child could imagine. You knew nothing of the world and you followed your brother and sister anyway. You have been beaten, humiliated, and exhausted but you still haven't given up."

"What good will it do, if I cannot free them when I find

131

them?" Vinan retorted. "If I cannot learn how to fight with the sword then it will be for nothing."

"It doesn't matter," she replied. "You will not be alone when you get to Qiriq."

She pulled Vinan around so his eyes met hers. Her hands gripped his shoulders so tight he thought she was going to dig her fingers into him.

"I promise you," she said earnestly, "I will help you get them back. I will not leave you until they are safe with you again."

Vinan saw something else flash in her eyes before she released her hands suddenly and turned away.

"You don't have to do these things alone." she said as her usual voice returned. "Don't be a hero and die for nothing. Stek and Kirru need you to save them. Coming all this way after them is heroism enough."

Crissa returned to her work on the rigging and left Vinan alone with his thoughts. He looked down at his sword again and sheathed it. He walked back towards the cabin to get some food.

"Your skills with the blade are better than you think," the old Raq said to him. "The Shai is a swordsman of incredible ability. Do not compare yourself to him. "

"I won't be fighting him when the time comes," Vinan said.

"No," the old man. "It is your nerves that you must control. You must focus on winning, not on your shame or your fears."

"Let me know when we are at Qiriq," said Vinan. "I will be resting."

And so, he retired into the little cabin, awaiting the sight of greater civilization and the markets of the slavers.

***

Evening overtook the land with a golden sun setting against a red-streaked sky. The little boat drew ever closer to the trade city of Qiriq. The two children aboard slept in the cabin, leaving on deck only the two warriors of Kodumaa and the Raq Horde. Silence had been the peace these two men had kept, preferring to keep the old wounds of history covered. That silence could be held no longer as the power of simple curiosity collapsed the rampart.

"How does a Raq war rider of the plains find himself owning a boat?" asked the bemused Shai. "I always heard your people are famously terrible at seafaring."

"Men change," the old Raq replied. "When the owner of a sword finds a hundred more arrayed against him for every one he cuts down then he must ask himself, what good is it to keep himself in the fight? For what does he fight?"

"You have a daughter," the Shai said. "Would you not take up the sword for her? Or is your war-rider spirit truly dead?"

"It was because of her that I put aside my sword forever," said the former war-rider. "After the war in Rhanijad, I saw no reason to ride, and then word that I had a daughter soon reached me. To protect her, I left the horde and took her to lands far from the wars. But war... war reaches all lands in which man dwells."

"What happened in Rhanijad?" the Shai asked pointedly.

"What happened?" the old Raq repeated as if confused.

"The legends of Farken-Raq end in Rhanijad. He struck down its High King in battle, scattered their armies, and then..."

The Shai waved his hand.

"He died. A thousand tales tell his death differently. He fell in battle with the Empire, his brothers killed him in battle, assassins killed him in the night, or he drank himself to death. You, who rode beside him, must know the truth."

The old man sighed. "I will not tell you how he died, but he indeed died in Rhanijad where I buried him secretly in a grave where no man would find."

"Then he is dead."

"Does this disappoint you?"

"I can never slay the man who destroyed my home. My blood oath to avenge my people will never be fulfilled."

"Tell me," the old man asked, "why must you fulfill it?"

"Why should those who did such evil live free?"

"Why must you dwell upon their evil rather than building something good?"

Silence hung in the air as the Shai had no answer.

"What have you done to rebuild Kodumaa?" the old Raq asked at length.

The Shai silently stared towards the setting sun.

"You are childless," the old Raq continued. "You have no home to call your own, no wife to build your home, no children to teach the ways of the Shaii'. What will you leave behind in the end but some bones and a beautiful sword?"

"That life was not for me," the Shai replied. "The day the Raqs destroyed Kodumaa was the day those dreams forever died."

"No," the old Raq shook his head. "You killed them in your heart. You forsook any hope of joy by choosing to dwell all these years on obtaining revenge. You seek vengeance now, but what will that gain you? There is no honor in it. It will not bring you peace, pay the blood-debt of your people, or silence the wails in your memories. "

"A Raq would not understand."

"No, Shai of Kodumaa, I understand better than you think. I took my vengeance when I rode with Farken-Raq in the sack of Kodumaa. I took my vengeance when we rode into Rhanijad to slay its High King. But with my bloodlust answered and my wrath fed, I was still not filled. Vengeance cannot fill the heart of man. It will leave you hollowed, as I found myself in Rhanijad."

"And," said the Shai, "what did you do after Rhanijad?"

"I left Farken-Raq in Rhanijad, to let go of the man I was. I died with my old friend."

"Did you?"

"Perhaps not entirely, but I did live on to protect my daughter. I will leave her behind when I mortally die and perhaps she can bring goodness to this world just as I once brought death."

134

Silence again hung over the two men in the yellow twilight of the plains.

"Old Raq," said the Shai, "you helped slaughter my people. You rode to war beside the monster Farken-Raq. By the blood oath I swore many years ago, I should slay you in justice for my people."

He turned to the aged war-rider.

"But," the Shai continued, "I see that you are a man of honor and a man of true mettle. You and your daughter have helped En'Shai in his hour of need. For that you have my gratitude and my respect. I would have never thought I would be honored to fight beside a Raq, and yet here I am."

"Will you give up your revenge after we help the boy?" the old Raq asked. "Will you at least attempt to live in peace when this is over?"

"I promise nothing. My life is too full of promises that I failed."

"Do you still plan to leave nothing behind when you are passed from this world?"

"No," answered the Shai with a smile, "in that cabin is a noble En'Shai who will one day far surpass you or me as a warrior or as a man. In him, I hold my hope that men can be good. In him, I see heroism reborn into this wicked world. Perhaps he will be my legacy."

The old Raq gave a knowing nod and he watched the sun set upon the Shai. As night fell, the way forward remained still as uncertain and black as ever it had been.

CHAPTER 14

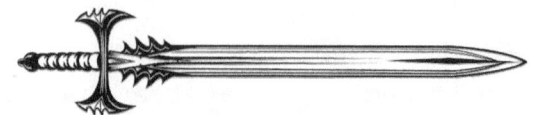

City of Misery

Vinan had never seen so many people and so much misery in one place. He had never smelled so much human filth. After leaving the docks and passing beneath the tall white walls he found himself harangued by men, women, and children in tattered clothes begging pathetically for coins to any who passed. He stared at a child for a moment, a gaunt little girl that reminded him of Kirru. He stared a moment too long, for the beggars now approached him from all sides. Fortunately, the Shai was paying attention to him and forced his way through the throng. He grabbed Vinan by the arm and pulled him out of the throng.

"Pay no attention to beggars, En'Shai. Do not look at anyone longer than you need to."

They proceeded unmolested with the Shai and the old man leading the way through the crowded main streets. Vinan noticed as much activity and business in the side street as in the main but whispered business instead of the competing shouts of the eager street vendors all around him.

"Fresh cooked meals here!"

"Jewels from the east! Fine jewels for your pretty women and girls!"

"Come here to see your future! Peer into the opportunities that life has for you!"

Vinan found the noise nigh unbearable. So many people, so many voices, so much pushing, so much smell, and no sense to any of it.

"Are you alright?" Crissa asked him in a low voice.

"I am," he answered while putting on a strong face.

"Just a moment ago you looked overwhelmed and in pain," she whispered. "Are you that worried about your brother and sister?"

"No, that's not it."

"Then what is it?"

There was no pretending to be strong with her. He decided he might as well tell the truth.

"How can anyone stand this?" he asked

"The city?"

"Do you smell it?"

"It's impossible not to. It's why I wish I could live in the mountains far from here."

"I wish I could too," he said downcast.

This silenced Crissa and ended her wistful dreams of snow-capped peaks. Vinan almost immediately regretted having done so but saw no purpose in any further regret. He could do nothing but be silent and continue.

The old man led them into a section of the city where the streets were lined with vendors and merchants on both sides, using aggressive tactics in their attempts to draw the attention of people from the streets. Vinan heeded the Shai's advice by ignoring them all. He did, however, see a comfortably dressed man leading a woman and two children with a rope tied around their necks. He could not take his eyes away from the spectacle, with the heads of the leashed bent down following the man who held the rope. Crissa noticed it as well.

137

"A slave-owner," she said. "That woman and her two children have just been bought."

If Vinan had hated the idea of slavery before, it sickened him uncontrollably now that it stood plainly before him. He thought of Kirru and Stek with ropes around their necks. He had to find them and fast.

"How far until we get to the slavers?" Vinan asked aloud.

"The auction blocks are not far ahead," the old man answered. "There is someone I know who may be able to help us."

"A former soldier of the Raqs has contacts in the slave trade," grunted the Shai. "Why am I not surprised?"

The old man ignored the barb and walked on until they came to the slave market. There were fifty or more wooden platforms in a giant open square of the city. The shouting of the merchants here was just as loud as before, but their words sent chills down Vinan's spine.

"One strong and sturdy young man in the best condition! Perfect for any labor!"

"Captured warriors! Several captured warriors from the Kingdom of Rhanijad! Fine assets for any pit-masters in need of fighters!"

"One pretty and untarnished young woman sold for her debt! A pleasant and pleasurable addition for any household!"

It was one thing to hear about slavery, to think about it and imagine it. It was another thing entirely to see it in action and watch hundreds—thousands—accept it as nothing, just another routine part of life. It made Vinan want to burn down this filth-ridden city and everyone who lived in it.

The old Raq walked to a block where a dark-haired man with a trimmed and oiled thin mustache sat. His robes were cheap, but gaudy, to give off the appearance of luxurious extravagance while his hat was a strange sort of cylinder the likes of which Vinan had never seen. He held a small sack that appeared, from the way he held it, to be very heavy. Behind him, almost motionless as a specter, loomed a broad dark-skinned man with a sword whom Vinan had no intention of fighting.

But fighting did not seem to be anyone's intention, as the old Raq walked to the platform and hailed the merchant.

"How is business, Masath?"

The merchant recognized the old man immediately and seemed both a little surprised and aggravated by his presence. He appeared to be in a hurry to leave. Vinan wondered if the sack he held or the fact that he seemed to be selling no slaves at this time were reasons for that.

"My block is closed for the day," the merchant said. "Come back tomorrow."

"Come now, Masath," the old man said. "You know I have no interest in buying what you sell."

"I know," he sneered, "so do not waste your time once again trying to convince me to give up the trade."

"That is not why I am here, though I do hope you give up the trade someday."

"Unfortunately for your hope, I have a family to feed. Why are you here? I thought you had left this city behind. And who are these two?"

He pointed to Vinan and the Shai.

"Just travelers I met," the old man replied. "They seek some people who may have come through this market."

"Oh, do they?" The merchant stroked the black hairs on his chin with interest. "What sort of people?"

"A boy and a girl, and they look something akin to him."

The old man pointed to Vinan.

"I did, in fact," Masath said. "I bought the girl for next to nothing from her slavers."

"Where is she?" Vinan blurted out.

Masath smiled, his eyes gleaming at the sight of a new opportunity, and raised his hand.

"The girl is no longer here," he said, "but I can tell you where she is now. I can also tell you what happened to the boy."

"Tell me!" Vinan said eagerly.

"Not so fast," the merchant grinned while wagging his finger. "Here, when services are given, payment is expected. You will give me payment if I tell you?"

"You will be repaid," the Shai assured him, flipping him a coin in the air. "Now speak."

And he did.

"Two days ago, a party of armed slavers arrived in the city seeking to sell some things they had picked up in the wilderness. There were about ten or so in total, but you likely only want to know of the two wild children.

"The boy had been bound tight and had signs of beatings on him. Even in his state he looked at all of us with hatred in his eyes and struggled against his bonds. I passed him over to look at other opportunities as several other merchants were already outbidding one another for him.

"The girl was frightened. She would not stop crying, no matter how much the slavers barked at her to stop. No one wanted her, so I bought her for two coppers. I was sure I could treat her well enough to get her to stop crying and sell her for a small profit. Unfortunately, calming her proved nearly impossible, despite my best efforts. Fortunately, it did not matter as I made good money on her anyway."

"Then what became of her?" asked the old man.

"I sold her to Seren-Raq the next day."

"Seren-Raq visited your stall?"

"Indeed," Masath answered. "As he passed through here, the sad girl caught his eye and he stopped. He offered me more than I imagined the girl would ever bring me. Of course, I accepted his offer immediately."

"So, she is in the temple now," said the old man.

"That is most likely," Masath confirmed. "Seren-Raq is

known for treating his slaves well. They almost never leave the temple and serve him hand and foot."

"What of the boy?" the old man asked.

"Rejak bought him," the merchant pointed to the man selling slaves two blocks adjacent. "Rejak deals almost exclusively with men and boys for the fighting pits. Everyone who wanted the boy wanted him for that purpose."

"Thank you for your help," the old man said. "You may not know it, but you have done a good deed by telling us this."

But Masath was not finished. "A moment... What of the rest of my promised payment?"

"Your reward," answered the Shai with menace in his voice, "is that I do not permit En'Shai here to cut you from belly to neck for selling his sister like cattle."

The slave merchant's bronze face turned white with terror as he beheld the Shai's glare. Vinan observed that the dark-skinned bodyguard had readied his stance to fight, but also that if the Shai wished to kill Masath where he stood, then his guard would be of no help. And Masath knew this.

"Apologies for my friend, Masath," the old man said to break the tension, "but you must have known that this business can make enemies capable of killing you."

"It is not my fault," Masath whined, "that I must feed my family and that reselling slaves makes that so easy!"

"Seren-Raq paid you generously?" the old man asked.

"He did."

"Good, then take your gold from him and put it to good use. We are finished with you. Our business is with him now."

Masath collected himself and almost regained his composure. He tried to put on the most welcoming smile he could.

"Pleased that I could be of assistance," he said as he bowed and departed. "May you have good fortune in finding what you seek."

He motioned to his guard and they made their way from the

market together. The four seekers spoke in low voices among themselves.

"Your sister is in Seren-Raq's temple," the old man said to Vinan, "and your brother is somewhere in the fighting pits beneath the city. The first will be much harder than the second."

"How?" Vinan asked. "We don't even know where Stek is."

"The pits are easy to enter," Crissa said. "But the Temple of Plenty is one of the most guarded palaces in the city."

"How guarded?" the Shai inquired.

"You might as well attempt to sneak into the Palace of the Benefactors," she answered. "Seren-Raq guards his slaves, his treasures, and his home with both a cohort of the city guard and a band of battle-hardened Raq fighters."

"And the pits?" asked the Shai.

"A few underpaid drunken slobs with swords," she said.

"Good," the Shai smiled. "Then they will be easy to bribe or overpower."

"How are we going to get into the temple and save Kirru?" Vinan interjected.

"One thing at a time, En'Shai. Your brother is within our grasp. After that, we can decide how to overcome Seren-Raq. What do you know of him?"

This last question was directed at the old man, who answered thus.

"The last time I met Seren-Raq he was only a child. Since then, I have only heard that he is a decadent lover of women who has fought no battles nor raised a sword. He remains mostly in his palace enjoying the perks of being one of the twelve rulers of Qiriq. The farthest thing from the sort of Raq warlord you wish to cut down, warrior of Kodumaa."

Vinan wrestled in his mind which course he wanted to take, regardless of what the other three said. On the one hand, Stek would apparently be easy to rescue. Though, if it were that easy then perhaps it would not be long until he freed himself. Kirru, however, could not free herself, especially not from a citadel so well guarded. Kirru's need was greater. He had to free Kirru.

"We are freeing Kirru first," he declared aloud.

The other three stared at him stunned.

"Why so?" asked the Shai.

"If the pits are as easy to get in as Crissa says," Vinan answered, "then Stek can probably escape by his own hand."

"You have never been in the pits," Crissa objected. "You don't know that."

"Stek can manage," Vinan said. "And if he can't, he still needs our help less than Kirru."

"Do you even know what the fighting pits are?" Crissa asked with incredulity. "Your brother will be put in a pit to fight to the death against other boys and men. They may put him there as soon as tomorrow for all we know."

This forced Vinan to reconsider. Stek fighting to death terrified him. Stek could die because he did not save him soon enough. And then he thought back to Kirru. Defenseless Kirru, scared Kirru, Kirru in a palace surrounded by savage soldiers, Kirru wondering when her salvation would come and if it would come at all...

No, Kirru's need was still greater as far as he was concerned.

"Stek knows how to defend himself," he said.

The Shai looked straight at Vinan and spoke before Crissa could get a word in.

"If that were true, En'Shai, then we would not be here to save him. You overestimate your brother."

"It sounds like the Shaii' of Kodumaa," Vinan shot back, "overestimated their own abilities as well."

The Shai gave Vinan a dark look. "Do not speak of what you know not, En'Shai. It is because of their mistake that I do not misjudge my enemy. I learn from my mistakes and that is why I am still alive. You have yet to understand this."

Vinan and Crissa, with tempers high, were both prepared to

speak but they were immediately cut off.

"Enough!"

The old man commanded with more force than Vinan had ever seen him use. It was enough to silence the three of them for a moment.

"Enough," he repeated gently. "It should not matter in the end who we save first, for we will save them both in good time. We should eat now and decide after some thought who to rescue first tonight."

At that moment, the crowds began to suddenly herd in the same direction and push into them. Vinan and his companions had to cease their conversation immediately and begin walking to avoid being swept up in the crowd. Crissa made every effort to stay close to Vinan while the Shai pushed aside anyone who entered his space. That wasn't many people, as few were stupid enough to get too close to the large and powerful swordsman.

"What is all this?" the old man asked a woman past forty winters of age.

"They are clearing the bazaar," she answered, bereft of breath. "The masters are coming!"

"What?!" Vinan shouted, hoping for more.

"The masters of the city," Crissa said to him as they continued with the crowd. "They rule the city and are going to speak in the slave bazaar. Follow me!"

Vinan did as she said. She slipped through the crowd and led him to an alley on the left side of the street, then turned right into another alley, then left into a truly empty alley.

"Wait here," she said. "I'll let you up in a moment."

And with that, she began to climb up the stone wall of the building with almost as much skill as Vinan had seen in squirrels climbing up the trunks of trees. Within a minute she had scaled the building to its top, all thirty feet of it. Vinan waited at the bottom wondering how she planned to let him up. He was sure he could climb the building, even if not as nimbly as she had done, but he was open to an easier way of scaling it. Two figures approached the alleyway and Vinan turned to them.

"Vinan," the old man said. "Where has Crissa gone?"

At that moment, a rope dropped from the high roof as Crissa leaned over the edge above.

"Grab that and climb up here!" she shouted over the side.

Vinan pointed up for the old man, grabbed the rope, and began to climb.

"I am too old for that," said the old man. "I will wait down here."

When Vinan reached the top he was greeted by Crissa who had tied the rope to a large stone atop the roof and was holding it securely. He felt a hard tug on the rope as he let go of it and then he looked over to see that the Shai followed him and Crissa up the wall. He took hold of the rope.

"What are you doing?" she asked.

"Helping you," he said. "The Shai is coming."

"It'll hold," she said. "Let go."

Disinclined to help those who did not need it, Vinan did so. The Shai proved quick in making it to the roof; when he was there Crissa untied her knot, rolled up the rope tight, and put it back in the sack she carried over her shoulder. The three walked to the other side of the roof and leaned on the edge to take a good view of the slave market.

The center of the bazaar had been cleared of loiterers, beggars, and all potential buyers. They formed the great throng that gathered on the edge of the market which was held back by guards with spears and armor made of metal links. All that remained in the main area were the merchants, their slaves, a company of better-armed guards in the center of the bazaar, and lastly, twelve men in various impractical and colorful wardrobes sitting atop camels and magnificent horses. Vinan quickly surmised that these were the masters of the city.

"That is Seren-Raq," Crissa said, pointing.

145

Vinan looked to where she pointed.

"Which one?" he asked.

"That one. On top of the black horse. Do you see him?"

Vinan did. His black horse was the largest Vinan had ever seen and the boy was surprised the man could sit atop it as masterfully as he did. The man himself was slender, bronze-skinned, and with hair bright yellow as the sun and cut in an odd way that was short—almost nothing—everywhere except the uncut top that was combed to one side and held in place by some sort of oil or ointment. His luxurious attire was a striking black and orange that exposed his slender muscled arms and his smooth hairless chest. Vinan found the entirety of it, from the hair to the attire to the idea that a man would shave his chest, beyond absurd. It baffled him that a man would ever go to so much trouble for appearances, especially to look like that.

"That is not what I expect to see," said the Shai, "when I hear of a son of the Great Raq."

"He has never been a warrior," Crissa replied.

"Then what is he?"

"The chief priest."

"The chief priest of what?"

"The goddess of luxury and pleasure."

"No wonder he has no desire to fight," the Shai scoffed with disgust and amusement.

Several men in the square blew ram-head horns simultaneously. The din silenced the crowds. When they ceased, one of the eight began to speak to all present.

"People of Qiriq!" the fat bald man shouted. "Uthal-Raq has utterly vanquished the armies of the Kingdom of Rhanijad and driven them behind the walls of their capital! He approaches our beloved city laden with captives and gold from his conquests! Do not fear when his army approaches, for he comes in peace and generously wishes to share his spoils with us! Wealth and prosperity will flood into this city when he arrives and there will be two days of free bread for all citizens of Qiriq!"

Rapturous sounds emanated from the crowd below, first fear of Uthal-Raq and then joy at the promise of free bread. Whispers became murmurs, and murmurs became gleefully spoken news as those in the throng passed the news down.

"More wars. More slaves," murmured Crissa as she hit her hand angrily on the edge of the roof. "More children with dead fathers. More captives sold like cattle in the streets. When, in the name of every god that exists, will it end?"

But the Shai was not listening to her. Vinan looked at him and saw a darkness hanging over him worse than any Vinan had seen. His eyes stared forward, burning with hatred and death. As if the Shai who had helped Vinan all these days had left and something like Kror stood in his place instead.

"Uthal-Raq..."

The manner in which the Shai said this froze Vinan in place with terror. He had never seen the Shai like this and did not know what the man would do next.

"Uthal-Raq," the Shai repeated without changing his tone. "Uthal-Raq still lives..."

CHAPTER 15

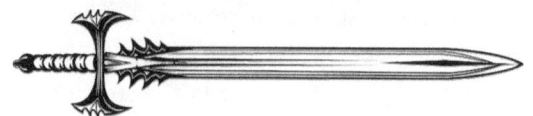

The Siren Call of Vengeance

"**S**o, Uthal-Raq approaches Qiriq..."

The old man sat in the alley and stroked his beard as he thought intently on this, entirely indifferent to the brooding of the Shai.

"Do you think...?"

Crissa began but stopped. Her eyes darted to the Shai, then to Vinan, and then they focused on her father again. Vinan had noticed, and so had the Shai.

"Does he think what?" asked the Shai. "Finish your question."

"Do you think there will be," she glanced at the Shai again, "trouble when he arrives?"

"One can never predict these things," her father replied. "One can never know what other men plan to do and how their plans may turn out when they attempt them."

"It does not matter," Vinan said. "I don't care if Uthal-Raq comes. I am saving Stek and Kirru."

"It does matter," said the old man. "The city guard will be on watch even more than usual, for there are those in the city who would kill Uthal-Raq."

"Good," said the Shai. "It seems there are some who still remember which men deserve death."

"Well," said the old man, "if there are, then I would say there are some men they are forgetting."

Vinan had no more patience for all this talk about the Raqs, vengeance, and the old man's philosophical opinions.

"I am rescuing Kirru tonight," he asserted. "If you want to help me, then help. I don't want to hear another word about Uthal-Raq"

"Vinan," Crissa pleaded, "I still think we should free Stek first. The under-city is easy to infiltrate."

"I am saving Kirru," he said undeterred. "If you want to get Stek instead so we free them both, then do it. I will be forever grateful."

"You will both be dead," said the Shai. "Neither of you know as much as you think you do about these things."

"Then come and help me get Kirru," Vinan said with exasperation. "I am going into the temple to save her whether you help me or not."

"Wait," interjected the old man. "You need more than just bravery. We need a plan. We need to know where to go and when to go."

"I have been to the under-city many times," answered Crissa. "But if we are going to the temple, then I will need some time to watch before I move."

"A good idea," said the old man. "Why don't you take Vinan and do that while I think a little?"

Crissa looked to Vinan to gauge his opinion. With nothing to propose or add, he nodded to resign himself to this plan for now.

"I will go," he said.

"Good," the old man smiled and pulled five copper coins from a purse on his belt. "You two should find something to eat while you do that. Be sure you are not seen."

"I know," Crissa said as she took the coins.

"Plan, scheme, and watch as you wish," said the Shai. "I will meet you in the Plaza of the Ancient Kings before the sun sets."

"Where are you going?" Vinan asked.

"To drink and to think," the Shai answered. "What else?"

"You would drink at a time like this?" Crissa asked.

"When a man has just learned that Uthal-Raq still lives after all these years, what is he supposed to do?"

The Shai turned and walked off.

"Come," Crissa said to Vinan. "Let's go watch the temple."

Vinan followed Crissa as they left her father behind to think. She navigated the alleys and streets with as much familiarity as Vinan used to in the mountains near his home. Vinan stayed wary of all the people he passed, especially the vendors and beggars who watched him. He then saw that Crissa seemed to be paying no one any heed while also keeping her distance. She walked forward quickly and with purpose, which appeared to make those around her keep their distance. This made him consider that maybe this was the way to handle himself in the city.

Finding the Temple of Plenty was not difficult. Its first identifying mark was a long over twenty-foot-tall stone wall that emerged before them. As Vinan took in how far it went to both his left and right, he began to understand the sheer scale of the temple. The walls went a great distance before they curved to a rounded corner and the next wall. Vinan and Crissa circumnavigated the outer perimeter of the great white barrier— stopping only to buy two pieces of meat on a stick for four of the old man's coins. The vendor had demanded eight and Crissa had only offered two at first, but both of them eventually came to an agreeable price. The meat tasted of bad quality and no amount of herbs and spices could hide that fact from Vinan's tongue, though he found the copious seasoning strangely pleasant.

The temple was one of plenty indeed. Plenty of feet of wall that stretched on to cover the palace and gardens behind, plenty of wealth and artisanal craftsmanship that had been poured into its construction and plenty of guards manning the walls to defend it all. Vinan observed that these were considerably more dutiful guards than he had seen loitering or marching in the streets. He would have to avoid their watch if he were to get into the temple, for he was not certain he could fight them if it came to that. These were not some indolent and unskilled paid mercenaries like he had dealt with on the river. There was a purpose in their step and a look in their eyes that revealed both their discipline and that they had shed blood before.

Vinan glanced past the open gate as he and Crissa passed. He struggled to divert his eyes from the lush gardens and flowing fountains within and tried to get a feel for how penetrable the area was. To his discouragement, there were more guards by the gate than anywhere else along the wall; and that also seemed to be where their living quarters had been built within the grounds. Men in half armor and no armor sharpened their weapons, polished their equipment, and lounged around in leisure by the gate. No, this was not where he would enter the temple. His heart sank still further when he looked upon the smooth wall that had no out-jutting stones to grab or holes to clutch. He did not know how Crissa could possibly climb these walls.

"The guards are especially concentrated by the gate," Crissa suddenly said to Vinan in a low voice.

"I saw," he replied. "Can you climb the wall?"

"Possibly," she said, "but I will need to time it perfectly and do it under the cover of night."

"You can climb that with your hands?" he asked incredulously.

"No," she replied, "I will need some rope."

They continued on inconspicuously. Vinan finished his food quickly while Crissa nibbled the brown meat on the stick. Vinan followed her as she made a short turn into a side street a little ways after they had fully circumnavigated the walls.

151

"Did you see a good spot?" he whispered.

She nodded.

"Are we going tonight?"

She nodded again.

"Do you know what is inside the walls?"

"Besides the guards?" she asked.

"Yes."

"Seren-Raq is in the main palace of the temple. A great number of servants and some priests, but they will most likely be asleep in their quarters. Lastly, there are all the slaves."

"And where are they?"

"Close to Seren-Raq's rooms, or in them. I would guess that Kirru is where most of the other slaves are. Only a few are likely to be in Seren-Raq's quarters."

"The women slaves?"

"Most of Seren-Raq's slaves are women, concubines but also cleaning women. Kirru will be with the common household slaves, who are also mostly women."

Vinan thought about this. If Kirru was housed with many other slaves, then it was likely that his entrance would not go unnoticed. Kirru would jump in his arms, with her usual lack of quiet, and who knew how the other slaves would act? To say nothing of the possibility of the guards seeing him or Crissa before then and raising the alarm.

"Vinan," Crissa said, "you know we don't have to do this now. Taking Kirru will have Seren-Raq looking for us, but few will care if Stek escapes. Those who bought him will be easier to handle."

"No," Vinan said firmly. "I am getting Kirru tonight whether you help me or not."

She sighed as if to resign herself to the fact that Vinan was never going to relent on this. The two stayed silent as they walked down an empty alley. The hairs on Vinan's back stood up shortly after and he began to sense the approach of someone. He turned around.

The second man of Ancar's party stalked behind them. Vinan's heart pounded as he turned around again and dashed forward.

"Run!"

He shouted to Crissa needlessly. She was already in full sprint just behind him as they tried to escape the slaver. They turned hard into a winding narrow street lined with tiny houses and Crissa knocked over several pots and vases as she passed them. This did little to slow the man, as his steps seemed to keep pace with the two of them, neither gaining nor losing ground.

They turned again into another side street but ran into two burly shirtless men who stood as if waiting for them, or anyone. They took an interest in both Vinan and Crissa immediately.

"Well now," said the first, a dirty black-haired man with a carpet of hair on his chest, "where are you children running?"

Vinan hesitated a fatal moment as he tried to think of what to do. The second man in the alley, bald with a gold ring in his ear and a glass eye, held a short, curved sword in hand and had been playing with it before the encounter. Vinan knew these were men he could not beat quickly, though he knew he could outrun them.

So preoccupied with them was Vinan that he had forgotten Ancar's slaver. The man flanked them on the other side of the alley.

"Well, slaves," he said, his knives drawn. "You did well escaping us and killing my brother. I think it is time I took you back to the markets where you belong!"

"So that's what this is," said the first of the alley-men.

"We are not slaves!" Vinan shouted.

"Half the money if we help you," said the second alley-man.

"Done," answered the slaver.

Vinan's protest did not matter. Apparently, the truth never did. What did matter was that Crissa had already reached under her cloak and procured her two curved daggers. Vinan drew his sword as the three closed in.

He did not have time to intelligently pick his target. He struck at the first enemy before him, his blade making contact with the first alley-man's stomach. The man fell to the ground holding his belly in his hands. Vinan ducked to avoid the swing of the second alley-man's curved sword and delivered a strike in passing. The man grabbed his bleeding leg and fell to the ground. Vinan turned to see that Crissa had been faring poorly against the slaver. She had lost one dagger and Vinan watched as the slaver grabbed her wrist, twisted, and yanked her to him. Crissa's dagger fell to the ground as the slaver held his to her throat.

Vinan lifted his sword and stepped forward.

"One more step and I cut her throat," said the slaver.

"Do that," said Vinan, "and I will kill you. Let her go, and you live."

"You misunderstand," said the slaver with a smile, "I am offering you the girl's life and freedom. You are the one who's already enslaved or dead."

Vinan gripped his sword tight. The slaver reckoned he had shocked the boy, so he continued.

"You see, when you killed Ancar, you sealed your fate. You did not know that I, Berthar, was his brother and would swear a blood oath on both you and the Shai."

"I too have a brother who I am trying to find," said Vinan, "and you are in my way."

"You won't find him," said Berthar. "You can drop your sword now and let me take you to the slave markets... or you and the girl can die here. It is your choice."

A sword end suddenly pierced the front of Berthar's chest and then withdrew itself. The stunned slaver dropped everything he held and collapsed to the ground on his knees. The form of the Shai revealed itself behind him. The free and surprised Crissa quickly gathered herself and her knives.

"It will be Berthar, brother of Ancar and slaver, who dies here forgotten," said the Shai.

He stabbed downwards to finish Berthar. He had barely wiped his blade on the dead slaver's clothes when a new voice made itself heard.

"What is all this?!"

Two guards appeared at the entrance of the alley. Small men, but well-armed with both the weapons and the authority of the city's government.

"What happened here?" one demanded. "Who killed these men?"

"They tried to rob these children," said the Shai. "That's three fewer robbers that plague your city."

"Where did you get those?!" the guard asked Crissa as he pointed to her ornate curved daggers.

"A gift from my father," she said.

"Your father, right," said the guard. "You stole them, didn't you? You must have escaped from the markets."

As he unsheathed his sword, he suddenly took the Shai's knife in the throat. The other guard turned to run in panic, but the Shai proved too fast. His sword came down on the man's shoulder to knock him to the ground. The stunned guard's armor did not save him for long, as the Shai grabbed him by the helmet and stabbed him with a knife in his exposed throat.

"Let's go, En'Shai!"

Vinan and Crissa rapidly followed the Shai from the alley. Vinan's heart raced in his chest, as he realized two guards were dead by their hands.

"Where are we going?" Vinan asked.

"To the old man," said the Shai. "He knows more about this city than any of us."

"But we just killed two guards."

"No," said Crissa, "we didn't. We saw nothing that happened in that alley."

"The girl is right, En'Shai. We heard noises in the alley and

155

we ran away."

Vinan shut his mouth as they continued. He knew far less of this city and its ways than the other three. Let them handle this mess, he would save Kirru tonight as planned.

The afternoon sun had sunk below the sky's peak, leaving a great many tight and enclosed areas of the city in shadow. After some minutes Vinan began to recognize some of the streets they walked down. They found the old man sitting on a bench outside a rowdy tavern.

"Did you find what you need?" he asked as they approached.

The smile on his face dissipated as the three came closer.

"What happened?" he asked.

"Nothing," said Crissa. "Some thugs and guards got into a fight. There were wounds dealt."

"I see," said the old man.

"Take us to the real under-city," the Shai said firmly but quietly.

"The real under-city is a myth," said the old man.

"So it is," said the Shai. "And it never existed. Now take us there."

"I can find you lodging for the night," said the old man with a muted sardonic chuckle. "Follow me."

"Where are we going?" Vinan asked

"To some friends of mine. They can give us a place for some time."

Once again, Vinan found himself being led through the winding streets of Qiriq. This time the old man led with Crissa beside him. Vinan and the Shai followed closely, with Vinan peering around his shoulder. Every moment he expected to be followed again. Any moment he expected one of the guards they passed by to stop them or take special notice of them.

"Hide your worrying, En'Shai," whispered the Shai. "It will attract less attention."

Vinan did his best, hiding his hand beneath his cape and

clenching it tight into a fist. He still could not shake off his fear as easily as the Shai and Crissa had apparently done. In the mountains of his home, he had known fear many times, but it was always against things he knew. Here, he found himself so unaccustomed to the way things were that he did not know what to even fear. The unknown was to him as great an enemy as Seren-Raq or the men who now kept Stek in the fighting pits.

They came to a small clay hut where the old man stopped. He knocked on the wooden door three times in succession, twice slowly, and three times rapidly again.

"There is nothing for you here," said a woman's voice inside.

"There is nothing good for us outside where blood is shed and flesh is bought," replied the old man.

"That is no concern of mine."

"That is the concern of Qiriq, especially those who seek for goodness."

"Goodness is dead."

"Goodness can never die as long as it lives in the heart of one."

"But the goodness of Qiriq is dead."

"And reborn shall it be."

It was here that Vinan realized that this was no mere banter. This was a planned mantra like those his mother and the other priestesses used constantly in their ceremonies.

"Broken is the conscience of the people of the city," said the voice inside.

"So protected shall ours ever be," the old man replied.

"The wings of hope are your folly."

"Hope's talons are my deliverance."

A bolt was undone from the inside and the door was opened. The old man entered and beckoned the others to follow. Crissa went first, the Shai after her, and Vinan entered last into the secret gathering.

"I thought you had gone," said a voice inside.

157

"I thought so as well," replied the old man.

A black-bearded young man sat in the corner of the room across from the beautiful, black-skinned young woman who had opened the door. Both were dressed in simple clothes, which fit the simple house with its simple furnishings.

"Why have you come back here?" the woman asked.

"To sleep," said the old man. "My companions have business in this city and need a place to stay."

"Most business in the city is unpleasant," said the bearded man.

"My business," interjected Vinan, "is rescuing two slaves."

"Not an unworthy endeavor," said the man. "What kind of slaves?"

"Children," said Vinan.

"Friends of yours?" the woman asked.

"My brother and sister."

"I am sorry," said the woman.

"They are fortunate to have a brother such as you," said the man. "Come, we will get you a place to rest."

He pulled back the plain green rug in the corner of the floor and lifted a trapdoor, revealing a hollow space beneath.

"You can stay here," said the man.

Crissa accepted an oil lamp from the woman and descended into the hole without hesitation. The old Raq followed his daughter down the creaking wooden stairs as Vinan stared down into the basement below.

"What is the matter?" the bearded man asked Vinan.

"Nothing," he answered.

"It is just a hole in the ground," said the woman, "But it is the best we can do. We will bring you food and blankets for the night."

Vinan nodded and walked down the stairs, each one creaking as he stepped on it. He was soon in the basement, surrounded by closed barrels and the scurrying of a rat away from the light of Crissa's oil lamp. The Shai immediately followed him into the cellar.

"We will bring food soon," said the woman. "Stay here until then."

The old Raq suddenly shouted to the bearded man above. "Aranthas!"

This alerted Aranthas, who looked to the old man.

"What are you going to do when Uthal-Raq arrives?" the old man asked.

"Whatever we must," the man replied.

"You will fail," said the Shai.

"The Shaii' of Kodumaa had their chance against him," said the man. "The Brothers of the Talon will succeed where they fell short."

The Shai and the man looked at each other in tense silence. After a moment, the woman began shutting the trap door.

"Wait here," she said. "We will return."

And with a screech of hinges, the four were left in the cellar with an oil lamp illuminating what little it could.

"So, you are among the Brothers of the Talon, old Raq," said the Shai.

"I was in the room when they were formed," he said. "I do not know how you know of them."

"I have seen much of the known world," said the Shai, "and some of the world that most men do not know. Qiriq is known to me and the Brothers of the Talon are its worst kept secret."

"Who are the Brothers of the Talon?" asked Vinan.

"Men who fight for justice and freedom in the darkness of Qiriq's nights," answered the old man.

"Idealist cutthroats and fools," said the Shai. "They stand no chance against Uthal-Raq."

"Perhaps," said the old man. "Perhaps they have a plan. I cannot know until they make the attempt."

"Whatever the case," said the Shai, "I will rest until the food arrives. Try to stay quiet and get some rest yourself."

Despite what the Shai had requested, Vinan and Crissa conversed in whispers after some time. The Shai did not complain and was loudly snoring soon enough.

"You have been here before?" Vinan asked.

"I know these people and knew of this place," she answered. "This is the first time I have used it."

"Who are they?"

"I would tell you their names," she said, "but you already know his. They are a husband and wife."

"And they are Brothers of the Talon?"

"Yes."

"What are the Brothers of the Talon?"

"They already told you."

"I want to know what you think of them."

"Rebels." Crissa shrugged. "Some fight to give Qiriq a king while others want a government run by the people. All of them are united in fighting the city masters. All of them oppose the slave trade."

"Would they help us get back Stek and Kirru?"

"I do not know."

"But your father is one of them?"

"He was one of them. He left years ago."

"If they could help us, I would take their help. I am getting Kirru and Stek tonight no matter what."

"And I am coming with you."

"I know. Thank you."

They sat in silence for a time before Crissa spoke again.

"Will you go home after this? Back to the mountains?"

Vinan realized that he had not thought far beyond getting Stek and Kirru back.

"I can't go back," he said. "I will be killed if I do. I will not throw my life away just to avenge my honor against Kror."

He looked to the sleeping Shai.

"Come with us." Crissa said.

"Do you know where you are even going?" Vinan asked

"Away from here. That is enough."

Vinan thought about it. He had to admit that the old man and Crissa knew more of the world beyond than he did. More importantly, Crissa had chosen to help him for no other reason than that it was right. In this world, where cruelty and betrayal reigned, someone like Crissa or her father were gifts from the gods indeed.

"I will save them," he said. "After that, we will leave Qiriq and go somewhere. If you and your father think you know a good place to go, I will come with you."

There was a sound of the rug being lifted above and the trapdoor was opened to reveal the candle-lit hut above.

"I have your food," said the woman. "You can come out now."

Vinan walked up the stairs and pulled himself up to the floor. He turned around, extended his arm to Crissa, and pulled her up. The old man and the now-awake Shai followed them.

On the low table in the hut there were several loaves of bread, a plate of fruits, and a stone pitcher of water. Vinan sat down on the floor and broke off a large piece of a loaf. He devoured it heartily and forgot for a few minutes about Kirru and Stek.

"Hungry, are we?" the woman said.

"It appears so," said the old man. "Thank you for everything."

"You will not stay long?" she asked.

"No," said the old man, "only as long as we need to get the boy's family."

"That is all good," she replied. "We can house you for as long as you require."

"It should only be a night or two."

"And you are freeing slaves?"

"Two," said Vinan. "Can the Brothers of the Talon help?"

The old man shot him a look as if he had said something he shouldn't, Crissa blushed with embarrassment, and the Shai smiled with amusement.

"I do not know of these Brothers," the woman lied. "But even if I did, I would guess they are already busy with a great many things."

It had been a desperate hope and one that Vinan had not counted on.

"We are going to save them tonight," he said. "First Kirru, and then Stek."

"I will be unable to accompany you," said the old man. "My strength and speed is sadly not what it used to be. I would only imperil your attempt."

"I will not be coming either," said the Shai. "My deepest regrets, En'Shai."

This hit Vinan with such shock that he did not fully comprehend what had been said for a few moments. When it finally sunk in, he said the only thing he could.

"What?"

"Do as you will," the Shai said. "I leave this city tonight."

The Shai silently glared at the young woman. She understood, and then exited from the front door.

"I am leaving to kill Uthal-Raq," said the Shai after she was gone. "I cannot help you."

"You are not helping me save Stek and Kirru?" said Vinan.

"You don't believe you can save them yourself, En'Shai?"

"I can."

"Good."

"But if you promised to help the boy," said the old man. "Why go now when you are so close to fulfilling that promise?"

"There is another promise I made long ago," said the Shai. "I swore a blood-oath against those who ravaged Kodumaa. As such, I must kill Uthal-Raq."

"But it was not Uthal-Raq who destroyed Kodumaa,"

objected the old man. "Farken-Raq led the invasion. Farken-Raq commanded the armies. Farken-Raq ordered the destruction of all Kodumaa."

"And Uthal-Raq carried out his orders with the greatest of cruelty," the Shai said. "Besides, Farken-Raq died many years ago and robbed me of that vengeance."

"Yes," the old man reflected. "I suppose he did."

The old man went silent and continued to nibble at some grapes on his plate.

"But you promised to help me," Vinan protested to the Shai.

"And I have. I brought you here and saved you from the slavers. You know where Stek and Kirru are. You can do the rest. Uthal-Raq is the last living man in my blood oath, and so I am bound by honor to kill him."

Vinan's anger rose at this third great betrayal of his life. First, it had been his brother, then his people, and now the Shai.

"Go then! Follow your honor!" he shouted to the Shai. "I do not need you! I don't need the help of any useless warriors!"

He slammed his fist upon the table. His eyes locked on those of the Shai and would not let go of their gaze.

"Warriors are useless, En'Shai?" the Shai said amused. "Even the one who saved your life?"

"All my life I looked to warriors for guidance," Vinan's glare did its best to bore into the Shai's broken soul. "All my life I prayed to their god and worshiped all that it meant to be one. All the time when I was a young boy, I did everything I could to become one.

"But now I see what they are. I see they are worthless, weaklings, followers of evil, selfish, murderers, liars, and breakers of promises."

A dead silence hung over the room. No one spoke. No one smiled. No one ate what lay before them.

"Farewell then, En'Shai," said the Shai at long last. "You need me no more. May the lessons I taught you be of some use to you."

And with that, the Shai snatched a loaf from the table, rose to his feet, and walked out the door.

After the Shai departed, Vinan took one more bite of bread and then rose to his feet.

"Are you going after him?" asked the old man.

"No," Vinan replied, "I am going to save Kirru."

"Now?"

"Now."

Crissa rose to her feet.

"I am still coming with you," she said as she followed Vinan to the door.

"Stay safe, Crissa," said the old man. "If nothing else, make sure you bring Vinan back alive."

"I will," she said, and then walked out the door into the night.

CHAPTER 16

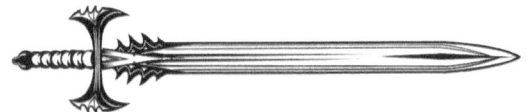

Reward for Kind Deeds

The beast closed in on his prey. He had ventured on alone, knowing exactly what he sought and what to not bother with. He had left the pack behind, for a cougar had no reason to congregate with the foxes. Let them chase after rabbits, he thought, for his catch would be the true prize.

The darkness of the forest concealed his approach. The traps laid therein failed to ensnare him. They had been laid for animals far lesser than him. Confidence that his prey would be outmatched by him had always been with the beast, but now that confidence had transformed into certainty. The shape of the hut emerged and the predator bared his deadly blade from its sheath. He made his way into the abode of the one who thought himself the apex hunter of this forest and threw himself to his task.

The predator raised his sword of Kodumaa high and swung down, bringing death to its target. The hunter's blood was spilled on the floor of his refuge. His sanctuary had become the den where trapped, he met his end. This gave momentary satisfaction to the beast, though it had not been the purpose of this hunt. The momentary thrill of bloodlust notwithstanding, the true prey lay prone on a bed of furs in the hut.

The child of the stars, the myth in the flesh, the corporeal manifestation of child's tales told in the same breath as giants, monsters, and faeries... she was here in this common hut in this remote forest. With mild illness and too weak to fight back, she had fallen into his hands without a struggle.

All that remained was choosing to which of his many would-be masters he would sell the child of the stars.

PART 3

The Warrior from the Mountains

CHAPTER 17

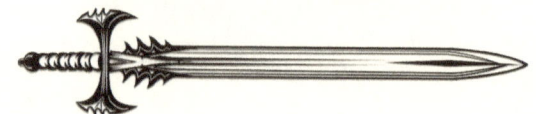

The Hedon Palace

Night fell upon the city of Qiriq, and the slave markets lay empty in the darkness. Vinan and Crissa hid in a deserted alley across from the Temple of Plenty. The walls lay directly before them across the empty street where they had been watching the guards march atop it for some time. As Vinan watched the same guard pass by the same section of the wall for the fifth time, he became ever more restless and agitated.

"When do we go?" he asked Crissa quietly.

"When I see a chance," she whispered back.

The guard passed by and continued to walk down the curvature of the wall. He would not be back for a few minutes and two other guards would pass by in that time.

"Now," whispered Crissa.

She ran out from the alley and into the open. Vinan quickly followed her across the barely lit street and stopped alongside her when they came to the wall. Crissa took out her rope—tied already into a noose on one end—and threw it upwards with her right arm. Her first throw missed the battlement at which she was aiming, and the rope came down gracelessly. Undeterred, she swung it up again. This time the noose slipped over the battlement allowing her to pull it taut.

"I'll go first," she said to Vinan. "Follow me as soon as I give the signal."

Vinan nodded. Crissa took hold of the rope and scaled the wall in a few moments. Vinan watched the rope until it rose a few inches with a sudden jerk—the signal for him to ascend. He followed her example and climbed as fast as he could, reaching the top only a little slower than she had. As soon as he was atop the wall Crissa slipped her rope off, wrapped it up, and put it back under her cloak. She then pointed to nearby stone stairs that led down into the courtyard below.

She whispered. "There. Quickly."

Vinan obeyed.

When they reached the ground, she darted behind the stone column that supported the stairs and beckoned for Vinan to follow—which he did. They were now hidden in shadow and behind stone with a clear view of the fire-lit courtyard ahead.

"The next guard is coming soon," she said, while putting her finger to his mouth. "We move out once he passes. Stay quiet."

As she had predicted, the heavy methodical steps of a guard upon the wall above approached and then passed over them. Crissa waited until the steps faded into the distance before moving out from under the stairs and looking to both her sides. She then motioned for Vinan to come to her side.

"Stay in the shadows," she said. "Stay out of the light."

Crissa and Vinan ran to a tree on the outside perimeter of the lit gardens and crouched low in the shrubbery. They now had a clear view of the lush courtyard with its ever-running fountains illuminated by lines of hung candle lanterns. A few guards paced back and forth in the gardens but were unlikely to see the two infiltrators where they hid. Vinan looked ahead to the palace and saw that the doors were flanked by armored and motionless guards with curved swords.

"We can't enter through the front," he whispered to Crissa.

"Not like this, no," she agreed with a nod. "Follow me. We need to get closer to the palace."

She crouched low to the ground and moved behind the bushes quietly. Vinan followed her example, crawling while keeping as silent as he could. He stopped when she did and waited for the boots of the marching guard to pass. He continued to follow her through and between the hedges. Twice they both had to risk running through a gap where there was a path between the hedges, and twice they crossed over rapidly enough to remain undetected by the guards. They remained in the shadows as they made their way closer to the palace in the center of the gardens.

They hid on their bellies in a spot between a rose bush and a tree sagging with overripe lemons, a perfect blind spot to avoid the sight of any passing guard. Vinan now faced one of the palace's corners and had a clear view of the front and one side. He watched the patrols march back and forth with their weapons on display and their backs straight. Had he not known better he might have wondered if these were not men, as he never saw them deviate from their determined path or break the pace of their steps.

"How do we get in?" he asked Crissa, still whispering.

"The palace has more than one door," she said. "No one would build it so all the soldiers get stuck in one doorway."

"That would be easiest for defending what is in there," said Vinan.

"That is what the guards and the wall are for."

And yet, here Vinan and Crissa were able to get past the wall but unable to penetrate the palace within. Vinan watched pairs of guards patrol to and fro before the palace. He looked to the tall, gilded doors that were the entrance.

"There," Crissa said quietly while pointing.

Vinan looked to where she pointed and saw it as well. A guard emerged from the side of the palace and a light suddenly emanated from where he came.

"There is a side entrance there," said Crissa. "He must be coming to relieve one of the others."

They watched the man walk on towards the wall.

"Now's our chance," she said.

Vinan did not question but followed her with all his speed and quiet as they dashed across the dimly lit path. They hid in the shadow of the palace's side wall with their backs pressed against it. Crissa began to slowly edge closer to where the guard had emerged and Vinan followed her every move. As they continued, they finally found a small doorway hidden in the darkness. Crissa inspected it and gave the door a slight tug.

"The door is locked," she said.

She reached into her cloak, pulled out a bent piece of metal, applied it to the lock, and turned. Vinan looked around for guards as Crissa fiddled with the lock. None were close by.

Click went the lock.

"It's open," said Crissa as she pulled the bent metal pick out and returned it to her pocket.

She pulled the door open slowly and peeked inside before opening it. She entered and Vinan followed.

"Where..." Vinan began.

"SH!"

Crissa cut off Vinan's question before he could finish and with good reason. His voice had echoed off the walls and reverberated through the arched chamber. Sound carried well in this palace and there was now real danger that he had been heard.

They ducked into the first doorway in the hall. It was a dead end, a crevice cut into the palace for seemingly no reason. While the halls in the main area were adorned with gold, carved with the art of craftsmen, and painted with striking images, this little room was still decorated in the plain stone and plaster with which it had first been built, as if it were an unfinished and forgotten afterthought among the other gilded rooms and halls.

Crissa leaned into Vinan's ear.

"You must be very quiet here," she said. "This temple was made so those within could be heard. Stay here while I find the quarters of the slaves. Stay in the shadows and do not move."

Vinan put his mouth by her ear.

"Will you even know how to find Kirru? You have never seen her."

"Are her eyes and hair like yours?"

Vinan nodded.

"Then it will not be difficult," said Crissa. "I know what her brother looks like."

And she went down the halls as silent and fast as a rabbit. Vinan was now left alone in a corner in the halls of the Temple of Plenty. He waited patiently for her return and kept alert. All around him remained an empty stillness, as no one seemed to visit this remote corner of the palace. He found the silence here eerie and honed in to listen closely to any sound at all.

He heard the faint steps of men in the halls some ways away. Two sets of feet with heavy and methodical steps, guards more likely than not. Their steps came closer for a brief few moments but then became fainter and more distant. Vinan knew this could not last forever as many guards had come through here before and likely would again. He only had to hope this side room was not inspected.

The silence was soon broken by the voices of women and a man. Vinan had not been listening closely so he could not at first make out what they said. Two women, one older and who spoke with calm poise and another who spoke in an excited and surprised tone. Vinan worked hard to concentrate and make out their conversation, even letting his head almost peek from the archway to the side room.

Finally, and after much difficulty, he could distinguish the words exchanged.

"Be gentle with her," demanded the voice of the old woman.

"Why?" asked the voice of a somewhat younger woman.

"Because our master commands it," said the old woman's voice. "The poor little thing needs sleep. She has spent many days in a slaver's cart and has been asking about her brothers ever since she came here. The guards found her wandering the halls."

"Lucky for her that our lord has ordered the guards to be gentle and that the captain has some sense," said the first woman. "Girl, you must go to bed. You will be awake early tomorrow and must be ready to do your work."

"But," said a little girl's voice, "I always wake early."

Vinan froze as he recognized the little girl's voice as his sister's. He had found Kirru at last.

He threw caution to the wind and left his hiding place to enter the gilded halls. He honed in on every hunter's instinct he possessed to try to find the source of the sound. But the labyrinthine layout of the palace soon thwarted his efforts as Vinan found himself turning corner after corner only to be greeted by empty passageways. The sounds were no more and he was left trying to navigate to where he believed it had occurred. He was certain he was going in the right direction, nevertheless. He had to convince himself of this.

He turned another corner and froze in terror. Before him stood two heavily armored guards on either side of the hall, motionless except for their eyes, which looked to the side and spotted the boy immediately. They both jumped to action in Vinan's moment of surprise. The first man drew his slightly curved blade while the second reached for his belt.

"A thief!" they shouted.

The first guard grabbed a twisted ram horn and blew into it. In the enclosed halls the sound bounced off the walls and echoed into a deafening shriek. Vinan panicked and ran down the halls the way he had come, holding his head in some pain from the noise. He turned a corner, turned a corner, turned another corner, ran down a long hall, and turned a corner again.

He was now in the entry of a wide-open golden hexagonal room illuminated in red candles. A great dome capped the ceiling, painted with the nude likenesses of various deities. This was a room Vinan knew he had never seen before even though he was certain he had retraced his steps.

He truly had lost his way in the palace.

The pursuing guard was now close enough to swing so Vinan ran into the spacious chamber to evade. No sooner had he done so than pairs of guards emerged from all six entrances. Vinan was trapped, hemmed in like an animal on all sides with no escape. He had to fight here.

He drew his sword and looked for an opening. None showed itself. The twelve guards all carried weapons and large circular shields; they approached Vinan cautiously to tighten the net.

A thirteenth man—an old, bearded veteran who walked with a dignified authority—entered the chamber. He was clad in armor covered with ornate trappings and his helmet had a red plume instead of a metal spike on the cap of the skull like the others. He approached calmly with no weapon drawn. Vinan observed that the twelve men held their positions and waited on this man without taking further action. In that moment Vinan saw something of Crissa's father in the commander, a wizened bearing chiseled from years of war.

"This is futile," said the leader. "Surrender now, boy, and you have my word you will not be harmed."

Vinan glanced at the immobile guards around him then looked past them to their captain with defiance in his eyes.

"Never!" was his answer.

The guards around him tensed up as if preparing to act, but did not yet move.

"Don't be a fool," warned the captain. "If you throw down your sword I will take you to Seren-Raq and he will hear what it is you want. If you don't, then I will be forced to take you prisoner or kill you."

174

Vinan knew there was no way out without battle, he tried the only thing he could think of to improve his chances.

"Fight me then," he said to the captain. "Fight me without the help of your men."

"Why would I do that?" asked the captain bemused.

"Are you afraid to fight a boy?"

"Your goading is beneath me."

"I challenge you!"

"Your challenge is of no consequence to me."

"I challenge you to fight me alone! If I win, I leave here with the slave I seek. If you win, I surrender myself to whatever you and Seren-Raq will do to me."

"This is a waste of my time," sighed the captain, now visibly annoyed. "I have fought and killed in many wars under the Raqs so you would not stand a chance against me in single combat. Your defeat is assured either way and you are already at my mercy. I ask you one last time, will you drop your sword?"

Vinan answered by lurching at a guard and trying to stab around his shield. He quickly came to realize how great an advantage was a shield as the guard pushed Vinan's blade aside and gave a counterstrike with his curved sword. Vinan easily backed away and dodged it but realized that the guards to his rear and sides closed in again. He hacked and struck again in futility, for his sword continued to land on the shields or glance off them.

But surrender was not an option for a warrior. It was not in his blood. He would rather die here trying to save Kirru than surrender.

"Take him alive!" commanded the captain.

Shields closed in on Vinan. He let loose a desperate flurry of blows on one guard's shield, hoping to overwhelm the man with sheer force. But he was instead struck by an adjacent guard's shield and pushed into the shield of another guard who also struck him. The guards now bludgeoned Vinan with their shields and it was all he could do to put his sword up and soften the blow of

175

every third strike. He had lost all momentum or advantage. The fight was now twelve grown and fully armored men overwhelming a single boy with a sword.

There would be no victory or escape for Vinan here, only captivity.

CHAPTER 18

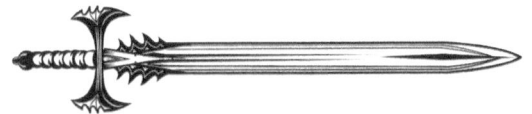

Darkness in the Temple of Light

For hours Vinan sat awake in the cell. For hours he stayed chained to the wall. For hours he stewed like a caged animal. The bruises of the guards' shield edges were fresh on his shoulders and back, bringing him pain whenever he sat against the stone of the prison wall.

Though beaten and imprisoned, he was not yet defeated. As long as he still lived and did not accept defeat, he could not be defeated. He considered this dungeon but another obstacle in a long line that had tried to separate him forever from his sister and brother. The slavers, the rapids, Ancar... he had overcome them all. He would overcome this.

But this time there would be no faithless Shai of Kodumaa to deliver him. He would escape this cell by his own strength and wits. If only he could free himself from the iron chains around his wrists.

He had never felt as helpless and frustrated as he did now. He pulled on the manacles again but found himself no closer to pulling his arms from the wall. Even if it was possible to get free that way, his strength was too spent. Perhaps if he could sleep a few hours then he could try again rejuvenated.

But every time he leaned to rest he found himself in too much pain to do so. The bruises on his body were still fresh and his arms were numb from being forced above his head for so long. His head tried several times to fall to his chest, but every time his neck prevented it and snapped him back to the world of the awake. His exhaustion could not overcome his uncomfortable position and take him to sleep.

The dim light at the end of the cell had flickered the entire time he was here. It glowed from a lantern around the corner, the last light Vinan's eyes had looked upon before the guards put him in chains and locked shut the grid of iron bars that separated his cell from the dungeon halls. That light was all that separated Vinan from total darkness in the windowless pit that was the prison under the Temple of Plenty. With only that light, Vinan could not know if the sun had yet risen. He could not know if the world above bathed in the light of day or the darkness of night, if the sky was clear or whether it showered rain, if the air was hot or cold. It occurred to him that maybe some had died in these cells while never knowing such things again.

And yet, the light also gave him hope that he could leave here and see both Kirru and the sun again. The sound he had heard of his sister's voice up in the palace was as faint as the edges of the light, but they both were proof of their source's existence. Kirru still lived, waiting to be saved. All Vinan had to do was escape his cell.

If only he could.

178

The light seemed now to burn brighter. Vinan at first believed it to be just his imagination, an effect of his overwhelming exhaustion. But he looked up and saw the silhouettes of three figures in the hall before him and one of them carried a lantern in his hand. They approached until the light was close enough to pain Vinan's eyes, unlocked the cage-like door, and entered the cell.

"He is still here and alive," said the voice of the captain. "I am pleased to see that you men are better at your duties than the fools in the gardens. Unshackle him."

Vinan felt the manacles come off and his arms dropped down in numbed relief. He made no attempt to escape or run, for even if he had his sword with him, he would have been unable to find the strength.

"Should we bind him for you?" one of the guards asked.

"Yes," the captain replied. "Even if he now seems too exhausted to resist, he is too savage for us to take any chances."

Another pair of manacles clanked tight on Vinan's wrists, with only a very short chain linking them. If healthy and rested he could have still fought with difficulty in these, but he was far from healthy and rested.

"Come with me quickly, boy," said the captain while grabbing Vinan's shoulder. "It seems that the priest wishes to meet you. You are not going to lie forgotten down here."

Vinan stumbled to keep pace as the captain pulled him through the stony hallway of the dungeon. A door opened before them and Vinan was overwhelmed with light.

Vinan had already known the palace was intricate, ornate, and the greatest wonder he had seen built by human hands. In the full light of day, with the high windows of the chambers letting in the rays of the sun, the temple took on a new level of beauty as the gold glimmered beneath the paintings of battling gods and sumptuous gardens where men and women feasted on an abundance of grapes. Brilliant colors burst from the walls in every direction to overwhelm the savage boy's eyes. Even as he marched to his judgment, the boy could have almost forgotten the dire circumstances in which he found himself while looking upon these halls.

The captain roughly pulled Vinan along until they reached an antechamber decorated in gold and bright blue. High windows let the sun in to drive out any chance of a dark corner while illuminating the silver throne at the end of the room. Seren-Raq—robed in a wine-red silk garment—sat upon that throne with a goblet in one hand and an ornate jeweled staff in the other. Around him stood several women clothed in very thin, almost transparent, white robes and bejeweled golden trinkets. The hair on their heads was of all colors and textures, from silky and yellow as the sunflower to black and entangled as a briar. Their skins ranged from the most milk-white Vinan had ever seen to black as the mountain panther. All of them waited silently as Seren-Raq observed the captain with his captive.

Vinan was pushed down to his knees by the captain about ten feet from the throne.

"My lord," said the captain. "This is the thief we caught last night."

"A boy slipped through walls and into the palace?" the enthroned man sighed with disdain. "Even the best guards this city can provide me are useless compared to Raq warriors."

"The guards who were on duty will be scourged for their

failure," said the captain. "Ten lashes for each man should improve their discipline a little."

"Will it?" Seren-Raq mused. "Will the sands of the desert ever be graced with lush jungle trees?"

He rose from his throne and stood aright. He handed his goblet to a young pale-skinned woman with golden hair and walked towards Vinan, stopping just before the boy. Vinan looked up at the man's smooth face and silky hair with scorn and said nothing.

"Interesting..." said Seren-Raq.

He turned around and went back to his throne. He reclined in it, took his goblet back, and took a long gulp of its contents.

"So, savage boy," he said. "It should relieve you to know that I have no intention of punishing you any more than what you have suffered. However, I do wish to know... why did you go to all the trouble of infiltrating this temple?"

Vinan said nothing; he only glared unmoved at the hedonic priest. Seren-Raq visibly took note of this and continued.

"Whatever your reason," he said in a voice pleasant and almost musical, "you showed yourself to be quite brave, foolish, or ignorant to try to steal from the Temple of Plenty. Did you not know that this palace is one of the most guarded places in the city or were you that desperate? If the latter is true, you could have come begging and received something to help you. Or have you heard nothing of Seren-Raq's generosity?"

Vinan had heard of no such generosity. He had barely heard of Seren-Raq.

"Tell me," the enthroned priest said, "what is it you seek

here?"

Vinan said nothing. His jaw remained clenched and his eyes stayed defiant.

Seren-Raq pressed on. "You must wish for something. One does not break into a palace this well-guarded for nothing."

He received no satisfaction from Vinan.

"Captain," said Seren-Raq, "did you cut out this boy's tongue?"

"If he wants to speak, he will," the captain answered, unintimidated. "He spoke well enough last night."

"So, you say," Seren-Raq said with feigned skepticism. "Tell me again, what was it he said?"

"He challenged me to combat."

"No, the other thing."

"What thing?"

"Didn't he demand something else as well? I seem to remember you saying something to that effect..."

"A slave?"

"Yes," said Seren-Raq while waving his finger. "That was it. Odd of him to demand a slave..."

He looked down to Vinan.

"Boy," he said, "there are no slaves in this temple. Everyone here is free to leave when they wish. Perhaps you broke into the wrong palace by mistake. Perhaps you are just a common thief. Until you are willing to speak I cannot glean your intentions. Perhaps I should send you back to the dungeon and deliver you to the city guard for justice."

Vinan thought about this. If Kirru was free to go when she wished, then why not put that claim to the test? Perhaps it was time to end his silence.

"Take him from here," said Seren-Raq with affected disappointment and frustration. "If he does not speak then he will receive nothing from us. Tell the guards to show less mercy if we catch him here again."

The captain put his hand on Vinan's shoulder, but the erstwhile motionless boy suddenly brushed it off with violence. As he stood only a hair's breadth from being cast out and possibly losing Kirru forever, he decided that the time for defiant silence was over. The sounds of swords being unsheathed rang through the gilded halls as Vinan finally spoke.

"I am Vinan, son of Bheif!"

Seren-Raq stretched out his hand and the guards stopped mid-stride. A tense stillness overcame the room where once there had been calm.

"So, you do speak..." mused the Raq.

Vinan planted his foot on the ground and rose from his knees. He stood straight, bound though he still was, and looked Seren-Raq unflinchingly in the eyes.

"I am Vinan, son of Bheif," he repeated. "I come from the ancient mountains forged by the gods when the world was young. I come for my brother and sister who were taken from me. I pursued the men who took them through the forest, down the river, across the plain, and to this city. Many men have tried to stop me and I have defeated them all. I know my sister is in this place and I will take her back."

Vinan could not see that the captain smirked with satisfaction at watching the soft Seren-Raq confronted with such an act of savage and blatant defiance. His hand rested patiently on the hilt of his sheathed sword but he was in no hurry to draw it. The boy was hardly a threat to anyone in his current state and with his hands restrained.

"Vinan!"

The exclamation from a familiar voice and the pitter-patter of little feet on the tiled floor heralded the presence of Kirru. Seren-Raq raised his hands with open palms to signal his guards to stand down while Vinan turned to the sound of his sister. No sooner had he turned than he found himself in the embrace of her skinny arms. She spoke excitedly and with much happiness.

"Vinan! I knew you'd come! They said they killed you and Stek believed them! I knew you were alive! I knew you'd come for us!"

All the while, Seren-Raq stroked his chin with interest.

"I see," he said. "So that is the truth..."

He looked to the captain.

"Captain! Free him."

The captain walked back to Vinan and unlocked the manacles. Vinan was too bewildered by his freedom to take advantage of it, or even to return Kirru's embrace.

Seren-Raq motioned to the serving women and they left immediately. He rose again from his seat to approach Vinan.

"I apologize for the rough treatment you have endured, Vinan, son of Bheif. I offer you the full hospitality of the Temple of Plenty. When you are rested we will speak again."

Vinan could not answer. In a few short moments, he had gone from captive to guest. He had found Kirru safe and unharmed. He was exhausted and had not slept for two days...

He collapsed forward and remembered nothing more.

CHAPTER 19

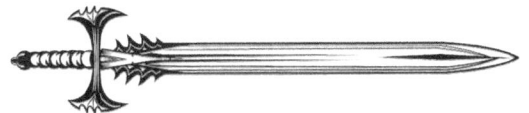

The Fighting Pits

Crissa had left Vinan where she thought he would be safe. She thought he would remain there while she found the quarters of the serving women. She believed she would be able to find Kirru, bring her to Vinan, and escape before anyone noticed.

She had been wrong.

The halls of the palace began to confound her by the fifth turn she made. The black and white tiles on the floor were identical in every corridor and every room. The blue and gold walls weaved a pattern to strike and bewilder the eyes that looked upon them. Only the mosaics on the ceiling—portraying different scenes of drink, debauchery, and worship to the temple gods—gave any unique indication of which hall or room was which.

How to return to Vinan was something she would have to worry about later. Her concern now was to find the servant quarters where there would be a little girl with a resemblance to Vinan, and then somehow convince her to come without being seen or heard by the guards. Crissa's steps made no sound on the tiled ground as she had already wrapped her feet in the cloths she always carried for this purpose.

This was not the first time she had sneaked into a palace and neither was this the first time she had evaded the guards of the city. In the many years she and her father lived in Qiriq she had made her way out at night with other children to climb into the windows of palaces. Back then she would take easy loot from the city masters who were too careless to find capable guards and too rich to bother guarding a few spare coins or trinkets. In those days, she had protested to her father that she and her friends had only taken that which would not be missed and had put it to good use. Such arguments had never moved him. His reproach still burned as new in her memory as the day he had given it.

I did not raise you with honor so you could hang as a thief.

Crissa shuddered as the memory of the reproach burned, not with its original approach but as a prophecy of the terrible things that had happened to Sander. It had been three years since, but still, his desperate cries rang in her head as loud as when he had screamed them. She had been warned against the path but had taken it regardless. It was poor Sander who had suffered the consequences.

The same feeling in her stomach, the twisted churning excitement that killed all appetite for food or sleep, was here now as it had been just before that fateful day. It had intermittently been tormenting her since the day she chose to help Vinan in the tavern. Yet she had chosen to risk all, even now sneaking into the most guarded place in the city, to help him.

Madness.

Crissa stopped at a corner and peered around it quickly. On either side of that hall was a spear-armed guard in chainmail who bore a large round bronze shield. She had to go back, as going forward would only ensure her capture. But, she thought, what if the servant quarters lay just beyond them? What if that passage was the way to the sleeping quarters of Seren-Raq's priestesses?

What if it was? Did she expect to enter the sleeping quarters of the priestesses without awakening any of them?

Yes, for that was certainly not impossible for her.

What then? Did she believe she could wake a small girl without awakening any of the priestesses? Did she consider that she had never seen Kirru nor Kirru her? What about sneaking that same girl past all the guards and out of the palace?

It was only now that she realized how much impulse and little thought she and Vinan had acted upon when they set out into the night.

I did not raise you so you could hang as a thief.

Madness.

Crissa backed away slowly as she heard footsteps approaching from the other side of the guarded hall. She slipped behind a nearby corner where she could see who was approaching the guards. Once they passed, she would gather her thoughts and rethink the plan.

Two white-clad priestesses, a young one with brown hair and an older woman with grey streaks in her once-red hair, escorted a young girl of maybe ten years. Though clean and finely clad in the white garments of the temple's entourage, she had an unrefined manner and a wild look in her eyes that was entirely foreign to the city of Qiriq. However, Crissa recognized that look immediately. It was the same familiar manner of Vinan that set him apart in this city no matter how much he restrained himself. This girl was a barbarian to this city. She had to be Kirru.

Crissa ducked behind the corner but did not run away yet. Conversation among the people began and she wished to stay and listen.

"Why did you let this girl past you? She needs to rest, not wander the temple."

This accusation was from the voice of a more mature woman, likely the one with the fading red mane, and Crissa guessed it to be leveled against the two guards.

"It is our master's orders," a man's voice replied stoically, "that all the priestesses be given freedom to wander the halls."

"So, we must do all the work of watching little children," said another voice, this one exasperated and distinctly feminine.

"Enough," interrupted the elder woman. "Take the girl to her bed."

The younger woman gave a disgruntled guttural sound while the little girl moaned in surprise and a little pain.

"Be gentle with her," demanded the voice of the old woman.

"Why?" asked the younger woman.

"Because our master commands it," the older woman replied. "The poor little thing needs sleep. She has spent many days in a slaver's carriage and has been asking about her brother ever since she came here. The guards found her wandering the halls."

"Lucky for her that our lord has ordered the guards to be gentle and the captain has some sense," said the younger woman. "Girl, you must go to bed. You will be awake early tomorrow and must be ready to do your work."

"But," said the little girl, "I always wake early."

"Then be awake when our lord asks us for our services in the morning," said the older woman. "You will need to serve him his breakfast and tend to the palace like all the others. Good night, my dear."

The footsteps continued down the hall past the two guards and further away from Crissa. Stealthy as she had learned to step, she had no means to become invisible or slip past the sentinels. She most certainly did not have the brute strength to surprise and overpower them.

There had to be another way to the quarters. Crissa would find it, convince the still-awake Kirru to come with her, and bring her back to Vinan. They would think about how to escape this palace after that.

She had barely turned to proceed down the hall she had ducked into when a clamor and a shout echoed through the corridors a distance away. The screech of a ram horn pierced her ears and left them ringing. She held her head disoriented but found the presence of mind to slip behind a pillar as the two guards rushed down the halls and away from her. Sound and shock bounced off the walls as footsteps rushed to the source of the horn blast. The once-tranquil palace had come alive with the cacophony of war.

No! Crissa thought in panic. *Not now! Why now?!*

I did not raise you so you could hang as a thief.

Madness.

The sounds of armored men charging through the halls came from every direction as the guards converged toward the source of the horn blast. Crissa remained hidden and still behind the pillar as she contemplated what she could do next. Perhaps it was time to return to Vinan and escape the temple while they could? Perhaps they could return for Kirru another day?

Yes, that did seem to be the best option.

She carefully made her way back to where she had left Vinan. The sounds of guard armor clanking and the boots thudding on the tiled floor came from the opposite direction from where Crissa headed. She used her memories of the frescoes on the ceilings to retrace her path back to Vinan, back to their entrance from which they would now escape the temple.

But when she arrived, Vinan was not where she had left him. The alcove was empty and the boy had left no trace of being there. The sounds of weapons echoed across the temple halls as Crissa realized with sinking dread that Vinan had probably run off to find Kirru. He stood no chance of finding his way there, or out of the palace. She had to find him.

But then she realized that she had no time to find him and escape. All she would accomplish would be to be captured alongside the boy.

But the thought of Vinan meeting a similarly gruesome fate...

I did not raise you so you could hang as a thief.

Madness.

She had to escape now. She would return for Vinan and Kirru soon, but now her only concern was to get out of the palace alive. To escape the way she had come was unthinkable now. The guards outside must have been alerted and they would be deployed out in the gardens in full strength. To escape, Crissa would have to walk brazenly in the open.

A moment of inspiration came over Crissa as she realized the guards had abandoned the way to the priestess' rooms. She quickly—albeit carefully—retraced her steps to where she had seen Kirru for the first and only time. As expected, she found the hall empty when she got there. The way to a priestess' room and her means of escape was now plainly before her.

At least she could get out safely tonight.

Crissa slipped into the doorless and empty bedroom of a priestess, barely making note of the woman's lack of privacy, and made her way toward the clothes that lay on a wooden shelf. She held up a robe to her own body and determined that her own size was close enough to that of the absent priestess. She snatched an armful of attire and slipped away from this section of the palace before the guards returned to their posts and the panicked priestesses to their chambers.

And return to their posts the guards were sure to do, as the clamor from across the palace had finally ceased. Vinan, if he were found and captured, would be taken to the dungeons beneath the temple.

No, Vinan was alive. Vinan had to be alive. She would find him and return for Kirru.

But Crissa knew she would need to return for him later. She returned to the very alcove where she had told him to stay so she could dress herself as a temple priestess. She found the thin white robes almost embarrassing to wear and was glad to have a cape with which to put over it. The brass-banded shoes that wound up her leg were absurdly impractical for any life other than one of luxury. She longed to be rid of them as soon as she was out of the palace.

When she was finished she took her old clothes, folded them, and stacked them neatly. She carried them in her arms and walked back out into the halls. She moved deliberately towards the exit, no longer burdened by the fear of being detected. She was a priestess now. She could come and go as she pleased. Those were the orders of Seren-Raq after all.

After she slipped out of the side entrance she walked down the center of the garden path. In her arms, she carried her old clothes, boots, and the rags she had used to cover her feet. Her daggers and rope rested concealed beneath the pile where she hoped they would remain hidden from view.

She glanced side-to-side as she continued, noticing that all the guards had been awakened and called out to guard both the courtyard and the walls. A few watched her closely while most simply gave her a brief glance before continuing on with their duties. The attire of the priestess was fulfilling its purpose well.

She was but twenty feet or so from the gate when a captain nearby held out his hand and gave her a command.

"Stop!"

She complied. He approached her alone while the sentinels at the gilded gate remained at their posts.

"Where is a little priestess like you going in the middle of the night?" he asked.

Crissa did her best to suppress any fears she held within her. She looked up at the tall, wide, brutish, olive-skinned man and answered him with the confidence of one who was under orders to be exactly where she stood at that moment.

"To deliver these clothes to the orphanage," she answered. "The one in the Al'wetaya district has need of them and Lord Seren has instructed me to deliver them."

She prayed her knowledge of Seren-Raq's charitable diversions would give her story the credibility needed to convince him. He stroked his black chin beard briefly while looking down at her.

"You chose an interesting time to attend to your task, girl," he said. "An intruder has been discovered in the palace and half my men are dead drunk on that horse urine they serve to us and call wine! I can't afford to give you an escort now."

"Then I'll deliver them alone," she retorted.

"Qiriq at night is no safe place for a little girl."

"It may be safer than being trapped in the palace with a thief or murderer. I know my way around the city and I will be back quickly."

"I am not about to have Lord Seren lose one of his priestesses..."

"You could disturb Lord Seren," she interrupted, "or you can let me pass and then I can get you some better wine that won't give you these headaches your men have."

And with that, she had staked everything on one promise that she had no intention of keeping. She hoped only that it would work.

The captain smiled.

"Will you promise that?" he asked.

He was apparently not a smart man.

"Yes," said Crissa.

The captain stood aside and motioned to the guards at the gate. They remained motionless as Crissa walked past them, through the gate, and into the streets.

She was free. And that trick would never work again.

The shadowy streets of the Qiriq night loomed hauntingly empty before her. A veneer of silence had long settled over the metropolis, as it did every night. Dirty narrow streets gaped open invitingly into near blackness, broken only by the faint glimmer of an occasional oil lamp. So full of crime and violence had the reputation of the streets become that even the hardest of Qiriq's criminals had abandoned them. This left even the darkest alleyways mostly deserted in the dead of the city's night. Ironically, this meant that Qiriq's streets were safer than they had been in Crissa's earlier lifetime. The thieves, the robbers, the smugglers, the enforcers, the peddlers of mind-destroying tonics, and all other scum of the city had descended into the infamous "undercity". It was a labyrinthine complex of bone-decorated catacombs built by the ancient race that had lived in these plains ages before the first stone walls of Qiriq had been erected. It was there that the dark business the city masters did not acknowledge was done. It was there that the fighters of the arena were kept locked away by their masters.

Crissa stopped before a lamp-lit corner to gather her thoughts. Though relieved that she had escaped unscathed, the disappearance of Vinan racked her with disquiet and fear. Worse yet, she had abandoned him in the palace without her knowledge to evade and escape. She thought about going back for him, despite every instinct she had screaming at her against taking this action. She fought the idea back. She felt that she had to return to find Vinan and deliver him from the belly of the temple. Her excuse to come back for him had been just that, a justification made up in the terror of those moments when the alarms had filled the halls of the palace with the din of rushing guards and clanging weapons.

Perhaps it was an excuse, but it was an excuse that had kept her alive.

But what had sounded the alarm?

Crissa had not had time to consider it before, but now she asked it to herself and gave it serious thought. Why had the guards been alerted from their posts? What had possessed one of them to blow the horn of alarm and what was the scuffle that had occurred from across the palace?

And why had Vinan not stayed where he was?

The horror of realization came over Crissa as she put these two things together. It would be fortunate for Vinan if he were even still alive. Those men within the palace were not mere levies taken from the Qiriq citizenry, clad in bronze and chainmail to perform the menial tasks of patrolling the streets. They were disciplined and hardened Raq warriors from the distant steppes. As fierce as Vinan could be in a fight, he stood little chance against one such man let alone a dozen or more.

And yet, she knew that he was impulsive enough to attempt it.

Crissa's survival instincts had been correct after all. She would have to return for Vinan and deliver both him and his sister from the grasp of Seren-Raq. This night that had begun in unity of purpose had ended in disaster. Where before two children of the mountains had been in bondage, now there were three.

The screams of poor Sander echoed in her head. The screams of pain as he writhed and rotted away from the disease carried by a rusty cut from a job gone wrong. For days he had howled, losing his senses and all that kept him human. It was with tears in her eyes that Crissa had plunged her blade into his neck to silence him. Those tears, held back since that day, returned with a sinking dread that the story was repeating itself with Vinan.

Crissa knew that only she could now do something to make things right and she knew she needed help to do it, so she began to walk into the shadows where few of the upright dared to traverse.

She would go to the undercity and find Stek.

***

The skulls that lined the walls of the undercity looked upon Crissa with empty sockets where their eyes had once been. There was no telling how long they had rested beneath the earth as the original catacombs had been added to by both the later inhabitants of the plains and, later, the city of Qiriq. For all she knew, any of the skulls could have rested here a hundred years or five thousand. Regardless, all of them sat one on top of the next to form a great mosaic of time and history embedded into the earth beneath the city.

Within this mosaic, between its walls of human remains, Crissa walked with purpose towards the cells of the arena slaves. She approached the arch that was obstructed by a grated door and guarded by a golden-haired and well-armed man.

"What are you doing down here?" he asked her as she approached, his square jaw grinning with amusement at the little girl who had lost her way in the deadliest part of Qiriq.

"That is between me and my lord, Northman," Crissa answered like an educated slave sent to do an important task. "My lord's business is with Rejak."

"He doesn't come down here," the barbarian guard scoffed. "Go home to your master and ask him for better directions."

"I do not think Seren-Raq will appreciate hearing how an uncouth barbarian turned away one of his handmaids," Crissa said.

This had some effect on the man, for his smirk lowered to a scowl. He seemed convinced now that Crissa indeed was exactly who she said she was.

"Rejak is not here now," he said. "He does not come here often."

"I doubt that," Crissa retorted, "especially on the night before Uthal-Raq's return and the arena games that will follow."

The man frowned.

"You know more about him than is good for you, girl," he said with some respect. "Wait here."

He walked down the passage on his side and spoke to another man in a low voice. Both men –the fair-haired gatekeeper and a thin, armed, young olive-skinned man—came back to the grate. A key from the blonde man undid a lock and the grate cracked open slightly to let Crissa through.

"Come with me," said the olive-skinned man whom Crissa considered incredibly handsome.

Crissa followed him down a narrow passage and a winding

staircase illuminated with cheap candles to a chamber where sat a man in relatively plain grey robes considering his wealth. Rejak was a well-built man several years older than forty, but looked ten years younger due to the thick black hair that showed no signs of balding or recession. A thin and meticulously trimmed beard covered his thick face that smiled when Crissa entered his chamber. Behind him was a tall and slender, black-skinned man who stood with his arms crossed above his ornately crafted scimitar.

"Well," asked Rejak, "to what do I owe the honor of Seren-Raq sending me one of his priestesses? And why one so young? And in the middle of the night?"

"My lord," she began, "has sent me to ascertain the fitness of the combatants for the upcoming festivities. He wishes to know if there is anything you require."

"Well, there is always the question of payment to ensure," he stroked the short beard on his chin, "that the games go as well as possible. I am also wondering if he will ever change his mind about bringing his priestesses here to... pray with my fighters and ease their pain."

The men around him laughed heartily at this last suggestion. Crissa did not react to it and instead remained fixated on her feigned mission.

"I wish to inspect the combatants so I may report to Seren-Raq that they are ready," she said. "This is what my lord has commanded me."

"Is that wise, girl?" Rejak asked. "Those are savage men I keep down there. Many have not seen a woman or girl in a long time."

"I know what they are," she replied, "and I am not afraid. I know not to get too close and I also know that it is in your best interest that Lord Seren's priestesses are not harmed while under your protection."

"You are quite bold and intelligent," said Rejak, "for one of

Seren-Raq's little pets. Take her there! See that nothing happens to her!"

This last bit was addressed to Crissa's olive-skinned guide, who moved through an arch to the right and wordlessly beckoned the girl to follow him. Crissa obeyed, all the while thinking to herself how perhaps she might have played it better by seeming a little less smart. It was too late to go back on that now.

She followed her guide down into the depths of the earth, into tunnels dug beneath most of the undercity; and it was here—past many well-paid armed men resting lazily—where Rejak kept his prized possessions and source of income. Within these dungeons, original ancient catacombs with recent additions of locked grate doors, were kept the most deadly and untamed of the arena fighters. The usual crowd favorites with their crafted muscles, pretty faces, and knowledge of how to cut a man to let out much blood but not kill him were mere showmen compared to the monsters here. Staring at Crissa from their cages as she passed and pretended to inspect them, were consummate killers waiting for their chance to escape and turn on their owners.

Crissa mused to herself why Rejak would keep them all together in the same place, but that was none of her business. While not every man here was a brute filled with raw strength all of them were immediately recognizable as deadly. Those who were awake eyed Crissa with curiosity but little interest as she passed while she, seeing that none of them were boys, gave each man no more than a glance. It was not until she and her guide were nearly at the end of the corridor that any cell's inhabitant caught her eye, this one a boy with dark brown hair and head bent down who sat with his back against the wall to which he was securely chained. She stopped at the cell and looked to the boy who looked up with a mix of exhaustion and fury caged within him just as he was caged in this subterranean prison. The flash in his eyes was immediately familiar to Crissa and she believed she knew why this was.

"A boy?" she asked.

"A young tribal hunter from distant mountains, or so his seller said," replied the guide.

"Why is he chained up?"

"Because he savagely attacked his handler. He has much potential in the ring, but no ability to be trained yet."

"Yet?"

"We have to break him first."

Crissa thought that if the boy here truly was Stek and shared his brother's resilience, then it would indeed take almost killing him to break him. That was, if breaking him was even possible.

"Let me see him closer," she requested firmly.

"You are as close as you can go."

"No," she persisted. "Let me inside."

"Did you not hear me when I said he attacked his handler?" Frustration began to build in the man's tone. "Because of that boy, a man has half of his face torn apart."

"I am not his handler," she said, "and you have seen to it that he is securely chained. Now let me inside to get a closer look."

The man gave a hesitated nod before reaching into his pocket and pulling out a key. The lock turned, the grate swung open, and Crissa's path was clear. She stepped in and tried to get a good look, but the darkness obscured the boy's face that barely looked up to her at all.

"Hand me the lamp," she said.

She opened her hand and the guide lent her the illuminating brass object. She held the steady flame forward and looked down. She finally made out the clear likeness of the restrained boy and knew immediately that she had found who she sought. Though bruised with black and green marks on his shoulders, chest, stomach, and face, the familiar look and determined fire in the boy's eyes were enough for Crissa to recognize the likeness of Vinan in him. He glared at her with a face of stone behind which burned much hatred, though none towards her.

198

This was undeniably him.

"I'd like a minute with him alone," she said to the guide.

"As you wish," he said, resigned, tired of haggling with her.

His footsteps faded into the surrounding darkness until Crissa was confident that she could whisper to the boy without being heard.

"Stek?" she asked.

The boy's seemingly implacable front cracked at the mention of a name he had not expected to hear. He stared at her no longer with a cold glare but with shock.

"What?" he gasped.

"Are you Stek?" Crissa asked after a shushing directed at him.

"Who are you?" Stek asked with an intense whisper.

"A friend of Vinan's," she replied, "and I have come to find you."

"Where is he?" Stek asked excitedly, while forgetting to keep his voice low.

"He went to find Kirru," Crissa whispered after another shushing. "Come with me and we can find him together."

"Then get me out of these chains," he said while tugging against them. "I have a sister and brother I need to find!"

"Alright," she said, trying to calm him, "stay still."

She stepped close to him and bent down, pulling a lock pick from her cape. After a few seconds of fiddling and twisting the manacle on Stek's right wrist was unlocked and, shortly after, the left one as well.

"Wait," she said in a low voice to Stek before he could sprint out of the cell. "We need to escape another way. There are too many guards back the way I came."

They had barely walked out of the cell and into the corridor when Crissa realized that there was a cell just opposite Stek's and that the inhabitant within had seen everything. He was a tall man with long chestnut hair and a beard of the same color. The sinewy

199

muscles on his arms, the scars on his body, and the build of his frame indicated to Crissa that this was a man who had survived many a battle inside or outside the arena. He stood at his grated door with a wide grin.

"That's a nice set of tricks you have with you, girl," he said. "Now, would you rather use them to help me or would you rather I shout to the guards?"

"If I let you go," she answered, "are you going to go at me or them?"

"My only plan is getting out of this hole and killing every damn fool who tries to stop me."

As Crissa looked into his eyes, she knew he spoke the truth.

"Can you use a lock pick?" she asked.

"I can figure it out," he replied.

"Here!"

She tossed him the bent piece of metal and was surprised when the lock turned just a few seconds later. He emerged into the hall and walked down the hall to another cell.

"You're free," said a voice within. "Is it time to break out?"

"Yes," he replied. "It is time to make the undercity bleed. Rejak is a dead man tonight."

Crissa looked to Stek beside her and saw that his attention was less taken now by the thought of escape and more by the imminent escape and slaughter unfolding before them. Bloodlust, wrath, and vengeance had all risen to his countenance from the innermost chambers of his soul. Crissa realized that she feared this small boy, for he had taken up a darkness that was absent in his brother. She knew she had to act now before he was swept up in the moment to join the freed gladiators in their bloodletting.

She slapped her hand on his shoulder and gripped it tightly.

"Let's get out of here," she said urgently. "Now!"

Stek hesitated a moment as his fire receded, then nodded in agreement as his demeanor became that of a boy again, the boy that Vinan desperately sought to reunite with. A boy that Crissa could deliver to him.

If only she could deliver Vinan from his own captivity.

CHAPTER 20

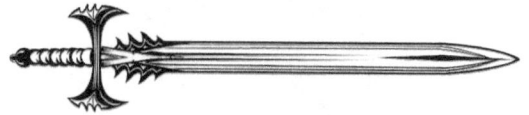

The Priest

Vinan opened his eyes to a brilliant ceiling of gold and plaster. The surface on which he lay felt softer than any he had ever known. There were pleasant scents of oils and fruits wafting all around him. He could not remember where he was or the last thing he had been doing before his presumably long sleep.

He remembered ceilings like the one above, paintings of men and women frolicking beneath giant overflowing cups of purple liquid that poured out of the top and drenched the merrymakers beneath the oversized goblets. He recalled walking through the halls of the temple in search of something, someone. He had come to bring her back, she was here, and he had seen her just before he had passed from consciousness...

Kirru.

He attempted to jolt from where he lay only to find very quickly that his muscles were not ready for it. With a shot of pain pulsing through his body and into his extremities, he fell back into the embrace of the soft bed.

"Vinan!"

That voice. Vinan would have recognized that voice even if he had forgotten his own name. The willowy arms of Kirru clasped about his neck and he raised his hand to run it through her hair. He was not dreaming. Kirru was here, in the flesh, and together with him again.

"Tell our lord that he is awake," said the voice of a woman.

Vinan heard but did not care. He lay there a moment more before he mustered the ability to speak to his sister since what seemed a lifetime ago.

"Are you alright, Kirru?"

"Yes," she said. "I am now."

"My lord treats all in his care with utmost generosity and good graces," interjected the woman from before, "even those who do not deserve such."

Vinan turned his head to his left and beheld a somewhat fattened young woman with golden hair standing by his bed. She was dressed in the same thin white garb that Vinan had seen on the other women of the palace. He observed that several more of them stood waiting in the chamber, but this one seemed to hold a position of authority over the others. Her blue-green eyes looked down from her pretty face on Vinan with condescension and disgust.

"Where are we?" he asked.

"You are in the hospitality of Seren-Raq," she answered, "High Priest of the Temple of Plenty. He has ordered that we treat your bruises and we have done so. We are here, at his command, to serve you as he wishes us to."

Vinan looked away from her and back to Kirru. He closed his eyes in relief because, for now, any immediate danger to himself or his sister had passed. It was apparent to him that Kirru had been treated well here and was being fed more than enough. He then thought of Stek and the pits where he was kept. He still had to save Stek. He had to save Stek while there was still time.

"Vinan? Where is she?"

Kirru's question brought Vinan out of his own thoughts.

"She?" he asked, bewildered. "Who?"

"Where is Enna?!"

It had been some time since Vinan last thought of the little girl of the wild. He remembered the last time he saw her, ill and recovering in the hut of the woodsman. That had been days ago, days before he tried to infiltrate this temple of luxury. He did not care to count how long it had been since he had looked upon those brilliant eyes bright as the stars. Not since the time he had spent in the deep hellhole beneath the palace or the unknown hours he had spent in this bed of perfume.

"She... she is safe," he managed to answer. "We will go back to her when I find Stek."

"That may not be long," the voice of Seren-Raq interrupted from the entrance of the chamber. "I have dispatched men to find him, buy him, and bring him here. Soon, your family will be whole again, Vinan, son of Bheif."

The priest entered while dressed in flowing purple-red garments whose softness could almost be felt by merely gazing upon them. Seren-Raq, High Priest of this temple of generosity or whatever it was. His skin was almost as orange as Vinan remembered it, colored and tanned so much that it barely resembled any shade of human skin known to Vinan. His golden hair was shaved short around the sides to leave an oiled and absurd crown of long locks. His face was shaven nearly clean, except for precisely trimmed patches of incomplete beard. As he sat down in a cushioned chair beside the bed he smiled at Vinan and Kirru with what seemed like warmness and concern.

"When you were recovering," he continued, "your sister told me of her home and her brothers. She is fortunate to have a brother like you. The courage you showed was equal to that of the greatest Raq warriors who served under my father and brothers."

"Your father and brothers..." Vinan repeated.

"Ah, yes," he said. "You don't know. The Great Raq

204

conquered many lands to which you have never been. His sons continued this and I am…"

"I know who you are," Vinan said curtly.

"Oh?" Seren-Raq cocked an eyebrow upwards. "Do you?"

"You are Seren-Raq," Vinan answered, "son of the Great Raq and lord of this temple."

"That is correct," Seren-Raq said with astonishment, though whether feigned or real Vinan could not determine. "Though, given the way you entered my home, it seems you know the name only and not my reputation nor what I do."

"I have heard much of the Raqs and what they have done," Vinan said.

"And so, it is always doomed to be," Seren-Raq sighed. "I am to be forever remembered for the bloody deeds of my brothers."

He looked at Kirru and smiled sweetly.

"Tell me, Kirru," he said, "is your brother always this way?"

"No," she answered innocently. "He usually does not sleep this much."

Seren-Raq laughed a musical laugh that made Vinan realize that this High Priest of the temple had a strangely entrancing, soothing, and pleasant manner with everything that emanated from his mouth.

"Well then," he sang like a songbird, "let us refresh his body and spirit with food and drink!"

He motioned and two women made their way to Vinan.

"There is a meal prepared for you," he intoned invitingly. "You must be famished after all you have been through."

The two women—both of them dark-haired, olive-skinned, and strong of grip—helped Vinan up to sit on the bed. The sheet fell to his waist and he realized he was naked beneath it. A red-haired girl approached with a blue robe and threw it around his shoulders. She slipped his arm into one hole and then the other.

Seren-Raq rose from his seat and turned to leave.

"Dress him and escort him to the dining hall," he said to

them. "I will be awaiting your company, Vinan, son of Bheif."

***

The robe the women dressed Vinan in was the most comfortable garb he had ever worn. The soft fabric of the blue garment was gentle on Vinan's bruised skin and its thin texture kept him from sweating in the warm air of Qiriq. As he followed the priestesses through the halls he had once sneaked through uninvited, he began to understand why Seren-Raq would wear them.

He contemplated to himself how much everything had changed so quickly. Was Seren-Raq truly his enemy? Kirru seemed happy here, or at least not unhappy. There was no sign that Seren-Raq had mistreated her at all. She seemed more filled in and better fed than she had ever been in her life. Indeed, she spoke to Vinan with more vigor than he ever remembered in her since they had left the mountains. He would have listened more intently, but she was speaking in awe about the art painted on the walls and ceilings.

"... and did you know that there is a very big," she stretched her arms to their full span, "painting on the ceiling of the big hall? It has this great big cup with naked people..."

Vinan did not want to be told about it. He had no interest in whatever decorated these walls, only that Kirru was safe within them. She seemed to be, and that was good enough for now.

Two brass doors opened before him revealing a spacious banquet hall. Upon an oiled and polished table of cedar wood, there lay a feast of meat, breads, and fruits of all shapes and colors. Seren-Raq, who sat in a chair at the head of the table, rose from his seat as Vinan entered behind the escorting priestesses.

"Welcome, Vinan, son of Bheif," the priest said. "I hope the meal is to your liking. I had one of my best lambs slaughtered."

Vinan nodded in an attempt to show appreciation. He was unsure yet how to address Seren-Raq. He did not know Seren-

Raq. He did not trust Seren-Raq. It was better, Vinan thought, to let the man show his intentions before showing his own. For now, Vinan took his seat at the table beside the priest and reached for the meat.

"Vinan!" Kirru shouted. "Don't grab the meat like that!"

Vinan looked at her with puzzlement. His hand had already grasped the leg bone that he had ripped from the carcass. He stood there bewildered.

"You are supposed to wait to be served," Kirru said. "They serve you the food."

Seren-Raq laughed heartily with amusement.

"It is alright," he said through his chuckling. "Your brother is famished indeed. He can eat that entire leg, no, the whole lamb if he wishes."

Vinan took the leg and began consuming it. He did not care if this was not the custom here and Seren-Raq certainly did not seem to mind. He was hungry and needed to fill his belly regardless of custom or etiquette. He ripped the meat from the bone with his tooth, he filled his plate with fruits, and he drank the water and purple "wine" that the women served him.

"Careful, Vinan," said Kirru. "Don't drink so much wine."

Vinan could see why very quickly. Numbness overcame his mind and his muscles as he was reminded of the drink in the Shai's flask. The same dulling of senses and relief from pain came as a result of the wine. Vinan drank it no more, instead choosing to eat the meat and fruits.

Sometime after Vinan had taken the last bite he was capable of taking, as he stared absently at a gnawed leg bone on the table, Seren-Raq rose from his seat.

"Well," he said, "are you ready to walk in the gardens, Vinan, son of Bheif? They are most beautiful at this time of the year."

Vinan rose, believing that a walk in the scenic gardens after that meal was certainly not the worst thing he had ever experienced since leaving his home in the mountains. He and

Kirru followed the High Priest out of the dining chamber escorted by an entourage of white-clad priestesses.

The gardens through which Vinan had crawled in the dead of night took on a new life in the brilliant hot sun of Qiriq. The branches of the groomed trees that lined the paved paths were filled with giant green leaves that provided welcome shade to the High Priest and his guests. Large yellow, orange, and green fruits hung beside the leaves above and some others had fallen to the ground as if to decorate the stones on which the walkers tread. The fountains in the center of the courtyard gushed forth seemingly unending streams of water beneath which a flock of strange pink birds were gathered. Vinan found the creatures striking and beautiful, despite their overpowering stench.

"Beautiful is it not, Vinan, son of Bheif?" Seren-Raq asked rhetorically. "When first I came to this palace these gardens were but an overgrown mess of tangled weeds with their pools of water long run dry. Really, a fitting metaphor for Qiriq itself... Is it not?"

Vinan remained silent, not wishing to give the High Priest any reason to believe he had been won over. Before him was a man who took great pride in his supposed accomplishments and received many rewards for them. Vinan saw no reason to feed the man's sense of worth.

"Yes," Vinan finally answered after a few moments of thought. "This place is as beautiful as the city outside is hideous."

Seren-Raq ceased to walk in an unnaturally natural way to disguise how abruptly he was actually stopping. He turned around and—to Vinan's surprise—the High Priest's face bore no sign of wrath or wounded pride. He smiled gently and looked down at Kirru.

"Go to the garden for a while, my dear," he said to her. "The birds are waiting for you."

Her face beamed with delight and two priestesses came forward with baskets of old bread. She turned to her brother.

"Please come with me, Vinan," she pleaded. "We can feed

the birds together. They are so beautiful!"

"In a little while, my dear," Seren-Raq said before Vinan could answer. "I wish to talk with your brother for a few moments."

As his little sister left towards the fountains with the two priestesses, Vinan stayed behind as the High Priest wished. Seren-Raq waved his hand to dismiss the others and leave only Vinan and himself in the grove.

"The flamingoes add an exquisite touch to the gardens," he said. "All guests inevitably spend much time admiring them."

"Fla-flamingoes?" Vinan asked.

"Those exotic pink birds there," Seren-Raq answered, pointing to the fountain. "It seems your little sister has taken a liking to them. Strange creatures."

He walked beneath a tree and plucked a ripe orange fruit from one of the low-hanging branches. He offered it to Vinan, who refused it.

"Tell me, Vinan, son of Bheif," Seren-Raq said while reclining in a stone seat, "do you hold hostility against me in your heart?"

Despite how deadly of a question Vinan knew this could be, he felt confident enough in his judgment of the High Priest's temper to make an answer.

"You bought my sister from slavers and did not hurt her," he said. "For that, I guess I should be grateful. I wonder though, why you let slavery continue when you have all the power you appear to have."

"It is not so simple," answered Seren-Raq. "Power in this city is shared among all the twelve masters, of whom I am but one. Even the might of my brother's army counts for little. They know I do not command my brother and that he despises me."

This caused Vinan to remember Kror, and Seren-Raq undoubtedly noticed.

"Tell me, Vinan, son of Bheif," said the High Priest, "why did you leave the mountains with your brother and sister? What your sister told me makes little sense."

"What my sister said...?" Vinan inquired with a poor pretense of puzzlement.

"A girl of the forest who needed to be returned to her people," Seren-Raq answered. "A girl named Enna with white eyes bright as the night stars. She said the three of you left to return her to her people and that you cannot return until it is done. A pretty story to tell a child, and I applaud you for convincing Kirru of it... but there is another reason, isn't there?"

Vinan stood frozen in surprise. He should have considered that Kirru would divulge what she knew to the first person in the outlands who delivered her from the slavers and treated her with any dignity. He also gained an appreciation for Seren-Raq's intellect at that moment. The High Priest was far more than the hedonist fool he let others believe he was.

"There is," Vinan said at length. "In truth, we can never return home. It was better not to tell her yet."

"To protect her?" Seren-Raq asked.

"Yes."

"Does Stek, your brother, know the lie?"

"He does."

"Admirable," Seren-Raq said as he peeled the orange fruit, "admirable that in this world there are families where the bonds of love are still strong."

"Yes," said Vinan as he thought of Kror, "admirable."

"Your family threw you from your home didn't they?" Seren-Raq said.

Vinan stared at him in silence.

"Do not be so surprised," said Seren-Raq. "My family knows nothing but betrayal and fratricide. I know the look on your face too well. I know the pain that lies behind it."

"My brother," Vinan answered, "murdered the High Warrior, accused me of it, and cast us out. He rules our people now. I have no wish to ever go back."

"I see that I am not the only one with wicked brothers," Seren-Raq reflected.

Both of them were silent for a time in the peace of the gardens until the High Priest spoke again.

"This Enna your sister speaks of... who is she?"

"Just a girl who became our friend," Vinan replied.

"Your sister said she has eyes bright white like the morning star. Is this true?"

"No," Vinan said as he remembered what had happened every time any others had seen the strange eyes of the girl. "I don't see that at all."

"You are a terrible liar, Vinan, son of Bheif." Seren-Raq said with a sly smile. "It doesn't matter to me though. Her eyes could be red as a sand demon's and I would care little. Nevertheless, it seems you have lost her."

Vinan did not answer. He only hoped that the girl was still safe with the woodsman where he had left her. When he, Kirru, and Stek left this city, he would return there. He was sure of it.

"Where she wishes to go, I care not. I fight for my brother and sister," said Vinan.

"It is good that you fight for something," said Seren-Raq. "Most men live and die having never accomplished anything or never fighting to protect something."

"And what do you fight for?" Vinan asked. "What do you protect?"

"I do not fight," Seren-Raq answered. "I leave that for men with blood on their hands and desire for death in their minds. I build. I have built for myself all in this palace a tiny haven of peace and serenity. Here, there is no war. Here, these women do not have to fear any violence against them."

"But there is slavery outside the walls of your palace," Vinan shot back. "I have seen the city and it is terrible. I have seen the slaves and the people of the city who do not live as you do. Why haven't you helped them?"

211

"Outside the walls of the city," Seren-Raq began, "there are lands ravaged by my brothers and by other such men of the sword, lands torn apart from without and within. Lands where mothers and fathers kill their children to spare them the pain of cursed life. Compared to that, a life in the safety of Qiriq is a blessed one indeed."

"And you don't give this blessed life to the rest of the city?" Vinan interrupted.

"They would not know what to do with it," Seren-Raq answered. "You see, Vinan, most mankind desires slavery and bondage because of their own short-sighted desires. Have you ever wondered who the slaves are in the market? Certainly, some of them are spoils of my brothers' wars or kidnapped like your brother and sister, but slavery was alive and well long before Farken-Raq's horsemen reached this city's walls all those years ago.

"Go down into the city again and watch closely! You will see a father selling his daughter for a small amount of money. You will see a new mother abandoning her newborn child on a doorstep to be taken in or die in the street. You will see families starving because the father refuses to drink even a little less wine. Indeed, the eternal state of man is self-inflicted pain that is then forced by them upon others."

He paused for a moment and then stared at the wall before him as if he were looking miles into the horizon.

"If I had the power to end it" he continued, "and bring peace to all in the world, then I would. I do not have such power. Compared to the armies my brothers command, the kingdoms and empires they battle, and the enormity of suffering in the world, I am quite small. I must content myself with doing what little I can and helping where I can."

There was something different about the High Priest now. There was fierceness that Vinan had never seen in him. Was it possible that this man was far more than a simple lover of pleasure

212

and beauty?

"If such power did exist, though," said Seren-Raq, "I would seize it without hesitation and put it to use."

For the first time, Vinan began to think differently of this man. Was it possible that this priest truly bought the women and girls here so they could live a better life? Why did it matter that they served him hand and foot if that meant they lived in the luxury and safety of the temple? Vinan had already seen the streets of Qiriq. He knew what the alternative to this was for all the women in this temple. Perhaps it was better to save a few than none at all.

Perhaps.

A man suddenly ran breathlessly towards them with a scroll in hand. He knelt before the High Priest with reverence before being signaled to stand up.

"My lord," panted the herald with the scroll in his outstretched hand, "Uthal-Raq is ten miles from the city. He requests the presence of his most serene brother, the High Priest of the Temple of Plenty."

Seren-Raq took the scroll from the messenger's hands, opened it, read it, and put it aside. He rested his chin on his hand for a minute.

"Tell the captain we are riding to meet Uthal-Raq," he commanded. "Tell him I want the usual horses prepared and one more besides."

Seren-Raq rose from his seat with purpose and looked to Vinan.

"Come with me, Vinan, son of Bheif," he said. "Let us leave Kirru here for a little while and go out to meet my brother. I want to show you what sort of men you and I stand against in this world."

CHAPTER 21

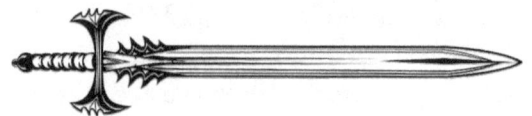

Imminent Collapse

Crissa's father sat running his fingers through his beard, contemplating.

"Strange," he said. "Strange, yet not surprising."

Crissa stood quietly beside Stek and waited for her father to make a decision. Any course of action had to be preferable to her immediate instincts. It was through an action of Vinan's and hers that Vinan had been taken prisoner while Kirru remained in the palace of Seren-Raq. The rescuing of Stek was the one bright mark of a night of failure, and the boy now stood there in the safe house with them. Crissa desperately sought her father's counsel now, having told him all that had happened.

"You have managed to trade the freedom of one brother for another," the old man said to his daughter. "This is not the worst that could have happened."

He put his hand on her shoulder and smiled. This reassured her only a little, as the capture of Vinan weighed heavily upon her. Nevertheless, it was good that her father showed no anger or disappointment. That had never been his way.

"So," he looked to the boy, "you are Stek, brother of

Vinan?"

"I am," the boy answered with a look of mistrust, "but I do not know who you are."

"I am but an old man who met your brother and promised to aid him," Crissa's father answered. "This young girl is my daughter and tried to help Vinan save Kirru last night."

"I heard," said Stek. "I want to know how we are going to save my brother and sister now that I am here."

Crissa realized that little had changed. A boy from the mountains stood among them, having undergone many hardships, seeking to be reunited with his brother and sister. As she looked at Stek, she realized he was going to be no more reasonable or patient than Vinan had been. If her instinct told her anything, Vinan was probably the more reasonable of the two brothers.

"We know where they are," said Crissa's father. "From what I understand, your sister is in little danger. Vinan however..."

He could not finish.

"What will happen to my brother?!" Stek demanded.

"I cannot say," the old man answered. "I have little knowledge of Seren-Raq, whether he is cruel or merciful. The rumors say he is far more merciful than his brothers."

This appeared to appease Stek little, if at all. Crissa mused that if Stek knew of the other Raqs' mercy, then this would have been of even less comfort.

"I do not care that he is merciful," Stek said angrily. "I will go into his house and get Vinan and Kirru back."

Not again. Crissa thought with dread.

"We tried that already, Stek," she said. "That is why Vinan is there."

"I will not be captured like him," the defiant boy answered.

"Then why were you captured by the slavers while he wasn't?" Crissa's father asked poignantly. "While you were restrained, your brother traversed the wilds to find you. If you think you can do better than him then you know little of your brother's

215

abilities, or your own."

"Quiet!" Stek snapped, giving Crissa's father a look of contained rage and wounded pride. "I will not wait here. I am leaving."

Before this could continue any longer, the door burst open and three men dressed in the uniforms of the city guard marched into the room. Crissa recognized Aranthas in the middle, dressed in the outfit of a captain, and put away the dagger she had instinctively drawn. Two other young men in guard attire followed Aranthas with spears in their hands.

"So," Crissa's father said with a resigned sigh, "this is your plan, Aranthas?!"

"Why are you still here?" Aranthas demanded as his eyes scanned the three. "Where are the others and who is this boy?"

"The boy is one of the reasons we are here at all," the old man replied. "Where the others are is out of my control now."

"You'd best find them soon, old man." said the "Things are moving far faster than we had hoped."

"Oh?" Crissa's father put his hand on his chin. "Has something happened?"

"You have not left this house, have you?"

"No. Enlighten me."

"Rejak is dead. Murdered by his pit fighters."

"Good!" Stek said suddenly and without any prompt.

"No. It isn't," Aranthas shot back.

"I see," said Crissa's father. "I hadn't thought you would resort to allying with him."

"Do not look down on me, Raq warrior," the young rebel said with indignation.

"I certainly don't," the old man said. "Rejak had many resources you and your men desperately needed. I always thought you were too proud to bribe him for them."

"He was integral to our designs," Aranthas said. "Without him, we have to act while we still can."

"He was a slaver and an animal," Stek interrupted. "I'm glad they killed him."

Aranthas looked to Stek, unable to ignore him any longer. The boy's appearance caught the man's attention as his eyes studied him.

"Who are you, boy?" the rebel leader asked.

"I am Stek, son of Bheif," Stek answered with defiance and indignation. "I was born of the mountain warriors and will not be treated as a child!"

"That is most interesting," said Aranthas. "Seren-Raq's guards have been searching for a barbarian boy from the distant mountains. They almost uncovered some dangerous things and interfered with our own plans."

He motioned with his finger and his two men pointed their spears towards Stek. Aranthas gave a sly smile.

"In fact," he continued," word on the street is that Seren-Raq left the city a short time ago with a mountain boy. I thought that he was the one, but the guards' search continues. The priest's men will be appeased for at least a few moments and distracted if the city guards give them what they want."

Stek struck a defiant pose and glanced around the room for a weapon. Though there was none for him to use, Crissa could see in his eyes that it made no difference. His fighting spirit was no less fierce than his brother's.

She would have to draw her dagger to defend him.

"Please, Aranthas..."

Her father rose from his chair to be greeted by a spear-point. He allowed the interruption, gave every appearance of meekness, but did not back down. Aranthas motioned to his follower, who withdrew the weapon away from the old man.

"Consider what you are about to do," Crissa's father pleaded. "Would you sacrifice the ideals of everything for which you have fought? Would you deliver this defenseless boy back into the captivity he escaped?"

The rebel thought for a moment as those in the room waited in tense silence. His reply came in a tone full of regret.

"I have made many sacrifices and many compromises. Too many to throw everything away with the end so close. Captivity in the hands of Seren-Raq will be one of the safest places in the city while we do our work."

"I understand," the old man said with resigned sorrow.

In barely an instant the seemingly meek old man incapacitated the young leader with a strike of his hand and seized the spear from the guardsman closest to him. A well-positioned strike from the blunt end left the guard in a pathetic heap on the floor with his hands on his groin. The final man had time to react and direct his spear against his aged opponent. However, the Raq warrior—old though he was—outmatched his opponent with his many long years of martial experience. It did not take long for his superior spearplay to leave the other man disarmed and on the floor beside his companions.

"Go!" the old Raq exclaimed to the children. "Go now!"

All three ran into the street, after the old man disposed of his spear and Stek paused to grab it off the floor. They ran quickly around many corners and through many obscure alleyways until they were nearly out of breath.

"That is far enough," Crissa's father said through heavy but controlled panting. "It will be a good while before those men recover from their pain."

"You... you didn't kill them?" Stek asked.

"It was not my intention," the old man replied. "Had I wished to kill them, they would be dead."

"But you didn't!" Stek said incredulously. "Why?"

"I have spilled more than enough innocent blood for one lifetime," he answered. "I had no need to kill those men when incapacitating them was all that was needed."

"You lacked the will to kill them." Stek muttered. "Warriors do become soft with age."

218

"To simply kill is not strength, young warrior. I pray you learn that one day."

Crissa's father said this with such authority, sternness, and sorrow that Stek was silenced immediately. Crissa, meanwhile, remembered the words of the rebel concerning Seren-Raq's guards and realized that they needed to leave the city with all haste.

A sudden commotion and stampede of feet came from the direction of the main streets. The din made Crissa turn her head instinctively as she wondered the reason for it. Had the rebels put their plan into motion? Had Uthal-Raq already arrived at the head of his army? Was blood about to be spilled in the streets of Qiriq?

Stek sprinted down the alley without warning.

"Wait!" Crissa cried. "Stek!"

It was already too late. She had no choice but to follow him as quickly as she could. This time, however, the footsteps behind her assured her that her father would stay beside her. She would not lose Stek as she had lost Vinan.

When she reached the end of the alley by the main street, Crissa was surprised to see that Stek had stopped suddenly as if shocked.

"Stek?" she asked.

The boy snapped out of a trance and looked at her.

"Kirru," he said excitedly. "I saw Kirru!"

"Where?" Crissa asked.

"She was with the white robed women," he pointed in the direction of the city gates. "She was riding with one of them,"

"The priestesses of the Temple of Plenty are leaving the city," Crissa's father pondered as if suddenly unsettled. "Why?"

Screams echoed from another direction of the city. The screams were joined by a tumult of voices and then by the smell of smoke.

The city of Qiriq burned.

The old Raq shouted to the children as he sprang into action. "Follow me!"

219

Crissa grabbed Stek by the shoulder and pulled him along. In the throng of terrified and confused citizens, only the old man and his daughter seemed to be moving with any plan or purpose. She followed her father through the city, easily moving past any bystanders. A paralysis seemed to have taken hold of the bewildered populace as the distant sounds of violence and smell of fire inched ever closer. Helplessly did the people of Qiriq wait for a sign or direction as all the business in the city ceased abruptly.

Three men dressed as guards stormed into the middle of the street. One man led and the other two dragged a finely garbed man forcefully by his arms. They threw him to the ground in the middle of the cobbled path. The well-groomed, balding man of fifty or so years slowly pushed himself up to his knee and whimpered something inaudible.

The leading guardsman shouted. "People of Qiriq, look and behold!"

He drew his sword and pointed it at the man's throat. The whimpering ceased and the magistrate fell as silent and motionless as stone.

"Citizens!" the soldier announced with arms spread. "This is the true form of the masters. This is who has ruled us all these years. These are the kind of men who keep us in slums."

He delivered a sharp kick to his helpless prisoner and raised his sword aloft.

"Freedom for Qiriq! Death to the masters!"

Crissa did not wait to watch the grisly end of the master's life. She and Stek followed her father as he ran in the direction of the city gates, the same city gates through which the priestesses had exited. Crissa soon realized the object of her father's purpose.

A stable waited before them and she knew it was well stocked with good horses. She and everyone else in Qiriq knew that couriers and scouts, tradesmen and merchants, captains and magistrates all bought steeds from the *Unshorn Mane*. The owner was a reputable businessman who selected and bought only quality beasts. His connections with the nomads of the grass plain ensured that even an excellent stallion could be purchased in the urban maze of Qiriq, if the price was high enough.

But in these circumstances, would any price be high enough? Crissa's father pushed upon the door only to find it had been locked shut. He banged upon it with his staff until a small peephole opened at eye level.

"What is it?" a man asked gruffly from within.

"Friend," Crissa's father asked, "do you have a horse?"

"Go away," came the answer.

"Listen to me," The old Raq, with lightning speed, shoved his staff into the gap of the door slit before it could be closed. "Do you intend to wait here?"

"We will be safe," the man on the other side replied. "We have survived before. Leave us!"

"You won't be safe here," Crissa's father argued emphatically. "Not your stables. Not you. Not your family. You need to take what you carry and flee the city while you still can."

"So says the man who wants my horses."

"I only need two," the old man flaunted a bag of coins with his left hand, "and I have coin to pay you. Please let me buy two and I will leave you to do as you will."

He then withdrew his staff from the hole. To Crissa's surprise, the peephole did not close immediately. The man on the other side seemed to wait a few moments, considering, before closing it. Then the sound of a bar being removed came from within the house and the door was soon cracked ajar.

"Come on," said the man on the other side. "Get inside quickly."

The door was closed again and a large metal bar returned to its place soon after Crissa and Stek entered the house. The master of the stables loomed tall over them, the calloused hands at the ends of his muscled arms surely capable of defending himself and all he owned. The fear in his round face quickly faded when he confirmed that the three were but two children and an ancient man. He likely believed he could overpower all three of them with little effort, for they seemed of little threat to a hardened and strong man such as himself.

"Follow me." He said as he led them through the house and into the stables behind it. Crissa overheard the hushed sounds of the man's wife doing her best to put her children at ease with stories and play. Crissa could not help but hope that the mother's efforts would not be in vain as the chaos in the city spread.

The smell of horse dung filled the air inside the barn. Ten of the twelve stalls were occupied by beasts of varying sizes and colors. The smoke in the air outside had not gone unnoticed by the animals as they were all alert and agitated in the confined stalls. Panic had not set into their spirits yet, which was a relief for Crissa and her father.

"Pick any two you want." The stable master said.

"That one," Crissa's father pointed to a great black stallion fit to be a war beast before pointing to a smaller red and white mare only slightly larger than a pony. "That one as well."

He threw the bag to the stable master, grabbed a saddle, and strode to the black beast as if assured that the coins in the bag would be more than enough. The stable master only needed a quick look inside the bag to confirm that it was indeed a satisfactory payment.

Crissa bridled and saddled the red and white one with no trouble. Her father, once a Raq warrior, had taught the skill to her long ago. Like most things he taught her, she had never forgotten it.

"Get on." She said to the hesitant Stek once she was mounted. Following her example, he put his foot in the stirrup and lifted himself onto the saddle behind her. It was more than she had expected of one who had never been on the back of a horse.

"Hold on to my back," she told him, hoping that his first ride upon a horse would not end with him falling hard to the ground.

The stable master prepared to open the heavy barred gate that led to the streets.

"Ride out of here as fast as you can," he said. "I want to keep this gate closed."

"We will," Crissa's father answered. "If you can, take your family and whatever you can carry and flee the city. I fear this will be the great conflagration that finally destroys it."

The stable master gave a gruff wordless acknowledgement and said no more. The gate opened and Crissa's father spurred his black mount as if riding into the battles of his youth. Crissa kicked hers and followed her father into the streets.

They escaped Qiriq through the yet-unclosed gates and began their pursuit of the priestesses and Kirru.

CHAPTER 22

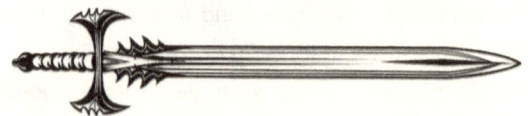

The Boy and the Warlord

The brush grass of the plain stretched for miles with no end in sight. Were it not for the occasional ridge that broke the flatness of the horizon, Vinan thought he might have been able to look into the distance and see the hills and the forests he had escaped. In contrast to his old home, he found this a hot, barren, brown land that barely knew the blessing of trees or the welcome shade.

Vinan began to accustom himself to sitting on his horse. He sat in the leather saddle with no more fear of falling off. Though he held the reins, Seren-Raq's captain—with the bridle firmly in his grasp—directed the animal. Vinan was amazed at the ability of the man to ride his own beast so easily while guiding another.

"Have you ridden horses long?" Vinan asked the captain inquisitively.

The captain glanced at him, seemingly surprised that the boy had the courage or desire to attempt small talk with him. But, nested within that surprise, Vinan detected what he guessed to be a hint of respect.

"Since I was a boy half your age," the man answered. "I was

born on the steppe. I rode alongside the Great Raq before he was known by that name. My life for years was war in the saddle beside him, even if my last days have been spent guarding the palace of his son. I could no more forget the saddle than you could forget how to walk."

Perhaps Vinan should have been able to tell that this man was no mere hired guard. He possessed something that was lacking in the guards of the city, something Vinan had not seen in a man since the Shai or the men from his home. The pride of a warrior, the honor of a man ready to give his own life to defend what he valued. Vinan considered that perhaps he could have respected and liked this man more had they first met under different circumstances.

The entourage stopped abruptly as a lone horseman dashed towards them. He was dressed as the Raq warriors in Seren-Raq's palace, with extraordinarily simplistic and practical armor but ornate jewelry around his wrists and arms. A curved scimitar hung from his belt and a yellow cloth was wrapped over his head to protect it from the oppressive midday sun. As he came closer, the captain let go of the bridle of Vinan's horse and rode to the front of Seren's cavalcade. The captain drew his curved sword for the first time that Vinan had seen and its metal glimmered as it reflected the sun's blinding rays.

"Halt!" the captain demanded. "That is close enough, rider."

"Am I mistaken or is this Seren-Raq who you escort?" the rider said as he stopped.

"Who do you serve, rider?" the captain asked, ignoring the rider's question.

"I am but a scout for the army of the mighty Uthal-Raq," he answered, "just as you serve his venerable brother."

"In that case, Raq warrior," Seren-Raq interjected as he rode to the front, "we have come to visit and congratulate my brother on his victories in Rhanijad. I wish to be taken to his camp."

"My master," the scout replied, "is not at his camp. He

marches with the vanguard to Qiriq. If you wait, he will be here soon."

This disturbed Seren-Raq and it was noticed by all, no matter how hard he attempted to conceal it.

"In that case," the priest said, recovering as best as he could, "we will await your master's approach where we stand. Will you send word to him?"

"I serve my lord with all obedience," answered the scout. "He will be very pleased to know that his brother has come to greet him."

He turned and rode off the way he had come. Seren-Raq sat silently atop his mount in deep thought. The captain noticed and looked to his lord.

"What is it?" he asked.

"It's nothing," said the priest with false bravado. "I am only wondering why Uthal-Raq is coming to Qiriq ahead of his army. Something must have happened."

"We will know soon enough," the soldier answered stoically.

It was not long after that shapes emerged from over a distant ridge and began to approach the small band of horsemen. Clouds of dust arose and the earth trembled at the approach of Uthal-Raq, his guard, and the great beasts of war. Amidst the shaking of the ground and the whinnying of nervous horses, only Seren-Raq seemed unaffected atop his steed. Vinan's pony shook beneath him as the war-beasts approached, causing even the captain to exert much effort to keep his own mount from panicking. Yet, only the priest and the horse he sat upon remained calm before the storm of dust, men, and strange beasts that approached the riders.

Vinan beheld the vanguard of Uthal-Raq's army. A line of armored spearmen in red armor approached, marching in perfect cadence as the sun's rays reflected off their bronze shields with blinding glare. Awed as he might have been by the sight of the force of men, it was the nine mighty war-beasts in the front that captured Vinan's attention and his terror. The behemoth animals were easily as tall as three or four fully grown men, and each was large enough to carry six or seven men on its back. They walked on all fours, with legs as thick as old trees that pounded the earth with each heavy step. A long snout drooped from each one's thick head almost to the ground and beneath the origin of that snout there were two tusks like those of the mountain boars Vinan had hunted in his homeland. Only, each tusk was easily the size of his body from foot to head. Vinan thought that there could be no other beasts as great and powerful as these and was in disbelief that any man could have tamed them.

The force halted when it was nearly upon Seren-Raq and his entourage. The beast in the center crouched after a shouted command from its rider. A lone man stood atop the animal's back to look down and tower over the riders before him. He was a wide-shouldered and well-built man with a square jaw and a long thin black beard that hung down to his bare and muscled chest. A helmet of shining bronze with a black horsetail plume protected his head and an elaborate curved sword hung from the belt around his waist. A cape of purple and gold covered his shoulders and waved in the wind.

"Brother!" he shouted in a booming voice. "You come early to greet me in my triumphant entrance! Your loyalty is noticed."

"I come at your bidding, great Conqueror of Rhanijad," the priest replied in a regal, if insincere, tone. "The Temple of Plenty has offered many prayers to the gods for your victory and safe return."

Uthal-Raq jumped from the back of the beast and landed feet first on the dirt. He stomped towards the riders with his dust-covered, once-black boots trampling upon the earth. Though he stood beneath the riders, there was no sense that anyone towered above him in authority. This man feared nothing and respected nothing.

A chill ran down Vinan's spine as he was reminded of Kror.

"Tell me, Seren," Uthal said with menace, "did you really believe that you could hide anything from me?"

The question momentarily caught the priest by surprise, but he immediately recovered.

"I have no designs against..."

"Enough!" shouted the warlord.

He turned around and waved his hand. Six men with dark red armor approached, their faces concealed by their helms that left only two slits for the eyes to see through. When Vinan saw who they escorted, he froze in terror. The third man from Ancar's slaving party, with his blue eyes as unyielding and ruthless as Vinan remembered. In his left hand, he held a rope which had the stumbling small body of a child on the other end, wrists bound tight in front. The child's head was concealed by a sack and Vinan could not know why, but a sick feeling entered his stomach that moment as he guessed.

"What is this, Uthal?" Seren-Raq asked.

"The temple of the star-ancients," Uthal-Raq replied. "I know of it and I know of your interest in it. You will no longer conceal your designs of that place from me."

"The temple is an ancient religion which I study to amuse myself," the priest protested. "It has no power now, if ever it did to begin with. It would bore you as it bored Farken. The star-ancients are but myth and the temple is of interest only to me and others who wish to study the past."

"Is it?" the warlord exclaimed. "Only a myth?"

He walked to the bound child and suddenly pulled the hood off. Familiar black hair fell down the child's face and Vinan did not even need to see anymore to recognize her. Regardless, Uthal-Raq pulled back her hair to show the glowing white eyes. All present were in awe and aghast except for Vinan. The look of terror on Enna's face as she frantically looked around her struck Vinan to the core and drove the young warrior into a rage.

"This mercenary," Uthal-Raq pointed to Ancar's former

partner, "found her in the woodlands under the care of a hunter. Fortunate for us, but not so fortunate for the poor woodsman."

Vinan's wrath was further kindled when he looked to the mercenary and received a knowing smile of recognition from him in return.

"Ah," said Uthal-Raq to his brother with a sly smile, "you are fascinated by her. We will take her to the shrine and she will show us the secrets of her people."

"Indeed," the delighted Seren-Raq returned with a sinister smile. "You will learn of the full power of the star-ancients, my brother."

Vinan's rage could be contained no more. It shamed him that a part of him wanted to let the girl remain with the Raqs. He had his sister. Seren-Raq would find his brother soon enough, or so he said. He knew then that he could choose to be silent, let the girl remain a prisoner of the Raqs, and be reunited with his siblings again.

But he knew that that would have been the act of an unworthy coward. He had sacrificed too much pain, blood, and effort to protect the girl only for her to be used by this warlord that stood before him. Worse, it would be a betrayal of Kirru who desired to be with her friend again. But, more than anything, Vinan realized that he had grown to care for the little girl and her safety.

No, this had to end now.

"That girl is mine!" Vinan shouted.

"*Vinan!*"

Enna looked at him with hope, tears streaming down her cheeks, as Vinan approached Uthal-Raq. All were stunned by the gall of the unknown boy who rode alone to challenge the triumphant warlord and the might of his army.

"What?" Seren asked incredulously. It seemed Vinan had finally managed to surprise and unsettle the priest.

"It doesn't look like she is yours," Uthal-Raq answered. "Now

229

be silent, return back to where you came from, and I will forgive your insolence. The girl is mine."

"Enna!" Vinan shouted as he dismounted.

"What?" Uthal-Raq said, visibly annoyed.

Seren-Raq tried to intervene.

"Vinan, what are you..."

"Her name is Enna," Vinan interrupted as he stood upright with defiance. "And she is with me. I am taking her with me."

"Is that a challenge?" Uthal-Raq asked.

"If you will not give her back," Vinan drew his sword from its scabbard, "then it can be nothing else."

"Who are you, boy?"

"No one," Seren-Raq interjected. "Just some wild boy I..."

"I am Vinan, son of Bheif," Vinan said. "I have travelled far and fought many men to protect that girl. I will not leave here until she is returned to me."

"Damned primitive fool," mumbled Seren-Raq.

"Do you know who I am, boy?" Uthal-Raq asked with little amusement.

"I know," Vinan answered with a face of stone and a voice of ice, "and I do not care. I do not fear you."

Uthal-Raq smiled with sadism and relish. He unlinked the golden latch on his cape and threw it aside.

"Then prepare to die here." he said to Vinan as he drew his curved sword and charged.

Vinan tried to evade the aggressive charge of Uthal-Raq and swung at the man's unarmored stomach. But the power behind the warlord's assault threw Vinan off-balance and he missed his mark as he ducked to avoid his enemy's curved blade. Neither of them landed their first strike as the duel shifted to a race toward exhaustion.

Vinan quickly realized that the first strike had been his best chance.

Uthal-Raq rained down furiously upon him with fast and

powerful blows. Against this onslaught all Vinan could manage was to avoid being cleaved in two. No opening presented itself for him to attempt a counterattack. The warlord knew how to kill men and had such confidence that he did not fear facing Vinan with most of his bare skin exposed. Vinan continued to retreat on his back foot, raised his own sword to defend against Uthal-Raq's, and then continued his retreat as another swing came down upon him. The warlord allowed him no time to strike back.

Vinan received a sharp kick in his stomach from Uthal-Raq's boot. So focused had he been on the curved blade raining blows down upon him that he had neglected to watch the rest of his opponent's movements. He fell to the ground on his back but immediately jumped back to his feet despite the pain in his gut. He took a blow of a fist to his face and fell again. The curved sword came down at him again and he raised his weapon to protect his face. It was in that brief moment that he realized he had been given something he lacked until now, an opportunity. He kicked at Uthal-Raq, who jumped back to avoid Vinan's foot. This gave Vinan enough time to get to his feet again.

Now the two stood apart, each with their sword in hand and each waiting for the other to move.

It was foolish. It was madness. It meant certain death. Nevertheless, Vinan let his fury take control and charged headlong at Uthal-Raq. He tried to make one great blow to end it all and put all his energy and strength into it. The warlord turned away effortlessly and twisted the blade away from the boy's grip. The sword went flying several feet away into the tall grass. Uthal-Raq suddenly lifted Vinan up with one arm and slammed him back-first into the ground. His right arm was soon pinned to the ground by the boot of the warlord, who stood over him triumphantly with sword in hand.

"I could kill you now, boy," Uthal-Raq said, "but I see no point in staining my sword with the blood of a little rabbit."

Futile fury rose in Vinan's chest. Of all the animals the

231

warlord could have chosen in that moment, why did it have to be a rabbit?

Uthal-Raq made a motion and two of his faceless guards approached.

"You four will escort the mercenary and his prize to the Temple of the Star-Ancients," he commanded. "Wait for me there, for I will return after I tend to business in Qiriq."

The men did as commanded. Enna was pulled away by the mercenary and Vinan lost sight of them, only able to focus now on the oppressive strength of the Raq's boot that kept him pinned to the ground. That pressure was suddenly eased as the warlord looked to the two guards.

"Execute him," he commanded.

The blade of one of the men quickly unsheathed, flashed through the air, and buried itself in the gut of Uthal-Raq. As the warlord slumped to the ground in a bleeding heap, the guard pulled out the sword and struck down his stunned companion.

Before Vinan had time to take in or comprehend what had just happened, a familiar and unexpected voice came from the man in the armor.

"Run, En'Shai!"

CHAPTER 23

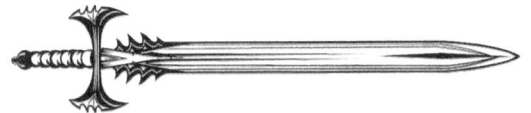

The Shrine of the Star Ancients

V inan fled.
    He knew his sword lay in the grass... Just over there, right where Uthal-Raq had thrown it. He only had to survive long enough to get it and he would be able to escape from here.

He found it and frantically turned around to face the enemies rushing at him. But there were none. To his surprise, he realized that no one was pursuing him or paying him any heed. A chaotic melee had broken out where once there had been an orderly line of shields, armor, and spears. Spears and swords clashed and men fell to the ground. There were footmen and horsemen, men donned in the garb of the Raq army, and men dressed in simple cloth. Arrows were fired into the struggle from every direction and the nine war-beasts panicked, trampling over men, or forcing them to open a path for the frenzied animals.

One suddenly charged headlong toward Vinan, who froze in terror. The rider of the beast had lost control of it and now clung to the saddle on top with every ounce of effort in him. It wasn't until the animal was nearly upon him that Vinan regained his wits and turned to run. He was suddenly tackled from the side and pushed into the grass. The beast continued on its own path and left Vinan behind. The man who had tackled Vinan stood up and held out his hand. Even though covered head-to-toe in the red armor of Uthal-Raq's guards, Vinan knew the man immediately.

"Are you hurt, En'Shai?"

Vinan shook his head and readily accepted the hand up.

"Good," the Shai said. "Let's get out of here."

The Shai strode—bloodied sword in hand—back towards the madness.

"Why are we going back?!" Vinan screamed.

"To get a horse."

A rider upon a horse rushed towards the Shai. He was clad in white and carried a scimitar in hand. Only his eyes were visible beneath the hood of his linens. The Shai stood in the path of the sprinting horse unmoved, appearing even to welcome it. Vinan watched as the Shai pulled out a knife from his belt with his left hand and threw it at the rider. The knife buried deep in the chest of the man and the horse stopped on its hind legs just before Vinan and the Shai. The Shai seized the reins of the horse and calmed it. He jumped upon its back and outstretched his hand to Vinan again.

"Mount, En'Shai."

Vinan took his hand and was pulled up to the saddle. He sat behind the Shai and held him firmly around the waist as the warrior of Kodumaa spurred the horse on at full speed.

They fled from the battle and into the plain. The long grass brushed against Vinan's legs and the warm wind that swept across the prairie swept through his long hair. The swiftness of the horse's gallop made his stomach jump into his chest. The exhilaration from moving at such speed was a feeling Vinan had never imagined before now. For a brief moment, he forgot why he was here and the horror of losing Stek, Kirru, and Enna.

And then it all returned to him at once.

"We have to get back to Qiriq," he said to the Shai.

"Qiriq is likely bathing in blood right now, En'Shai," the Shai answered as he slowed the horse to a canter. "Those were the Beshar nomads of the plain attacking the Raq army. The Sons of the Talon have likely begun their planned assault on the Masters. There is nothing for us back in Qiriq."

"My sister and brother are there," was Vinan's laconic response.

"Damn you, En'Shai," the Shai grunted.

The Shai steered the horse hard to the left and Vinan had to squeeze the animal tighter with his legs to stay mounted. Vinan feared for Kirru now that Seren-Raq had left his home and war had begun. He only hoped he could arrive in time to take her far away from here.

As the Shai took the horse around a hill, two other horses with riders atop them emerged from seemingly out of nowhere. The Shai's horse reared and Vinan could not hold. He fell to the ground on his back and lay there dazed for a moment before getting back to his feet.

"Vinan!" called a familiar voice that Vinan had not heard in a while.

Stek jumped off the back of Crissa's horse and ran to his brother. Vinan had barely enough time to comprehend his brother's presence before he found himself gripped in Stek's ecstatic embrace. Vinan returned it and held his brother tight to convince himself he was not imagining this. Stek was safe and here with him. After all that had just happened, Vinan found himself now on the verge of both laughing and weeping.

"You actually came," Stek said quietly. "You followed us here."

"I told you I would do anything to protect Kirru," Vinan answered as calmly as he could. "That goes for you too."

As this occurred, the riders steadied the nerves of their horses and took in the circumstances. There were three horses all told.

235

The old Raq warrior was the first on a black stallion, with his daughter Crissa on a red and white mare behind him. The Shai sat atop his brown horse, stolen from the desert warrior, and stared at them with bemusement.

"So, old man," he said, "I see you found the other mountain boy."

"And you found the one we lost," the old man replied. "Did you find what you sought?"

"I did, and I slew him like the dog he was."

The old man sighed and bowed his head in solemn silence.

"What?" the Shai mocked. "Mourning the death of your fellow Raq?"

"Where were you going with him?" the old Raq warrior asked while ignoring the taunt.

"Back to Qiriq to get the sister," the Shai said.

"She is not in Qiriq," said Crissa. "We are following her."

"Kirru?" Vinan asked. "You saw her?"

"I saw her ride through the gate with many women," Stek answered, "before the killing started."

"The priestesses left the city in a hurry just before the bloodshed began," the old man interjected. "The palace guards are taking them somewhere. Someplace Seren-Raq has already arranged."

"He knew this would happen," the Shai said with dark realization. "He knew and let it all happen."

"Or he even ensured it would happen," answered the old man. "But we need to know where the priestesses are headed. There is nothing in this grassland."

"Seren-Raq left before the battle began," said the Shai. "I know not where he went."

Vinan remembered the last exchange between the warlord and the priest before the former had fallen to the Shai's sword.

"The Shrine of the Star-Ancients..."

"What did you say?" asked the old man.

"The Shrine of the Star Ancients," Vinan repeated. "They took Enna there."

"Enna?" the Shai asked.

"The girl!" Vinan exclaimed in exasperation. "The girl of the wilds! Uthal-Raq and Seren-Raq ordered them to take her there. That is where the priestesses must be going."

Vinan did not know why he believed that, but he did. Perhaps it was because it was the only answer he could guess.

But now it was the old man who had been taken by a sullen darkness. For the first time that Vinan had noticed, he was visibly unsettled and disturbed.

"Farken-Raq ordered that place sealed many years ago," he said. "Why is it open again?"

"You know the place?" Vinan asked with hope.

"I do," he said. "So did Farken-Raq, and so do his brothers apparently."

"Then we have to go there," said Vinan as he returned to the Shai's horse to mount it.

After Stek followed Vinan's example and returned to the saddle of Crissa's horse, the old man sighed and looked into the distance. It was as if he knew of a dark secret concealed many long years ago and now had to face it again. His face bore the weathered look of a man who had once looked upon and buried a hideous thing that others were now bringing back into the light.

"Follow me," he said to the other riders. "I will lead us to the place best left forgotten."

***

It had been many years ago when Farken-Raq had sealed the ancient ruin. The old captain had been there when it happened. He thought a moment and considered that he was likely the only one still alive who had been there that day. When his new lord, Seren-Raq, ordered it reopened the captain had made his opinion

237

known. He agreed with Farken-Raq that some things were left buried forever from the eyes and hands of men.

But Farken-Raq was dead and had disappeared into oblivion since the first war in Rhanijad. His own end was lost to history and would never be known by anyone. Seren-Raq was now the lord the captain had sworn to serve.

The captain may not have afforded the young priest the same reverence that he had shown to the elder brother who had ground many kingdoms and empires under his heel and reduced them all to dust, yet he felt a strange compulsion to protect this young man who had rejected the ways of his brothers. Even the brilliant Farken-Raq's accomplishments amounted to the effectiveness with which he could bring about annihilation and death. In Seren-Raq, the captain saw a man pained by the wanton destruction all around him, a man driven by the desire to bring forth light and life into a darkened world.

Thus, when the tomb of the lost civilization was reopened and the priest looked upon it with child-like wonder, the captain's fear of the place had been challenged. Over the years, the priest continued to visit the shrine and the captain watched. He watched as Seren-Raq used his position as High Priest to abate the suffering of slaves and the poor in Qiriq. He watched as the Temple of Plenty was restored to something worthy of its name, transforming into a refuge for those seeking a temporary haven from the suffering that came with living in Qiriq. He watched as Seren-Raq began to understand the long-lost knowledge of the ancients and command powers beyond human comprehension.

No, this was not a man driven by the desire for war and the power he could win from it. This was a man who looked for something loftier than simple pleasure and gratification. Though surrounded by the many priestesses in the palace who waited on him, Seren-Raq provided for them far more than he asked of them in return. This youngest son of the Great Raq had no desire for conquest, glory, or the destruction of civilizations. He was a restorer, a caretaker, a protector, and a philosopher. As such, the captain was willing to follow him, serve him, and protect him in everything he did, just as he had with Farken-Raq.

And now he rode alongside the priest to the Shrine of the Star Ancients. Together they fled the chaos that followed Uthal-Raq's slaying and rode directly to the refuge of Seren's labors. Seren-Raq told the captain that now was the time for the secrets to be revealed. Now it could be hidden no more, for it had been found by those who should never touch it. The power of the Star Ancients was to be used now, lest it fall into the hands of worse men than he.

When they approached the outer edge of the shrine the captain was surprised to see the priestesses outside the entrance. All of them had dismounted from the horses they had used to arrive and were awaiting orders of any kind. They all had that look of confusion over what to do next that was ever upon people who had never lived free. It was also apparent that they could not enter the shrine themselves, or would not. Looks of relief washed over their faces when they saw their priest and lord arrive.

"My lord!" said the High Priestess, a buxom blonde woman who usually ran the administration of the Temple of Plenty. "It has begun just as you foretold."

"And all of you escaped?" the priest asked.

"Barely," she answered. "The gods have delivered us here, thankfully."

No, thought the captain, *it was my men who did that.*

He was thankful that he had moved his wife and sons from the city a month ago. With some foresight and luck, they would be safe from all that Seren-Raq predicted would happen when Uthal-Raq returned.

"You have not taken refuge within?" Seren-Raq asked.

"We can't," said a lieutenant of the palace guard. "Uthal's bodyguards are within and say that their lord will have the head of any who enter."

"I see," said the priest. "Take these women to Gelek for now. I will deal with the men here myself."

"My lord?" asked the bewildered lieutenant.

"See it done. And leave her with me."

He pointed to a little girl among the priestesses, the same little sister of the wild boy who had challenged Uthal-Raq. She was brought forward and Seren-Raq put his hand gently upon her head.

"You must come with me into this place," he said.

"Where is Vinan?" she asked.

"You will know soon enough," the priest lied. "For now, there is something which I will need you to help me with."

"What is it?" she inquired innocently.

"You will know soon," he assured her. "Follow me."

He waved his hand to the rest. The priestesses and the other guards mounted again and departed towards Gelek. Only the captain and the girl were left with Seren-Raq, who strode through the cavern's entrance and into the shrine beneath.

The caves they entered were a collection of rocks like any other cavern. There was no indication on the walls of the centuries-old mysteries that lay preserved beneath. Seren-Raq led with no need for a candle, lamp, or other light. The hint of an unearthly blue-green shone before them and illuminated the path ahead. It shone brighter as they approached until they turned into a room covered in the light. The true entrance to the Shrine of the Star Ancients.

It was here, surrounded by the shining words of the long-dead and nigh-mythical race, where the men of Uthal-Raq stood guard. All four were dressed in the same deep red armor. The sea-like blue of the room contrasted greatly with the blood hue of their battle-wear. Dressed as they were, with their faces concealed by their helms, they stood aright like haunting phantoms in a place they did not belong or understand. As Seren-Raq entered, they looked to him and moved their hands toward their swords.

240

"Where is our lord?" their leader demanded.

"Uthal-Raq is dead," the priest answered with a dismissive wave. "You can choose to serve me or leave if you wish."

The four drew their swords. Though Seren-Raq had not admitted to killing his brother, fratricide was so common among the Raqs now that the soldiers could not imagine any other explanation. The captain drew his own sword instinctively, though he knew even then that it was a futile action.

"*Deresamai, at el Mortis!*" Seren-Raq incanted.

The inside of the chamber mutated at his command and metallic tendrils emerged from the floor. Seren-Raq made deliberate motions with his hand, and the appendages wrapped around the shocked and screaming guards. Their panicked cries ceased with the priest closing his hand into a fist, the sound of crushing bones, and a shrill, terrified scream from Kirru.

The captain knew that they were still not alone. He had fought in too many battles not to know when there was a crouching enemy hiding in the shadows waiting for the chance to strike. Apparently, whether by the same instinct or through some power he had learned from the magic of the Star Ancients, Seren-Raq was also aware of this.

"Come now, mercenary," Seren-Raq said as a hundred tendrils hung idly in the air at his command, "we have no reason to fight. You have something I require and I have the power to generously reward you."

The golden-haired mercenary emerged from a corner of the chamber, still holding tight the strange girl with white eyes. His sword was drawn before him in defense.

"Enna!"

Kirru cried. She tried to run to her friend but the captain grabbed her shoulder and kept her in place with his hand that had slain uncounted men. He ignored her cries to let her star-eyed friend go, leaned down to her ear, and spoke quietly.

"Do you want your friend to die? Be quiet."

This hushed the panicking of the now terror-stricken Kirru, who sobbed in the captain's grip.

"They did not tell me," said the mercenary, "that this place was full of ancient sorcery."

"They did not know," Seren-Raq answered. "I am the only one who can use the power of this shrine, except for her..."

He pointed down at the strange girl. The captain saw that fear, horror, and defiance were all contained in her face. She looked upon Seren-Raq with disbelief, horror, and hatred.

"I need her to unlock the secrets that have been hidden from me," the priest continued. "So, I ask you, do you desire a reward in exchange for her? Do you wish to see more?"

"Are you out of tricks or is there truly more?" the mercenary asked.

"More than you can imagine, former Shai of Kodumaa." Seren-Raq answered with a smile. "*Erethas!*"

The wall behind the blonde man revealed a long straight crack from the floor to the ceiling and began to pull itself apart. As the two halves of the wall separated, a large inner room full of light was revealed. All stood in awe at this revelation. Even the hardened fighter froze in place, his blade pressed tight to the mountain girl's throat.

Seren-Raq strode past the mercenary and into the chamber.

"Bring her with us," he said to the mercenary. "Come, Kirru."

The captain let her go and waited at the entrance, guarding it once again. The inner chamber was Seren-Raq's domain. Within there, the priest faced no danger from the mercenary. The only duty left to the captain now was to guard the entrance as he always did.

CHAPTER 24

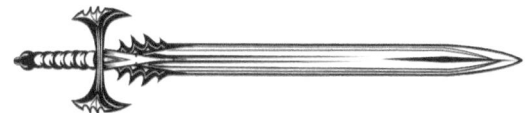

The Last Duel of the Shaii'

The old man led the others to a formation of boulders that stood out in the great rolling grass plain. As they approached, the largest of the stones loomed above their head and cast a shadow over them. The coolness of the shade would have been welcome but to Vinan the pitiless faces of the giant rocks only heralded dread within him.

They rode into the maze of stone behind the old man and stopped before a small arched opening in the side of the titanic center rock, large enough for only one man to pass at a time.

"This is the entrance," the old man said.

The Shai dismounted, leaving Vinan alone atop the horse, and crouched to the ground.

"A great many horses have just been in this place," he said. "They have already departed the way they came."

"Then we must follow them," Vinan said.

"No, En'Shai," the warrior of Kodumaa answered as he looked down and strode towards the opening of the cavern. "There are footprints of a small child that lead to the cave. Either your sister or the wild girl is down there."

The Shai drew his sword. "And we will follow them."

The old man, still silent, dismounted. He walked past the Shai and stood before the gaping entrance.

"Follow me from this point on," he said. "Only I have been to this place and only I know what lies beneath."

Vinan, Crissa, and Stek dismounted. Vinan drew his sword while Stek produced his newfound spear.

"You have lost your spear," Stek said to Vinan incredulously.

"I have learned to use this," Vinan answered, holding aloft his sword, "and I will take back Kirru with it."

The brothers' eyes met and for the first time, they fully realized that each of them had changed forever. Vinan saw the bruises Stek bore in his body, the wrath kindled by the betrayal of Kror and the captivity of the slavers, and the will to destroy all who stood in his path. Stek meanwhile beheld his brother as a warrior shorn of the traditions of his people, dressed as the outlanders, and bearing their strange weapon. The same accursed weapon Kror had used to destroy their lost home. He noticed Vinan's own marks left from beatings suffered during his journey, even one so fresh that the blood stains beneath Vinan's mouth were yet to be wiped away. Stek understood now that his brother had never once given up on finding him or Kirru no matter how many defeats he suffered or how much pain he underwent. It didn't matter how many times Vinan was knocked to the ground, for he would rise to his feet once more to fight again.

"Follow me," said the old Raq. "There is no opening to the shrine except through this passage. Anyone who entered is still here."

And the other four followed him into darkness, into the strange blue light.

***

"*Quera utra persalas!*" Seren-Raq commanded.

244

But it was of no use. The girl with eyes bright as stars refused to answer or pretended not to understand what it was he said. He began to wonder if she truly did not know the language of her people that was written on these walls. No matter how many times and in how many different forms he demanded in the tongue of her ancestors that she speak, she did not. She simply stared with longing sorrow at the shining blue writing on the smooth metallic walls.

"Answer me!" he shouted to her.

"She doesn't understand you!" Kirru pleaded, her arms wrapped around her friend. "She doesn't know!"

The mercenary, erstwhile, stood off to the side and laughed.

"So, you cannot unlock the power here after all, priest," he mocked. "The power of myths and legends eludes you."

Seren-Raq made a single twitch of his finger and the walls shifted. The blue runes that were scattered upon the metal surface like the constellations of the night sky glowed with blinding light for a moment.

"I tell you now, swordsman of Kodumaa," he said, "I have unlocked far more power in this shrine than most men believe even exists. If this girl were to reveal that which I have yet to unlock then anything is possible."

"Anything is possible," the one-time Shai repeated. "Anything and nothing."

Seren-Raq found this galling. He had not spent years reading and deducing the language and power of the Star Ancients only to be deprived of it when he needed it most. It was only a matter of time before he would be at the mercy of his remaining brothers. He needed to unlock the full power of this shrine now if he were to realize his dream, even if he was disgusted by the thought of what he must do.

He raised his hand and looked at Kirru. Two tendrils emerged from the floor behind her and wrapped around her arms, pulling her away from the girl of the Star Ancients. The terrified little girl of the mountains screamed and her friend reached out, seemingly to stop it, but was restrained when Seren-Raq made a motion with his left hand to command another tendril to wrap around her.

"Now, girl of the Star Ancients," he commanded, "reveal to me the secrets of your people! *Quera utra persalas!*"

***

The antechamber shone full of dancing blue lights. In the center stood the captain of Seren-Raq's guard and around him were four sprawled corpses dressed in the same red armor that the Shai wore. He drew his curved sword and blocked the path of the old man and the Shai.

"Stop where you are and turn back!" he commanded. "None shall pass beyond this point."

The Shai raised his sword for battle, ready to rush the captain and contest the ground. However, the old man raised his hand.

"How long has it been, Bortei?" he asked. "How long since we last rode together across the plains with the wind at our back? How long since we ate horse meat together as we slept under the night sky?"

The captain was visibly unsettled by this and stepped back in shock as if the ghost of a long-dead man were speaking to him.

"There are times I miss those days, Bortei," the old man continued. "Your sword looks as if it has become well-shined without blood to stain it. Is little Seren truly as peaceful a man as they say?"

"It is you," the captain rasped.

"Are your wife and sons well?" the old man asked.

"Strong and well, my Raq," Bortei answered.

"Please, old friend," the old man answered, "I am Raq of nothing now. Are you going to block my path?"

"Go your way," Bortei said. "I only wish I could have kept this place closed as you wished."

"Regret nothing," said the old man. "You served both me and my brother well. Are your wife and sons still in Qiriq?"

"No," Bortei answered, "I ordered them to leave the city a while ago."

"Go to them," the old man pleaded. "Take them far from here. Qiriq burns and the carrion swoop in to lord over the ashes. Leave before they come."

There was a moment of tense silence before the Shai lowered his sword and stepped aside to let the Raq captain pass. The captain walked between the old man and the warrior of Kodumaa to exit the cavern.

"Farewell, Farken," he said as he passed. "May the end of your days be spent in peace."

And he was gone.

Before anyone could go further into the shrine, the Shai pointed the end of his sword at the face of the old man. Vinan, Stek, and Crissa stood still, uncertain of what to do.

"I knew this moment would come," the old Raq said with resignation. "If you are going to end my life, Shai of Kodumaa, then do it."

The Shai stared at him, his eyes filled with wrath and bewilderment.

"Why are you alive?" he demanded.

"Because I lost all will to rule," the old man answered. "I lost it when I saw my little brothers kill one another while our father still lived. I rejected my father's place when I chose to take my child and go into hiding."

"They said you died in Rhanijad," the Shai said, as if doubting the old man's tale for a moment.

"But who killed me?" the old man asked with a smile. "How did I die?"

The warrior of Kodumaa looked back to him, eyes wide with realization.

"Now you understand," the old Raq continued. "Each of my

247

brothers needed to become the slayer of Farken-Raq to claim the title of greatest warlord, and so they all claimed to be. By my disappearance I robbed them all."

"Then you know full well why I have sworn to kill you," the Shai said.

"How could I not?" replied the old Raq. "I commanded the armies that conquered Kodumaa, I ordered that the Shaii' be eliminated, and I—knowing Uthal and what he was—let him have his way with your people. How could you not wish vengeance upon me?"

The Shai seemed taken aback by his old enemy's acceptance of the situation.

"You do not fear death by my hand here?" he asked.

"Why would I? Kodumaa is far from the only land that was brought to ruin through me. My death is long overdue. Had you and I never crossed paths it would take me in ten years or five. My days are nearly at an end and I only go on for the sake of my daughter."

"You think that mentioning the girl will make me pity you, slayer of children?" the Shai demanded angrily.

"No," answered Farken. "But I ask that, if you are to kill me, that you care for Crissa and protect her."

The Shai slowly lowered his sword in disbelief, yet the old man's face betrayed no emotion. Vinan felt he could breathe easy again and Stek lowered his spear.

"So, this is the legendary Farken-Raq," the Shai mused. "This is the sword, the right hand, and eldest son of the Great Raq. The man who trampled twenty kingdoms beneath his boot."

"And what did you expect to find?" Farken-Raq asked. "A monster who breathed fire, with reptilian eyes glowing, with bloodlust and long claws upon his hands? No, Shai of Kodumaa, I was only ever a man. A man who knew what I did. It is I, not Uthal-Raq, who deserves the punishment for what was done to Kodumaa and the other kingdoms. One does not blame the savage

248

dog who does what his master commands."

The Shai gave the old Raq a long testing stare.

"Keep what is left of your life, old man," he said. "The Farken-Raq I sought is long dead, if ever in truth he lived. We have two little girls to rescue."

They walked through the antechamber and into the sanctuary of the Shrine of the Star Ancients. When they entered they saw Seren-Raq on a raised platform atop a great many steps. All told, he stood about the height of two war-beasts above Vinan and his companions. Standing to his side was the golden-haired mercenary, the companion of Ancar the slaver, who watched Seren-Raq in fascination. A metal wire was wrapped around Enna's body, leaving her constrained and unable to move. Kirru, meanwhile, was lifted by her arms from the ground and suspended by the same metallic appendages.

"Seren-Raq!" Vinan shouted in anger as he entered. "Let them go! Now!"

Kirru cried as she watched her brothers enter. "Vinan! Stek!"

Seren-Raq turned around in surprise as Vinan, Stek, the Shai of Kodumaa and Farken-Raq approached.

"Vinan," he said. "I see you are still alive..."

"I told you that nothing would stand between me and those I sought to save," Vinan answered. "Now give me back Kirru and Enna!"

Seren-Raq moved his hand and Kirru was gently lowered to the ground. The tendrils did not detach from her and she remained in their grasp.

"Kirru I will give to you freely," Seren-Raq said. "She was always yours, and never mine to keep. However, this girl is needed for a greater purpose."

He pointed to Enna.

"Help me, Vinan," said Seren-Raq. "Help me convince her to unlock the secrets of her people and I will release her to you unharmed."

"She is a child! How can she be of any use to you?!" Vinan yelled. "My people saw her as a demon, the slavers saw her as an item to be sold, and you think of her as a key to knowledge. Why can't anyone see that she is just a girl like any other?"

"You do not understand, Vinan..."

"I understand perfectly," Vinan replied, pointing his sword at the priest. "Give me the girl or I will take her back!"

Wire-like metal tendrils began to rise up around Vinan. He brought up his sword to defend himself as they circled around him.

"You do not comprehend the power I wield here, Vinan, son of Bheif," Seren-Raq said. "With one swipe of my hand I could destroy you here and now."

"Seren!" Farken-Raq shouted. "Stop this!"

The tentacles of ancient power stopped for a moment as Seren-Raq looked incredulously at the long-dead brother he seemed to vaguely recognize.

But the two had no time to exchange words of greeting.

"Fallen Shai!" the Shai of Kodumaa yelled to the mercenary. "You dishonor your people! You dishonor yourself!"

All the rest in the sanctuary were silent and time stood still for them. The Shai walked towards the steps with his sword drawn, heedless of the powers Seren-Raq wielded.

"Kodumaa is dead," the golden-haired mercenary answered. "You follow the failed ideals of dead men, hypocrites corrupted by the very lust for power they preached against. Liars who enforced laws on their followers while doing the very things the laws opposed."

"As long as I live," the Shai replied, "the spirit of Kodumaa lives within me. The beauty and good that it stood for means far more than the men who failed to uphold it."

"Then you are stupider than I believed possible," scoffed the mercenary. "I now wish to fight you to end Kodumaa once and for all."

"Then let it be done," the Shai declared. "Seren-Raq, are you a man who keeps his word?"

"I am," answered the priest.

"Then I demand a challenge," said the Shai, "a battle to decide the fate of the white-eyed girl of the wilds. She is yours if I fall, but if I win, you will return her to us."

"So, it is agreed," said Seren-Raq. "So let it be done."

The Shai waited for the golden-haired mercenary to descend the steps. When they were both at the base they began to circle each other like wolves awaiting the right moment to strike. They raised and lowered their swords, shifted their feet, and feinted at each other though over ten feet separated each of them from the other's reach. No weapon had made contact, yet this last battle of the Shaii' had begun. Vinan had never seen swordplay like this.

Almost simultaneously, each of the men charged toward their opponent. Their swords crossed and counter crossed as they tried to strike each other down. They dodged around their enemy's blade with inhuman speed, seeming to dance with moves of unimaginable complexity. The momentum of battle shifted back and forth so rapidly that Vinan could barely keep track of it. First the Shai, then the mercenary, then the Shai again for a moment, then the mercenary, then the Shai once he found himself behind his enemy, then the mercenary when the Shai found himself on his back foot, and so on as the contest continued.

But soon all the intricate footwork of the duel disappeared. The two men angrily tried to bring down their swords on each other, turning the fight into a savage beating of steel on steel as steel tried to cleave flesh.

Then the blade of the mercenary found its mark in an unprotected spot in the side of the Shai's armor. The wounded man fell to his knees facing his companions, dazed and surprised as he realized that all was over. Vinan's gut sank as if suddenly filled with lead. He wished to scream in anger and shock but found not the voice with which to even whimper. He could only stand motionless with his mouth agape.

251

"En'Shai," the Shai gasped, blood dripping from his mouth.

He threw his sword down and it landed halfway between himself and the boy.

"Take the sword. You are more worthy of it than I," the warrior said with his final breath. His rival made a sweeping swing of his blade to detach the head from the body, which slumped lifeless to the ground in a heap of red armor and blood.

Thus did the last true Shai of Kodumaa meet his end with the memory and ideals of his homeland, for they died with him and would never rise again.

CHAPTER 25

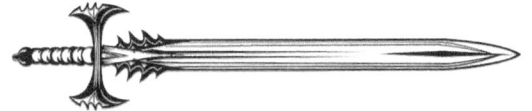

The Warrior Ascends

No one noticed Crissa slip away before Vinan and his companions entered the sanctuary of the Star Ancients. Only Crissa noticed a side passage to the left of the entrance. She knew she would be of little use in the battle ahead for she carried no sword. Even if she had one, she did not know how to wield it and had far less strength than Vinan. No, she would have to try to help another way. She hoped the unnoticed opening would give her that opportunity.

She moved up a winding tunnel narrow enough for only one to pass through at a time. Her feet trod softly upon the rock and made little sound as she ascended up the winding subterranean path. An end to the claustrophobic passage appeared to reveal brilliant blue light contrasted with shining metallic silver. Familiar voices shouted at one another and echoed from the chamber ahead.

"I understand perfectly!" Vinan cried. "Give me the girl back or I will take her back!"

"You cannot comprehend the power I wield here, Vinan, son of Bheif," Seren-Raq said. "With one swipe of my hand I could destroy you here and now."

"Seren!" Crissa's father shouted. "Stop this!"

"Fallen Shai!" said the Shai of Kodumaa. "You dishonor your people! You dishonor yourself!"

Crissa emerged from the tunnel beneath the titanic dome illuminated with illegible blue runes of an ancient and lost language. She realized that she was looking down upon the others present from an elevated position. Directly below her, at about a ten-foot jump, stood Seren-Raq surrounded by metal tentacles that had risen from the floor. Two little girls were held in their grasp, the first was the girl with eyes of stars that they had left with the hunter and the second was a young chestnut-haired girl. With one look Crissa remembered the sister of Vinan and Stek from the palace. She also realized that, as the metal vines began to rise around Vinan, she could save both the girls now in the grasp of the priest.

For, even with all the power Seren-Raq seemed to hold in this chamber, he had not yet noticed her presence above him.

She crouched to the ground to avoid being seen and crawled slowly towards the edge of the precipice. She peered over the edge and watched as the Shai of Kodumaa engaged in battle with a golden-haired mercenary. They fought so similarly that she deduced that the other man was a great warrior as well. The fierce and flawless battle dance of the two men ended abruptly when the golden-haired man struck down the Shai, who threw his sword to Vinan's feet in his last moments.

Seren-Raq held the power in the room. He held the two girls. His swordsman had triumphed. Two boys and an old man stood in opposition to a swordsman of incredible skill and a priest who wielded ancient powers beyond imagination.

But not one of them knew of Crissa's presence here and that she was in position to jump down and cut the girls free. She readied her daggers and silently waited for her moment to strike as those below dealt with the aftermath of the final duel of the Shaii'.

***

Vinan was too stunned to move, too numb to shout as the mighty Shai who had accompanied him through the wilds met an ignominious end. In one moment, the great warrior, and his friend, had been reduced to nothing.

Farken-Raq walked slowly to the corpse. The victorious swordsman raised his sword in threat but the old man did not heed him. He knelt by the heap of red armor.

"So passes the Shai of Kodumaa," the old Raq said thoughtfully. "May he rest in peace with his ancestors."

His hand reached down to the corpse's waist.

"What are you doing?" the golden-haired swordsman demanded.

"The dead will not need his scabbard anymore," Farken-Raq answered. "The sword is Vinan's now and he will need the belt and sheath."

"The boy can have the trinket," scoffed the swordsman. "No one has any need for Kodumaa's memories."

Farken-Raq rose to his feet and held the scabbard in his hand. He looked to his brother atop the platform.

"Seren," he said. "I do not know you well. I have only heard what men say of you, and they say you are a thoughtful and compassionate man who looks to the future. I ask you, then, please shut this place up and forget all memories of it."

"You are right," Seren-Raq answered with a smile. "You do not know me. You are a relic of our father's blood-drenched empire. You were his conqueror, his dog, and his prized eldest son who killed whoever he told you to kill. You were the reason every brother between you and I killed one another."

He pointed his finger accusingly at his aged brother.

"After you began your brilliant conquests," the priest continued, "how many wars did our brothers wage? How many nations did each one smash as they sought to match you and outdo the others? How many of them have ended their lives untimely while leaving a mountain of corpses in their wake?"

"Seren," Farken-Raq sighed, "listen to me..."

"No!" Seren-Raq shouted. "I have waited for my moment when I could use the power hidden in this sanctuary to bring men like you to heel. With this I will turn back the armies of warlords and empires to bring mankind into a new era of progress and peace."

"Seren," Farken-Raq pleaded, "there is nothing for you here. There is nothing the Star Ancients left behind worth using. There is nothing in this chamber that you can use to better mankind."

"You know nothing, Farken," Seren scoffed. "You did not study them nor did you seek to grasp their knowledge. You have not read the writing on these walls. You only saw that which your limited warrior's mind could not grasp and shut it away in your ignorance. The Star Ancients were a civilization of incredible achievements with power that men of today can only imagine. Indeed, we know not whether they were even from this world or whether they came from beyond the stars. Our ancestors once worshipped them as gods."

"And yet," Farken answered, "what is left of them but their ruins? Like all of us, they disappeared and their achievements passed into nothingness."

"Enough of this!" Seren-Raq exclaimed. "I will not argue with a man whose only accomplishment was the slaughter and destruction he left behind."

He looked past Farken-Raq to the boys from the wild.

"Vinan, son of Bheif," he said, "I have no wish to keep Kirru from you and your brother any longer. Help me convince this girl to give me what I want and I will return Kirru to you."

Vinan knew he had to answer. He was responsible for himself and his siblings now. The Shai was no longer here to aid him and would never be by his side again. He was the warrior now.

"And the girl?" he asked. "What of her wishes? What if she does not wish to tell you anything?"

The tendrils around Enna's arms tightened, causing her to cry in pain.

"No!" Kirru screamed, tears in her eyes. "Stop it!"

Vinan advanced but the golden-haired mercenary raised his sword. The two stood facing each other, each understanding that another step from Vinan would mean another battle. Anger boiled inside Vinan's gut as he watched Seren-Raq hold the two girls tighter in captivity. The smile on the priest's face, one that revealed confidence in his power here, chilled Vinan to the bone. There would be no peaceful way of dealing with this man. Despite Seren-Raq's conceits, Vinan now held him in no higher regard than he had held Uthal-Raq or Ancar.

"What will it be, Vinan, son of Bheif?" Seren-Raq asked. "Do you wish your sister to be with you again or not?"

Vinan gripped the hilt of his sword tight, ready to fight the battle he knew he would have to fight.

"I understand," he said, his eyes staring at the priest with a piercing wrathful glare. "I finally understand why those in this land suffer. It is because men like Kror, Uthal-Raq, the slavers, and you all believe that something makes it right for you to hurt the helpless and the innocent. There is always some reason why you believe you have the right to trample upon those who you think are lesser than you.

"I will never do it!" he shouted in defiance. "I will never become like you or them! If I fight it will be to help those who are weak like her from men like you."

Tendrils rose slowly around Vinan and he slashed one in two.

"Now give me both of them back!" he demanded.

A cloaked figure jumped down from a rock above Seren-Raq and landed close to him. The figure brandished a dagger, cut Kirru free, and grabbed her.

"Now, Vinan!" Crissa shouted. "I have her!"

Stek did not wait for Vinan and, spear aloft, charged the golden-haired mercenary.

"You!" exclaimed the wild boy. "Die!"

Vinan rushed aside Stek to attack the mercenary and keep him away from the fleeing Crissa and Kirru. The fighter evaded Vinan's and Stek's assault with little effort. Stek's spear jabs struck where he aimed but met only air. Vinan's sword blows were effortlessly swept aside by the mercenary's blade.

Despite this, Vinan felt confident enough in the distraction of his adversary that he looked to Crissa and saw her fleeing metal tendrils that rose from the floor. Seren-Raq had recovered from his moment of surprise and directed the room against the girl, who slashed at the metal appendages with her dagger while holding Kirru close.

The mercenary swung at Stek so Vinan responded by swinging at him. The more seasoned fighter pulled back his attack on Stek and redirected his onslaught towards Vinan. Vinan found himself on his back foot, warding off blow after oppressive blow from the former Shai until their swords met mid-air and locked in place. The fighter smiled and made a twisting motion with his arm that forced Vinan's whole body into a spin. The sword went flying from the boy's hand and across the room. The suddenly disarmed Vinan found himself evading the blade of Kodumaa with nothing to strike back with. Stek's furious attempt at an assault, which forced the man to divide his attention, was likely the only thing that kept Vinan alive.

Crissa and Kirru were now surrounded by the snake-like appendages that Seren-Raq commanded, and he motioned them to close in on them. Crissa fought back furiously with her daggers and covered Kirru to protect her but could not outrun the powers that the priest held in the sanctuary.

The once-Shai continued his pursuit of Vinan, knowing that the boy could only dodge his attacks for so long.

"And this is where your journey ends, boy," he said with complete calm.

Stek received a boot in his gut mid-charge and fell back momentarily stunned in pain. The fighter, now with the distraction out of his way, prepared to unleash all on Vinan. He pulled his arm back to prepare it for the slaughter and grinned at the unarmed holocaust before him.

"Farewell, mountain boy."

At that moment, his eyes suddenly shone with a bright blue. His sword dropped from his hand and clanged on the ground. His hands grabbed the side of his head as he bellowed out a cry of unrestrained pain and terror.

"MY EYES!" he screamed. "WHAT IS THIS?! STOP THE LIGHT! STOP IT!!!!!"

Vinan noticed now that the runes in the sanctuary shone brighter than ever before in the same shade that afflicted the once-Shai's eyes. The room lit up in a brilliant constellation of dancing ethereal blue, and it all settled on a focal point upon the raised platform across from Seren-Raq.

Enna, the wild girl from the forests, the girl with eyes bright as the stars of the night, stood bathed in the same blue light. It glowed about her, emanating from her with a powerful aura. Her hair rose up at its roots and moved as if by its own will. Surrounded by the ancient power she had unlocked and free of Seren-Raq's hold, she moved her arms deliberately as if preparing something far more grandiose than the others present could conceive.

Seren-Raq, once again, snapped himself out of his stunned state.

"So, you do know the power," he sneered.

He looked to the girl he had neglected and prepared more tendrils against her. The girl finished her movements with an ungracious and sudden swipe that sent a piece of the ceiling hurling down toward the priest. Seren-Raq jumped to the side and commanded some tentacles to block the path of the projectile. The piece of the ceiling crashed into the floor and several more chunks of the ceiling, on which runes of the ancients were written, broke off from their place. The girl motioned with her arm and the rune-stones hovered in the air at her whim. Seren-Raq answered with a command of his own that caused more vine-like appendages to rise from the ground around him.

"Vinan! Here!" shouted Farken-Raq as he tossed Vinan the sword of the fallen Shai.

Vinan caught the sheathed sword mid-air and drew it from its scabbard. He ignored the blinded once-Shai and rushed to Crissa and Kirru, hacking and slashing at the tendrils that surrounded them. He and the recovered Stek cut through enough of the metallic vines to create an opening and reach the girls. Crissa jumped through their opening, still holding Kirru tight. The tentacles made a halfhearted effort to stop them, as their master's attention was now absorbed in his battle with Enna.

Seren-Raq and Enna both moved their hands in furious exertion. Chunks of ancient rune-stone and metal tendrils smashed into one another. Blue light shone bright throughout the chamber and especially around the girl of the Star Ancients. The fight was evenly matched, or so it seemed to Vinan. Neither of the two knew the full power of the ancients, yet each possessed pieces that the other lacked. Standing across from each other atop the raised platform, they continued their struggle with Seren-Raq only occasionally pausing to command the tendrils throughout the room to impede Vinan, Stek, and the escaping girls.

Vinan and Stek ran aside Crissa as she bolted for the sanctuary's exit. Stek stabbed his spear tip furiously at the appendages as Vinan made wide swipes to sever them in two. Crissa and Kirru jumped through the sanctuary door and were now safe in the antechamber beyond the reach of Seren-Raq's power.

"Seren!" Farken-Raq shouted through the tumult. "Enough of this! Leave and forget this place! Live your life in peace!"

"Do not speak to me of peace, warlord!" Seren-Raq replied. "I will use the power locked away here to rebuild the world once I destroy the rest of our brothers! Any who seek to stop me will meet their end before this power!"

He strained himself, his eyes bulging in maniacal strain, and tendrils rose from everywhere in the room.

"The time of holding back is over!" he shouted. "Now is the time for you to submit to the power or be destroyed by it!"

Surrounded by the metal tentacles and in their shadow, Vinan and Stek stood back to back with their weapons ready.

"So, this is how we die," Vinan mused. "In battle together."

"At least we saved Kirru," Stek replied.

But then, piercing through the din and the tension of the struggle, there spoke a clear voice familiar to Vinan.

"*Vinan! Go!*"

Vinan turned to look at Enna, who now floated several feet above the ground and was bathed in the blue light of her people's magic. Her face was resolute and calm but her eyes betrayed an immense sorrow. Vinan at that moment could never have comprehended just how heavy a decision the girl had made. The shock of hearing her speak so clearly to him for the first time at the moment of her most fateful act would haunt him to the end of his days.

"*Go!*"

CHAPTER 26

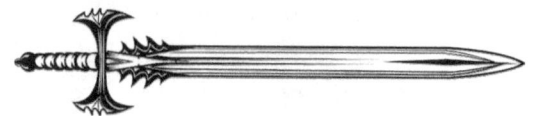

Farewell

Everlasting seemed the moment when the girl with eyes of stars ordered her friends to depart, and eternally it would be burned into Vinan's memory.

Her face was laden with sorrow, her body was strained by the power she wielded, and her eyes were heavy with the knowledge of what she was about to do. Tears streamed down her cheeks as she pointed to the door of the sanctuary through which all had entered. Never before had Vinan seen her like this. Never before had she spoken her intentions so clearly in words he could comprehend. From that day to the end of his days, the memory of that moment was always with him.

The blue of the room shone brighter than ever before. The lights of the ancient runes danced in the air and flickered like the stars in the heavens. The girl rose into the air surrounded by a brilliant sphere of that light and floated many feet above the ground.

And then she gave her final command.

"*Omna Termina. Omna Morta.*"

All the tendrils of the room rose up at the lifting of her hands and were ripped from the grasp of Seren-Raq. With a sweeping motion from her, the snake-like entities struck out in all directions against the very chamber that housed them. The once-elegant chamber began to break apart as pieces of the walls and ceilings separated from their place and smashed on the ground. Where some places had been hit, small fires began to ignite at the power of an unknown incendiary. The structure began to crumble as it tore itself apart around all those present.

Seren-Raq protested as his great hope was brought to nothing. He shouted that to destroy all this was a selfish act and that the power could be used to help mankind. He called upon the power he used before to stop the girl and her designs of destructive finality.

But his words fell upon deaf ears. The girl had made her decision and wielded all power within the room. The few tendrils the priest could control flung themselves up at the elevated girl and stopped just before her luminous being, unable to penetrate through the sphere of light.

Blood streamed from her mouth and down her chin. Tears poured from her eyes.

Vinan understood all in that moment. He ran to the exit, pausing only long enough to command Stek to run. He ignored Seren-Raq, who continued to flail in futility against the unstoppable resolve of the girl of the Star Ancients. In their rush to escape, the little tribe also ignored the blinded and weeping once-Shai, who now sat curled on the floor in a pathetic heap cursing both his existence and every god he did not believe in.

There was a cry into the chamber from Kirru to Enna. Vinan shouted to Crissa and Stek to take her and run. They did so, and Farken-Raq followed just behind. Vinan, assured that they would now be safe, was the last to depart. He left the sanctuary and prepared to run through the halls and out of the antechamber.

He turned one last time to Enna, the girl for whom he had suffered so much, the girl for whom he had done all this. He

263

looked to her and realized that he was leaving behind a true friend, a noble friend who had accompanied him all this time to save Kirru and Stek. He could not thank her, for any thanks he could give would never be enough. Water rose in his eyes as he looked upon her and said his final goodbye. She returned his gaze and tearfully returned his sorrowful farewell as best she could.

"*Vinan... Go.*"

And he did.

Vinan escaped through the caverns and came out into the midst of the rock formation. The sunlight beat down upon his head with oppressive heat as he continued to flee far from the collapsing ruin. He followed Farken-Raq, Crissa, Stek, and Kirru as they all mounted upon the three horses they had left outside.

Before they could ride away, the great stone collapsed into the earth. The implosion left no doubt and no room for hope that anything or anyone within the sanctuary of the ancients still lived or could be salvaged. All of it had been lost forever.

And thus did the girl with eyes of stars meet her end, at peace with the knowledge that the power of her people would never again be used and that her only friends in the world were safe at last.

CHAPTER 27

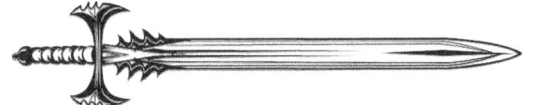

Family

T he yellow grass of the barren plain stretched for miles beneath the light blue sky. Five travelers rested as their horses drank from the clay-banked ponds left by the rare and precious rain. They sat and pondered what to do next, where to go, and who among them would stay together. All they knew was that blood flowed through the streets of Qiriq and they would all ride as far from that city as their mounts would take them.

Vinan stood in the prairie looking down at the ornate sword of the Shai. He contemplated the last gift the warrior of Kodumaa had left him and remembered the hard lessons the man had taught him in their days together. The Shai had indeed been right in that the world was cruel, uncaring, and full of those who sought to harm the innocent for the tiniest of gain. But Vinan remembered also the pain, the wrath, and the vengeance that the Shai held with him at all times. He knew that, like the Shai, he had lost his home and would probably never see it again. He also knew he would have to be vigilant lest he take on the worst vices of the Shai.

Vinan now realized that, despite all their time together, he had never known the man's name. Now he would never know it.

The man's tale had ended, his deeds lost forever as no one would write or sing them. But Vinan would never forget him or the girl from the wild—the child with eyes bright as the stars in the heavens.

Enna.

Vinan pushed the thought of her away. He was not ready to weep for her. Not yet. Night would come soon enough, and then the tears would freely flow. Now he had to refresh the horses and ride far away from here. He looked to Kirru and Stek as Crissa showed them how to water and care for the horses. She passed her water skin to the two children and gave them food from her pouch. Vinan remained content to watch his siblings from a small distance, confident that they were now safe.

"Where will you go now, Vinan, son of Bheif?" asked Farken-Raq.

Vinan stopped watching Kirru for a moment and looked to the old warlord who stood beside him also watching the children.

"I do not know," he answered. "The truth is that I do not know where the plain goes except back to the lands I came from."

"Do you plan to return to your old home?"

"Never."

"So, you only know where you will not go," the old man sighed.

"Yes." Vinan returned. "Now that Kirru and Stek are with me again, I will find a home where they can be safe."

"As long as you wish for them to be safe, you will have to fight. The battle to protect those you love will never end."

"And I will fight that battle," Vinan answered with resolve.

"I know you will. I will be there beside you as long as I can."

Vinan did not ask why and did not look upon the once-warlord with suspicion.

"I will take any help you can give," he said. "Thank you."

Farken-Raq nodded. "We should be going. The horses are ready."

"Where will we go?"

"That direction, I suppose." answered the old man as he pointed north. "It will be the best of our options. The land is not peaceful, but at least it is blessed with food and water."

"I will need to be ready to fight then?" Vinan asked.

"You might, young warrior, you might. That is true wherever we may go. There are lands beyond here where perhaps you can find a home for them, but it will take courage and a hand willing to defend all you possess."

"Then I am ready," Vinan assured him as he sheathed his sword.

The two of them returned to the steeds and all five mounted. It was then, in that ride to the north, that Vinan and Stek mastered the skill of horsemanship. Never again would they rely on another to carry them great distances upon the back of a horse. They were ready to defend Kirru as long as they could draw breath, this day and unto the end of their days.

EPILOGUE

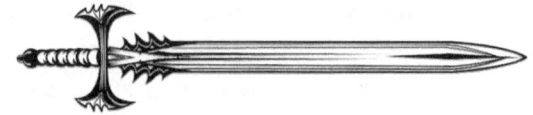

S o ends the tale of how Vinan left his home to save his brother and sister. So also begins the adventures of Vinan the Warrior, for many daring feats he would accomplish in his hope to find a new home for his family. Many battles would he be pulled into against his will, many villains would he slay by his hand, and many innocents would look up to see his sword raised in their defense. His deeds won him much renown through the known world until his people heard the tales and sought him, to convince him to return and challenge his brother.

But that day would not come for many years...

Vinan and his companions will return in
The Blood Sea.

ABOUT THE AUTHOR

David Standeven was born in the oil town of Midland, Texas. After graduating from the University of Texas at Dallas with a Bachelor's in Computer Science and a Minor in Business Administration, he began a career as a Software Engineer that has lasted 12 years and counting.

His first stabs at writing began in college, beginning as an insomniac hobby that refused to stop. In nearly fifteen years of writing, he has written works of Fantasy, Action and Adventure, Science Fiction, Speculative Fiction, Poetry, and Children's Stories. He credits this love of writing to his childhood love of reading that included JRR Tolkien, Alexandre Dumas, Feodor Dostoyevsky, Charles Dickens, Boris Pasternak, George Orwell, Aldous Huxley, and fellow Texan Robert E. Howard (since adulthood he has added Brandon Sanderson, Joe Abercrombie, Jo Nesbo, Stephen King, and numerous others to that list).

When not working, reading, or writing, David can be found smoking meat, learning to cook new dishes, sipping whiskey or slivovitz, or fermenting his own mead with local Texas honey. He lives in Fort Worth, Texas with his wife, daughter, and dog. He can sometimes be spotted at meetings of Fort Worth Writers or in the local libraries and coffee shops.

Progressive Rising Phoenix Press is an independent publisher. We offer wholesale pricing and multiple binding options with no minimum purchases for schools, libraries, book clubs, and retail vendors. We offer substantial discounts on bulk orders and discounts on individual sales through our online store. Please visit our website at:

www.ProgressiveRisingPhoenix.com

If you enjoyed reading this book, please review it on Amazon, B & N, or Goodreads. Thank you in advance!

www.ingramcontent.com/pod-product-compliance
Lightning Source LLC
Chambersburg PA
CBHW020817260626
47169CB00003B/710